HEIRS of ANTON

D0959034

Ekaterina

by Susan K. Downs
and Susan May Warren

Ekaterina

For more information about Susan K. Downs and Susan May Warren, please access the authors' Web sites at the following Internet addresses:
www.susankdowns.com
www.susanmaywarren.com

Acquisitions and Editorial Director: Rebecca Germany
Editorial Consultant: Becky Durost Fish
Art Director: Jason Rovenstine
Layout Design: Anita Cook

Published by Barbour Publishing, Inc., P.O. Box 719, Uhrichsville, OH 44683, www.barbourbooks.com

Our mission is to publish and distribute inspirational products offering exceptional value and biblical encouragement to the masses.

 Member of the
Evangelical Christian
Publishers Association

Printed in the United States of America

SUSAN K. DOWNS

Dedication:

To my forever-faithful heavenly Father—who always keeps His word. Thank You for fulfilling in my life the promises You made in Psalm 103. . .to forgive, heal, redeem, crown, satisfy, and renew.

Acknowledgments:

The thrill of seeing a new family born through the miracle of international adoption proved reward enough for those long hours of travel flying across the Atlantic. . .bouncing along un-paved roads. . .jerking over trans-Siberian rails. Still, I never would have guessed back then I'd see those exhausting Russia journeys as blessings in disguise.

Sincere thanks go to:

Lori Stahl, a special adoptive mother who, during her home-study interview, showed me a mysterious old graveside photo of her ancestors that started me thinking, *What if. . . ?*

Karen Jordan, Igor Korolev, Tatyana Terekhova, Marina Sokolova, and the rest of the team on the Russia side of our adoption work. Though we no longer work together, you'll always be like family to me.

My "Spit-n-Polish" partner, *Susan May Warren,* who shares my love of both Russian and heavenly things. I thank God for con-verging our paths.

Travis, Curtis, Kevin, Kimberly, and Courtney—whether through birth or adoption, when I became your mother, I knew I'd been blessed!

David, my beloved husband and partner in adventure, I can't wait to see where life's road takes us next.

Dedication:
To my Lord and Savior, Jesus Christ,
whose arms are always open. I am so grateful.

Acknowledgments:
Every book has a cast of "human angels" behind the scenes.

Luda and Gene Khakhaleva, Artyom, and Vova, who befriended us and helped our family negotiate the world of Far East Russia. We love you!

Cindy and Alexi Kalinin, my real-life Kat and Vadeem (only better, of course).

Costia Utuzh, our dear friend who spent his last days in Q and A sessions about the FSB and COBRAs. We miss you.

Yvonne Howard, missionary and critiquer extraordinaire. Again, what would I do without you?

Susan Downs, sister in Christ and writing buddy. Who knew a birthday greeting would turn into our wildest dreams?

David, Sarah, Peter, and Noah—my team at home who keep me smiling. I'm so thankful for your hugs when I push away from the computer.

And a special thank-you to *Andrew,* my strongest supporter, my hero, and my favorite person in the world. I love you.

CHAPTER ONE

His faithfulness continues through all generations."
—PSALM 100

Kat Moore stared ahead at the customs control booth and tightened her grip on the brass key in her jacket pocket. The key's teeth bit into her palm's soft flesh, but the pain shot courage into her veins.

She lifted her chin. Her journey, the one she'd waited for her entire life, could come to a smacking halt in about ten steps.

She tore her gaze away from the steely eyes of a Russian passport official and tried to find comfort in the faces of the other passengers. No one smiled or even met her gaze. Their stoic expressions stiffened a muscle in her neck.

The passengers from the KLM plane stretched in a haphazard line down a chipped, gray hallway in Sheremetova 2, Moscow's international airport. The smells of cement, dirt, and fatigue hovered like the presence of Big Brother.

A stiff wind, left over from some iceberg north of St. Petersburg, whistled in through the metal hanging doors and kicked up dust. Kat pulled her jacket around her and mentally flogged the person who'd written "warm and sunny in June" in her travel guidebook. They would probably describe the Arctic as "mildly chilly on overcast days."

The line moved one step forward. Kat shoved her backpack along the floor with a toe, just escaping a nudge from the young lady behind her, the one wrapped in a black leather jacket and sporting a fake blond hairpiece.

Nine more steps. Kat's stomach tangled, and she fought her racing heartbeat.

She'd obviously checked her sanity, along with her baggage, back in New York City. The shadows coloring the gray stucco walls did nothing to argue that point. This dungeon's gloom, barely fractured by a high-hanging chandelier, even barred entry to the rose-colored dawn she'd seen creeping over the eastern Moscow skyline as they landed. Kat couldn't delete the image that ran through her mind of prisoners lining up for execution.

Dust hung like Spanish moss from the ceiling, a steel canopy of what looked like discarded shell casings of a bygone war, and sent chills up her spine. *God, I sure hope You can still see me, because I could use a friend right now.*

She should have listened to Matthew. He was her common sense, the weight that kept her from taking off with her dreams. "You go hunting up the past, you'll just find trouble." His voice reverberated like a bass drum through her mind as she stared heavenward.

What had possessed her to think she could traipse around a country that still sent shivers down her spine when she heard the throaty growl of the word *Russhhha?* Shivers, yes, and curiosity. Somewhere, Mother Russia secreted Kat's family tree. The key in her pocket would unlock the mystery.

If Grandfather had been just a smidgen more forthcoming about the secrets surrounding her Neumann ancestors, perhaps she wouldn't be trying to resurrect her rusty Russian and dog-earing the pages of her passport with her thumb. Edward Neumann had always been a miser with answers to her questions like, "How did Grandmother die?" or "Did she have caramel colored hair like me and Mommy?" Of course, twenty years later, she discovered why he dodged her inquiries with the agility of a rugby player. Not that the new information ebbed her flow of questions.

However impossible, her mother had inherited Edward Neumann's stubborn streak, the one that kept Kat out of every meaningful conversation—especially the ones that ended with muttered sentences like "She's too young" or "It's too dangerous."

Now, as she looked for light in the overhead shadows, she wondered if they both hadn't been right.

The line moved forward. Kat dodged the woman breathing down her neck and nearly kicked her backpack into the heels of the well-dressed man in front of her. Tall and muscular in a black trench coat, he looked about fifty. Turning, he glanced at her pack, then at her, his dark brown eyes harsh. He wore his shoulder-length, gray-streaked black hair combed back from the deep forehead of someone with Slavic descent.

A blush burned Kat's cheeks. She offered an apologetic smile.

To her amazement, he smiled back, little lines crinkling around his eyes as he did it. "No problem," he said in English.

Relief poured through Kat. "Thank you." She flicked a look at the customs official. "Have you done this before?"

He gave a wry chuckle. "Too many times." A foreign accent laced his English, enough to give it an intriguing lilt. "Don't worry. The trick is to look past them. Fix on a spot behind their heads, and whatever you do, don't smile."

"Why not?"

He grinned and leaned close. "Smilers have a reason to smile. . .and usually it isn't a good one."

Kat nodded, eyes wide. Okay, so she still had a few things to learn about international travel. She thought she'd prepped pretty well. Russian guidebooks, novels, history textbooks, and insights into the Russian culture crammed the bookshelf in her Nyack, New York, apartment. She'd taken a refresher course in Russian and discovered that the language of her great-grandparents came back like an echo. She'd even purchased a travel water filter designed to keep Russia's bacteria out of her veins. But nowhere did it tell her not to smile. Her hand tightened around the key.

The line moved forward. Kat's heart moved up into her throat. She tried to swallow it down as the customs officer's glance settled on her. She stared at her new hiking boots, hoping she didn't look somehow suspicious.

If only she'd inherited the chutzpah that made her grandfather a World War II hero—a status he'd quickly deny. The Medal of Honor he kept tucked away in his nightstand probably had something to do with his stash of secrets. . .ones she was well on her way to unwrapping.

Weeks ago, when she'd received the rumpled package in the mail, she'd sounded out a halting translation of the Russian return address: T. Petrov, from a monastery somewhere near Pskov, Russia. She knew in her heart that this parcel, posted over a year prior and littered with more than a dozen different postmarks, held the key to her past. She just couldn't believe her eyes when an actual key fell out.

The brass key had already opened doors.

She even thought she'd seen a crack in Grandfather's permanently shuttered emotions. And when he'd met her at the airport before her departure and handed her a yellowing photograph, she'd glimpsed a sadness in his eyes so profound, her heart wept. Grandfather always said he'd lost his heart in the war, but she'd never seen the agony of his loss until that day.

Kat had memorized the old photo on the eternal flight over the ocean, hoping to see herself in one of the faces. Two women stood next to a grave, one of them supposedly a distant relation of hers. Their faces were drawn, as if they'd just buried a child or a father. The words written on the back, in Russian, gave no clues even when translated into modern day English: "For the

Lord is good and his love endures forever; his faithfulness continues through all generations."

Perhaps between the picture and the key, she'd find what she'd longed for her entire life—her family tree, her ancestors, her heritage.

The man in front of her stepped over the yellow line to the passport control booth. Kat hauled up her backpack, flung it over her shoulder—narrowly missing the beauty behind her—and shuffled up to the painted yellow boundary. One more step and she'd cross over into the past. She already felt like she'd stepped into a time warp, perhaps a World War II action movie, complete with soldiers wielding AK-47s and clad in iron gray uniforms. She wondered what it would be like to work as a spy or a covert operator in a foreign country.

Wouldn't Matthew cringe if he knew her thoughts? As an ER doc, Matthew's idea of off-hours' adventure consisted of ordering green peppers and onions on his plain pepperoni pizza. She smiled, then quickly smothered the gesture, lest one of the storm troopers decide to take her expression as a villainous sign. Still, the image of Matthew tickled a place inside her as she pictured his always-perfect grin dimmed at the thought of his innocent little girlfriend longing for a life of adventure. No, make that ex-girlfriend, as of two days ago.

"Slyedushi!"

Kat swallowed hard at the command of the beefy soldier standing next to the booth. Scraping up her composure, she stepped forward and shoved her passport through the slitted portal in the thick glass. A wide-faced woman snatched the document up without so much as a nod of acknowledgment to Kat.

Don't smile. Don't smile. She stared at the passport official. . . at her chubby hands leafing through Kat's empty passport. . .at her bushy gray frown as she scrutinized Kat's visa picture. The woman looked up to compare Kat's appearance to the photo. Kat met her gaze with a blank face and congratulated herself.

"Purpose of your visit to Russia?" The woman's wide cheeks jiggled when she talked. Kat blinked and searched for her voice.

"Uh, personal," she stammered.

The stamper clinked, and a purple circle appeared on the second page of Kat's passport. The woman handed it over. "Enjoy your stay in Russia."

Kat gathered her papers and held them to her chest, over her pounding heart. *Yes, oh yes...*

"Zis way." The uniformed soldier gestured to a security scan.

Kat thumped her backpack onto the rolling belt and stepped up to the scanner. She watched her bag pass through, then received a nod from the attendant.

Enter, she thought as she stepped under the gates, *your past.*

The harsh screech of the security siren stopped her heart cold.

She froze under the arch. The siren blared. Two security officials marched toward her.

The soldier behind them swung his gun off his shoulder.

A hand closed around her arm, yanking her back the way she'd come.

"Zis way, please."

She looked up into the cold gray eyes of the Russian militia.

<hr />

"Is he through?"

Captain Vadeem Spasonov pulled the binoculars from his eyes, blinking at the sudden change in vision. "Yep. Just before the siren went off." He scanned the crowd pushing against the glass walls that surrounded the baggage claim area. Families waiting for loved ones, drivers holding placards with names written on them, interpreters and business associates barking into cell phones and checking flight schedules, all hoping to catch a glimpse of the arriving passengers. "Any clue who he is meeting?"

Captain Ryslan Khetrov shoved his hands into the pockets of his leather jacket. Vadeem's partner looked every inch the FSB agent—a member of the international security force of Russia—with his shaved blond hair, square chin, dark eyes, and meaty hands that could probably wrap twice around a man's neck. Vadeem was never sure if that was a smile or a grimace on the man's face. He hadn't known Ryslan long enough to figure it out. Maybe he never would.

"Not a clue this time," Ryslan answered. "Keep your eyes on him." He turned his back to Vadeem. "I'll watch the crowd, see if anyone looks the type to hang out with an Abkhazian gangster."

Vadeem peered through the glasses. "He's more than that. He's looking to restart the war. He's already purchased an arsenal big enough to put a serious dent in the peace-keeping forces." He trained his gaze on the tall man in a black trench coat who had stopped mid-stride and now peered back at passport control.

Ivan Grazovich, the former general in the Georgian military and currently an Abkhazian thief bent on financing his country's revolution by unearthing Mother Russia's secrets, looked like a scholarly professor on sabbatical. Vadeem narrowed his eyes as the man turned, seeming to check for someone in the line.

Vadeem couldn't wait to nail this slime ball who unearthed Russia's riches and sold them to the highest bidder—most of the time back to the Motherland herself. Grazovich reinvested the cash in renegade Russian artillery, easily obtained through the Internet or from former comrades holding onto their own personal stash. The irony felt like a blow to the solar plexus. Worse yet, someone inside Russia was helping him escape the Motherland with his treasures tucked in his belt—someone with enough military clout to know where to send the general to shop for tanks and rocket launchers and, most likely, the same someone who knew how to woo Mother Russia into buying back pieces of her past while her children, her future, starved.

So far, the smuggler had been able to sneak out with a thirteenth-century icon of St. Nickolas laden with gold and lapis lazuli stones, a tapestry of Peter the Great woven in 1723, and an Ivan Lulibin goose-egg clock made of pure gold— national treasures they'd recovered at painful price tags.

Not this time. This time Vadeem hoped to catch both thief and traitor at their game. The assignment had Medal of Merit possibilities written all over it. Unfortunately, Grazovich and his traitor in crime were as slippery as month-old bacon grease.

Vadeem watched Grazovich stalk back toward the passport booth. "What's he up to?"

"Let me see."

Vadeem handed the glasses over to his partner. From their perch in the militia office overlooking customs control, they had an advantageous view of both passenger and greeter. Behind them, security officers scanned computer screens, giving every passenger a double scrutiny. Vadeem wondered if it was the officer behind him or the lady below who had set off the screeching alarm. He noticed rookie Denis Bogdanov leaning over the shoulders of the security team, casually reading each screen, supervisory in posture. Vadeem hid a smirk. The kid had enthusiasm pouring out of his ears and, dependable lackey that he was, he'd earned the right to prowl the corridors of the security department with his elders. The fresh-out-of-academy recruit with the short black hair and intense hazel eyes rather reminded Vadeem of his early days, when he'd been the wiry, astute, ear-to-the-ground soldier, waiting for the assignment that would make his career.

Vadeem was still waiting.

"He's walking back through the security arch."

"What?" Vadeem watched Grazovich as he ran toward a burly female security officer hauling off a terrified American woman. The traveler looked the color of chalk, and she couldn't quite keep pace with the elephant-legged stride of the guard. Vadeem stepped over to a junior officer manning a computer. "Who is she?"

"Nobody. Says her name is Ekaterina Hope Moore. First time in Russia, not even another country listing on her passport." The skinny corporal in a gray military shirt typed something. "Says here she's from New York."

"Immigrant?"

"Nope, born in Nyack, New York, in the U. S. of A."

"Klasna." Vadeem gripped the tightening muscles in his neck. "Just what we need, an American trying to hawk some retired military hardware."

"You think she could be Grazovich's contact?" This from Denis, who had popped into their huddle.

Vadeem watched the trio below as the guard pulled the American to a table and, throwing the backpack aside, began to frisk her detainee with the gentleness of a female wrestler. The lady from New York hardly looked like an arms dealer, but then again, innocents made the best mules.

"I want to talk to her."

"Vadick, don't scare off Grazovich." Ryslan grabbed his leather coat sleeve.

Vadeem shrugged out of his grip. "The general doesn't have a clue who I am. I could be a local taxi driver for all he knows."

Vadeem, however, knew Ivan Grazovich inside and out. He knew what he liked for breakfast, that he preferred Absolut Vodka over the Russian Smirnoff, that his last girlfriend had been found in a Dumpster in Amsterdam. Oh, yes. Although it had only been a month since Vadeem had joined the COBRAs, an elite, international crime-stomping task force of the Federal Security Bureau, or FSB, he knew Ivan Grazovich better than he'd known his own parents.

The thought made him wince. Even the little he could remember about his parents was fading after twenty years. He'd spent most of his life memorizing the daily habits of the current ward nurse in his orphanage rather than gleaning the finer points of manhood from a father. The difference meant he learned more about how to read people in a flash than how to build a relationship—a lesson he'd taken to heart and practiced well in his stint as a Red Beret in the new Russian army. He could count his close friends on his closed fist, and he liked it that way.

He'd learned at the sturdy age of eight the high cost of friendship and had veered an unwavering course around it ever since. Ryslan, his partner of three weeks, was the closest thing he had to a buddy, and even that thought wasn't appetizing when he had to choose between an unscheduled Saturday afternoon hike through Moscow's Gregarin Park or stacking shots of vodka at the local FSB night dive with Ryslan and his COBRA pals.

Not that belonging to the elite group of COBRAs didn't have its merits. With the right moves, he could have any number of women lining up to melt his cold exterior. But they only saw a man whose familiarity with the rigors of a regular PT schedule had left him with a muscular physique, and their brand of friendship left his gut pinging with emptiness. He'd pass on the ladies, the buddies. And as for the COBRAs, well maybe a high-profile arrest would do what the vodka shots and false camaraderie couldn't—earn their respect.

"Just keep your eyes on him." Vadeem shrugged out of his

leather jacket, reached over, and pulled a militia uniform jacket off a coat tree. Grabbing the hat off the corporal, he snuggled it down over his head. "If she is involved, I'll know."

Ryslan harrumphed as Vadeem left the militia booth.

Vadeem buttoned the jacket over his black pullover as he thumped down the stairs, hoping Grazovich didn't notice his black jeans and loafers instead of the standard issue military grays and black boots.

The American's confused voice lifted over the cluster of officers as she gestured to something in her hand. He approached the tallest officer, who stood a few feet back. "What's up?"

"An American. She set off the alarm with some sort of souvenir she had in her coat pocket."

"What is it?"

"Looks like a key." The official moved away, and Vadeem got a full view of the hapless arms dealer. She looked about as sinister as his grandmother, if he had one. Her tousled hair, the color of caramel, fell over her face in thick strands, and a button on her white blouse had come undone. Her jacket, a glaring red affair that screamed "tourist!" hung off her shoulders, weighted down on one side by a bulging backpack that skimmed the carry-on limit. Fear filled those big amber eyes, and for a moment they looked up and caught him staring at her.

Her expression was so desperate, it rattled his resolve to hike her back to one of the dusty offices and put her thumbs to the screws.

"Please, gentlemen, return this woman's key and let her be." Ivan Grazovich, smuggler and terrorist to the rescue.

Vadeem's eyes narrowed, seeing the way the gangster moved close and tucked an arm around the lady's waist. "She's with me," Grazovich said.

A tall soldier with gray eyes gave Grazovich a hard look. "And who are you?" Vadeem stepped closer, gaze pinned to the woman, and watched the way her amber eyes widened in shock—or relief?

Oh, she was about as innocent as Comrade Stalin.

"Leave the woman alone, gentlemen. Haven't you terrified her enough for one day?" Grazovich smiled. Mr. Goodwill.

Vadeem repulsed the urge to grab the smuggler by the collar of his starched white dress shirt, or his black trench coat, and wrestle the truth out of him with the blunt end of his Makarov.

Instead, Vadeem strode forward and hooked a hand around the woman's arm. "You can wait for her past customs," he clipped at Grazovich. Then, ignoring the man's glower, he towed Miss Arms Dealer through the crowd and into the inner sanctum of Militia Border Control.

Ilyitch stood in the shadows and watched the FSB agent tow the American into his custody. A sick feeling welled in his gut. She'd taken the bait, and now all their hard work, the waiting, the plotting would disintegrate under the scrutiny of Russia's finest. They would confiscate her belongings, ship her Stateside on the next available transport and, with her, destroy his hope of wiggling out from under the general's thumb. Every time Grazovich set foot on Russian soil, Ilyitch took a quick and painful survey of his rubles—no, dollars—and cursed the balance. He needed Grazovich to be right. Ilyitch didn't have time, patience, or luck to waste chasing after a fable.

Especially with the FSB on their trail. Ilyitch noticed Grazovich watching the FSB spectacle. An ugly smear masqueraded as a smile on the smuggler's face as the tall Captain Spasonov yanked his new suspect through the tangle of crowd while Grazovich looked on. Again, Ilyitch would have to yank the smuggler Grazovich out of the hole he'd dug. And then he'd have to baby-sit, hoping the general avoided trouble. . .like seducing, or worse, an American on her first day in town, at least until she helped them unlock the secrets of the monk.

Ilyitch turned and shoved his fists into his jacket pockets, ruing the day he'd met the general and every day he'd known him since.

CHAPTER TWO

Ten paces into custody, Kat's voice caught up to her. The first thing it addressed was the six-foot-two-inch military henchman's grasp on her arm. "Let me go!"

Her cry emerged in English—her Russian having deserted her—but to her utter shock, the bully bit out a terse, "No."

In English.

She stumbled along with him down the cold cement corridor, not sure what emotion won the battle—fear, anger, or shock. Her heart drummed a beat of terror against her ribs; her breath snagged somewhere in the land of freedom behind her.

"In here, please."

Again, English. . .and manners? She glowered at the creep, despite the fact her legs had turned numb, and let him muscle her into a room. Barren except for a warped wooden table and two decrepit chairs, the gray tomb reeked of KGB menace. Mr. Militia released her, and she stood, one hand nursing the tenderness in her arm, trying to dredge up a coherent thought.

"I'm an American. I have rights." Her voice sounded like it wanted no part of her words, the tone feeble and ready to race for the border.

He smiled, just enough to annoy, or perhaps, frighten her and motioned to a chair. "Please, sit down."

She looked behind her. He'd closed the door. A slit of a window high above her illuminated the dust clinging to the walls and ceiling, but did little to penetrate the cement room's murky shroud. She steeled herself against an involuntary shudder and wrestled in a deep breath. "Why am I here?"

"I just want to talk to you. Please, sit down." The officer sat down, folded his large hands on the table, and again smiled.

She narrowed her eyes. If he was trying the Good Cop/Bad Cop routine, she wasn't buying. The man might have incredible blue eyes and a bevy of solid power and strength poorly hidden under that ill-fitting gray jacket of his, but under the circumstances, those qualities weren't at all appealing.

His blue eyes felt as cold as a Siberian winter as they pinned her down. She rubbed her hands on her arms and took a calming breath, feeling anger knot her chest. "I'll stand, thanks."

The jerk pursed his lips, so arrogantly calm, she wanted to slap him. Except she wasn't sure that in reprisal he wouldn't just slap her into handcuffs and ship her off to the nearest gulag.

Did they still do that?

Her knees suddenly surrendered, and she reached for the chair. The officer smiled, as if in victory. "You don't have anything to fear from me, *Americanka.*"

Yeah, right. She'd feel safer with a scorpion.

"You know English," she said, finally latching onto her Russian. Somehow, speaking in another language felt like a barrier between her and reality.

One edge of his mouth tweaked, and his eyes held a hint of amusement. "Da."

He took off his cap and ran his hand through a swatch of black hair, cut short on the sides, unruly and curly-locked on top. It made the planes of his high cheekbones and angular face seem that much sharper, more dangerous. "Would you feel more comfortable speaking in your native tongue?"

"I'd feel more comfortable on my way to my hotel, thank

you," she snapped in Russian. "What is this about?"

He shrugged out of his jacket, which looked about two sizes too small, and crossed his arms over his black turtleneck. His bulging muscles made him appear every inch like a Russian mobster, ready to slice out her tongue.

"Let's start with your friend, Ivan Grazovich. How do you know him?"

She frowned, scraped her mind for any remnant of understanding. "Who?"

His brow pinched, his eyes darkened. "Do you think I'm stupid?"

Oh, how the latent rebel in her wanted to jump all over that comment. She bit back a reply and shook her head. "I have no idea who you are talking about."

He narrowed his eyes. "Why did you come to Russia?"

Kat exhaled a breath that felt like it started in New York. For the better part of two months, she'd been answering that question from various factions in her life—from her grandfather and her ex-boyfriend to her coworkers at the Heart-to-Heart adoption agency.

Even now, her answers felt unwieldy, slippery. To track down her identity? To unlock secrets that might account for a lifetime of deception? To unravel the riddle of her foggy ancestry?

To figure out who she was?

The answer to that question didn't seem so difficult at the moment—she could clearly identify herself as an in-over-her-head thirty-year-old teetering on the edge of tears, if not hysteria.

Under different circumstances, she might welcome the opportunity to spill her guts. She wasn't opposed to the truth, but the bully just might find sadistic pleasure in sending her home if he knew how desperation drove her. "I'm a tourist."

"Hmm. . . ," he said, his eyes narrowing. She did him the

pleasure of raising her chin and meeting his glower. She might possess the courage of a field mouse, but he didn't have to know it. Her recent escape from Matthew's hovering had taught her the value of masking her fear.

"Stay put." The man rose and stalked toward the door. "I'll be right back."

Oh, joy. Kat folded her hands between her knees as the door clicked shut.

Now what? She heard nothing but her heart beating a pathway to her mouth. The smell of her own sweat and the taste of fear repulsed her. Hadn't she scoffed at her grandfather's warnings of danger? Told him she could take care of herself? After all, she was the granddaughter of a World War II hero, the recipient of his gutsy genes and her mother's passion for truth.

C'mon, heritage of courage, kick in. Kat stood, crept toward the door, and tried the handle. Locked.

She slapped her palm against the metal door, furious, her bravado dropping to her knees. She had the sick feeling that whatever Mr. Military had left to do, it wasn't going to work nicely into her plans.

The door opened, and Kat jumped, leaving her heart behind.

Wide, Dark, and Menacing entered the room. Kat shrank back, suddenly giving merit to the Bad Cop theory she'd dismissed earlier. This version of Russian militia held her backpack in his meaty grip. Easily six-foot-four, with a black stocking cap, dark glasses, and enough body-builder bulk to match every KGB nightmare, he grabbed her upper arm in his bullish grip and yanked her into the hall.

Okay, *now* she was ready to spill her guts. Why had she played games? Where was Good Cop when she needed him? "Where are you taking me?" she asked on a wisp of voice.

He glowered at her, and she clamped her mouth shut. Her

heart in a pile of ash, she followed him down the hall, stumbling. Tears blinded her at his burning grip. Cop Number One had been downright gentle in comparison.

"Where are you taking me?" The words came out again in English, but this time her abductor ignored her. They cruised down the hall toward a door, and Kat's feet dragged. A cell? Oh, why hadn't she listened to Matthew? She'd drop to his feet in apology the next time she saw him.

The thug stopped. Opened the door.

The gray tones of the overcast morning dove into the dank hall. *"Ooidti."*

Leave?

She stared at Large and Mean, blinking. He shoved the backpack into her arms, then pushed her out the door. *"Beg-ee!"*

Run!

Okay, yes, she could do that. Her legs moved before her brain could engage. She streaked along the shadow of the building to the chain-link fence rimming the parking lot. Without a thought, she threw the backpack over and nearly vaulted the fence. She heard her pant leg rip as she straddled the top but didn't care. Freedom burned her lungs, pumped her heartbeat into her ears.

She landed with a thump, then took off through the parking lot, feeling like she'd just escaped from Attica, wondering how soon it would take the hounds to track her down.

And what they'd do to her when they did.

Vadeem stood in the empty interrogation room, his suspicions multiplying like fruit flies on overripe apples.

She'd escaped. He flung the can of Sprite across the room—the one he'd purchased hoping to woo her into unloading her secrets—and sprinted down the hall toward customs control. He skidded up to one of the militia. "Did she come by here?"

The man's blank look drove Vadeem to want to hit something, hard.

How had she escaped? He sprinted back to the room, glanced up at the window, then down the hall. The door at the end of the corridor hinted at her escape strategy. Palming his cell phone, he dialed. Ryslan picked up on the first ring.

"She's gone. Alert airport security."

"Who?"

"The American." He deliberately kept his voice low. "She snuck out while I was getting her a. . ." He grimaced. "Nothing. Just call security." He snapped the telephone closed and clenched his fist around it.

Sneaky, stubborn woman. Even if she wasn't a suspect before, she was now. And to think he'd been nursing feelings of pity. Something about the way she held in her fraying composure with a chin-up glower sparked his respect. And her eyes, the color of dark honey, had him second-guessing his gut feeling that she was hiding something.

Until now.

His telephone shrilled. *"Slyshaio,"* he snapped.

"Security hasn't seen her, but they're on alert," Ryslan reported, then added without pause, "we'll find her."

"Anyone watching Grazovich?"

"Denis has him. He just picked up his bag."

"I'm there." Vadeem slammed his phone shut and stalked toward the exit, following the sick feeling that once he'd found his smuggler, the renegade *Americanka* wouldn't be far behind.

Ilyitch stood on the upper concourse overlooking the parking lot, his legs wide, arms behind him as if in soldier stance, wishing all his ops played out with such precision. Miss America stood out like neon in the crowd, her red jacket screaming, "Bull's-eye!" as she stalked through foot traffic, trying to flag down a taxi. If it weren't for the fact that the general already had her in his sights, Ilyitch might entertain a spur of worry about the FSB agent hot on her tail. But the general knew his trade.

Ilyitch watched as the general's taxi cruised up and the passenger door opened. Ilyitch imagined her surprise, perhaps even her smile, as she greeted the general and, yes, accepted his ride.

She slid into the cab without hesitation. Ilyitch shook his head, his chest only slightly tight, knowing she had just, with a sigh of relief, embraced the devil.

A feeling he understood.

CHAPTER THREE

Kat sat on the day train, the hard wooden bench scraping away the last vestiges of her composure with every rhythmic jerk. She felt as if she'd been beaten like one of those floor rugs she'd seen some old babushka attack as they'd rolled through the last village. Still, the hard knot of terror in her chest eased with each passing kilometer. Who knew that angels dressed in black trench coats and spoke with an accent? God had surely been working overtime this morning. The Almighty must have activated a small battalion of unseen holy soldiers to yank her out of the grip of the customs officials.

Don't smile, and don't carry brass keys in your pocket. Any travel book worth its salt would have included those bits of advice, along with a list of pointers as to how to escape the clutches of the local militia.

Then again, who knew that angels came dressed not only in six-foot-four black, but in the garb of a friendly professor.

"Stopped shaking yet?" Professor Taynov turned around from the seat in front of her and smiled, the spidering lines around his eyes adding years to his youthful aura. Indeed, the history professor from Prague University, as he had introduced himself moments after scooping her into his taxi, mocked the definition of middle-aged, despite his graying hair. He had wide, strong hands, and his shoulders and arms filled out his trench coat. Even his energy when they fast-walked through the Moscow train terminal hinted at youthfulness. It wasn't just the hair tint and wrinkles, however, that stretched his age. . . . It was his eyes, as if they'd been plucked out of a battle-weary soldier and transplanted into his wide, chiseled face and youthful body. Eyes that looked right through her and made her shiver.

Of course it was only a guess. She'd known the man for a mere four hours. But after conducting home studies and interviewing prospective adoptive parents for the past five years, she measured herself a pretty good judge of character. That he'd also stopped his taxi and marched back into the baggage claim to rescue her suitcase confirmed the fact the man resembled a bona fide angel.

"Yes, I'm doing much better, thanks to you," she answered. She tightened her ankles around her suitcase, wishing she'd packed as light as the other travelers around her. She already felt like some sort of pampered movie star, attracting attention as she wrestled the bag onto the train. "Why did you intervene?"

Professor Taynov gave her a look of surprise. "Because you looked like you needed rescuing. Besides, I know that a woman with such a beautiful smile can't be a danger to Mother Russia." He winked, and Kat's eyes widened.

"Thank you," she stammered, wondering suddenly about his motives. Was the man really traveling to Pskov on happenstance, or had she suddenly found an admirer expecting more repayment than she would produce? She rubbed her arms and stared out the window, wishing again that her grandfather had consented to travel with her. Of course, this joint-jarring rhythm would have played havoc on his eighty-year-old bones.

She curled her hands around the backpack on her lap and instinctively checked for the brass key in the front pocket. Her heartbeat still jumped every time she glimpsed someone in black entering her airspace—a painful regularity in Russia. She kept conjuring up a posse of officers like the ones she had encoun-tered at the airport. She hoped that the man who'd freed her had also talked the passport officials into a full pardon. Who did they think she was, anyway? James Bond's latest hottie?

The fact that she'd purchased her ticket and made it onto the train without incident confirmed the hope that she'd been cleared. The militia regular—the one with the bone-piercing blue eyes who had nabbed her and dragged her back to the bow-els of customs—must have been some sort of renegade with a vendetta against naive Americans. A travesty one of his superi-ors quickly rectified.

Only, she wasn't quite so naive anymore, thank you very much.

The agony of the eight-hour ride loomed out into eternity, and the fact that her body was still ticking on New York time made the clack of the train beat inside her head like a gong. With God's providence, she would arrive in time to grab a cab and trek out to the monastery, inconveniently located some thirty kilometers from Pskov according to her now well-creased map. If it weren't for curiosity pressing her on like an overseer, she'd make a beeline for the Intourist hotel where, assuming they had a record of her Internet reservation, she would collapse. She felt like a kid on Christmas morning, sleep-deprived but wide-eyed at the pile of presents, hoping one was for her.

She rubbed her eyes until she saw stars, hoping to dissolve a film of fatigue. She would pay about a million rubles for a shot of hot cocoa and a bag of M&M's to put a kick into her adren-aline. Her energy level had taken a nosedive, jet lag crashing over her after the initial high she'd gotten from being yanked free of the militia's clutches.

It didn't help her altered brain cells that she'd been sucked back in time. The passenger train looked like something from her childhood history book. The wooden seat under her couldn't be more than a century new. And the smell. . .what was that?

She craned her head around and spied a woman wrapped in a wool headscarf as if it were January in Iceland and holding a mangy brown poodle. The dog's hair was parted around his eyes, and he blinked at Kat as if dazed by his own odor.

Across the aisle, a weary-looking blond holding a child in a snowsuit leaned her head against the grimy window. Her eyes were closed. Kat's heart turned in pity at the fist-sized hole in the woman's tights, just below her knees, and the string that bound her shoe heels to her shapeless loafers.

"So, why are you heading to Pskov?" Professor Taynov's grin seemed genuine. Kat scrambled through a haze of fatigue to sound coherent.

"I'm trying to find some relatives." Her dream sounded simpler when she put words to it. *"I'm trying to find out who I am"* seemed so. . .desperate.

He raised his black eyebrows. "You're Russian?"

"Partly. My grandmother was from Russia."

"So you've come back to the Motherland to find your roots." He shook his head. "Good luck. Russia's such a mess right now, you'd be lucky to find the sun in the sky on a cloudless day."

"I have some clues." Kat tried not to let his words dent her enthusiasm. "I got a letter from a monastery outside Pskov. From a monk."

"Really?" Professor Taynov reached out his hand. "Can I see it?"

Kat blushed. "Actually, there was no note, just the key."

"The one that set off the siren?"

She nodded, unzipped the backpack pocket, and handed it over. Professor Taynov examined it like an archeologist. "Looks old. Maybe a hundred years. Look at the cut—hand done. No lathe formed this key."

"What do you think it opens?"

He handed it back. "A door, perhaps, or maybe a chest?"

She shrugged. "I'm hoping the monastery has some answers." She went to slip it into her bag, then stopped. This and the picture were the only clues she had. Digging into her backpack, she unearthed a pack of extra shoestrings and pulled out a single lace.

"What are you doing?" The professor's brow furrowed. The look sent a chill up her spine.

"This key is the bridge to my past. I can't afford to lose it." She slipped the lace through the small hole in the key, then tied it around her neck. She dropped the key under her shirt, and the metal sent a jolt of cold through her as it touched her skin.

Professor Taynov nodded, his gaze resting on Kat's neck for a long moment. Then he turned around and said nothing more.

<hr />

Kat rolled her brochure into a tube and tapped it on her leg as she listened to the tour guide explain the three-hundred-year-old icon of St. John, the Winged Precursor, painted by somebody named Filatyev. Her Russian couldn't keep up, and she tuned out the drone of the leggy guide and moved to the back of the group. She was lucky to hook up with the last tour of the day. A brown-robed man, presumably a monk, had been less than helpful when she'd inquired after Brother Timofea Petrov and, instead, pointed to the "NO ENTRANCE WITHOUT A TOUR" sign. She took the hint and bought the last ticket. She could only hope God's intervention would hold out and she'd somehow find where they kept the active monks.

"Move this way and you'll find a chamber dedicated to St. George."

Kat shuffled with the group into a small room painted orange, red, and green, with an intricate mosaic of a young man slaying what looked like a dragon. While the rest of the group moved as close to the painted walls as the chains would allow, Kat slipped out of the room, quick-walked through the three prayer chambers of the monastery chapel, and stepped out into the sunshine.

The sweet redolence of a white lilac drifted on the breeze and the sun hid behind a scattering of pine trees to the west. Kat followed a cobblestone path past the chapel, deeper into the grounds. The chapel had obviously been one of the first buildings renovated since the Russian government began sinking money back into the church. She found the building in the brochure, then read about the library and the school. The grounds were set on a hill, the fresh aroma of the Velikaya River drifting up from beyond the sandstone cliffs. The path wound around three other buildings, perhaps housing, then disappeared into the whitewashed wooden fence that surrounded the grounds. She stopped at a statue, a bust of some monk who had obviously given his life for the monastery. She read the inscription, tracing the date, c. 1007, and marveled that the monastery could be nearly a millennium old.

Kat heard the cheery carol of a robin, and a gentle breeze lifted the hair from her forehead. The early evening sunlight sprayed off the golden cupolas of a community of green-roofed buildings and swept a kaleidoscope of color throughout the compound, reflecting a magnificent light display off the red-and-gold buildings and illuminating the centuries-old icons painted on the high gables. Kat closed her eyes. She felt light years removed from her morning battle with the Russian militia and easily believed God could be found in this place.

Now, if she could only find Brother Timofea.

Maybe he lived in the back buildings not listed on the map. The brochure did boast an "active" monastery. Curiosity and hope pressed her up the path toward the buildings. For the first time, she wished Professor Taynov hadn't left her with a "good luck" at the train station. He'd shaken her hand, pointed her toward a taxi, and hoofed off in the opposite direction.

So maybe he wasn't trying to start something she wouldn't finish. She blushed, even thinking it. She might be traveling alone, but she didn't need to suspect every person she met. A souvenir from living six years under Matthew's hover. Or perhaps simply a scar from her painful reception by Russian customs. Shame pressed down on her chest, and it didn't help that she'd now found the door to the first building and stood with her hand on the latch.

She sucked a deep breath.

"*Zhenshina!* Stop! Where you going?"

Her knees nearly gave out. She yanked her hand off the door and whirled, her heart in her throat.

"Are you lost?" She'd been nabbed by a monk, obvious from the brown robe he wore, but instead of softness, his dark eyes peeled layers off her deceitful intentions, leaving only the naked truth. She gulped, scraping up anything. Even a grunt would do. Giving up on words, Kat shook her head.

He gave her a shriveling look. "Can I help you?"

"Maybe," she squeaked. She scrambled for Russian, which had abandoned her again. "I'm looking for. . ." *What was that brother's name?*

"Come with me." He reached out and grabbed her by her shaking arm.

Okay, God could make an appearance right about now. The

Second Coming. Anything. She'd accept acts of nature, a finger-of-God tornado perhaps. She stumbled along, wondering how she'd managed to be apprehended twice in one day. Thankfully, the key was safely thumping against her chest instead of locked along with her bag and camera in the monastery coat-and-camera check.

She wondered if they had good food in prison. Her stomach was starting to clench.

The monk marched her into another unnamed building, down a hall, and into a wide, barren office. Two squeaky-clean, tall windows peered out across a graveyard. Beyond that, dark gray limestone rose like a wall surrounding the spiritual conclave.

"Yes?" An elderly monk sat behind a simple wooden desk, clad in the standard garb. The wrinkles on his face and his wide, shiny head betrayed his age as somewhere near Ivan the Terrible. He clasped his hands on his desk and raised his eyebrows, obviously accustomed to respect. Still, despite the reasonable tone of his low, aged voice and his slow demeanor, Kat came up empty when she searched his face for patience.

"I found this woman wandering around the grounds."

Kat rubbed her arm where the monk had held on and wondered how a man of God could have such a cruel grip.

"Are you lost?" The head monk frowned, and a chill ran through Kat's veins.

Looking heavenward, she shook her head.

Her own thundering heartbeat filled the silence in the room.

"What do you want?" The gravel in his voice rattled Kat's bones.

She found her voice, hidden right behind her cowering curiosity. It emerged as feeble as her courage. "I'm looking for one of your brothers. . . ."

The two monks exchanged glances. Kat took the opportunity to dig into her pocket and pull out the scrap of envelope that bore the return address. Like forensic evidence, it felt like the hand of justice, clearing her of her crime. "Someone from this monastery sent me something. Brother Timofea Petrov. I need to talk to him."

She held out the paper to the elder monk. He took it, and one bushy eyebrow tightened, angled down. "What did Brother Timofea send you?"

Kat hauled in a deep breath. The key did belong to her, right? Head Monk and Thug Monk weren't going to wrestle it from her, were they? "A key, Sir."

"Call me Father, if you please. Do you have it?"

Kat scanned a look between the two monks, who seemed now less sinister than curious. She nodded.

"Can we see it?" Father Monk stood, and his voice softened.

"If you tell me where I can find Brother Timofea." Kat crossed her arms over her chest and pushed against a betraying tremble. She lifted her chin and tried to stare down the father. A second later, she was examining the polished wooden floor, her pulse nearly too loud to hear the monk's quiet acquiescence. The sadness in his voice, however, rang volumes.

She watched his eyes as she tugged the key from beneath her shirt. They widened, and his expression changed. "So that's where it went."

Kat held the key in her palm, ready to white-fist it should they even sniff suspiciously. "Where is Brother Timofea?"

The father sent a small nod to the monk beside her.

"Follow me," he said.

⚓

Vadeem watched Ekaterina Moore trudge out of the monastery

gates, the low sun turning her hair rich amber. She'd obviously had a doozy of a day, and rightly deserved, the little escape artist. Still, her shoulders shook, and the fact that she was crying made Vadeem want to step out from under the full lilac and yank that awful rolling suitcase out of her grip as he muscled her into HQ. The bag rolled like a rummy behind her as she dodged ruts in the sidewalk. She stopped now and again to wipe her eyes, and once she turned and stared back at the monastery as if she'd left behind her soul and contemplated a dash back to retrieve it.

He'd have to dodge the effect of those amber brown eyes brimming with tears if he hoped to keep his eye on the prize. Namely, Grazovich. And after watching the smuggler scoop her up like a prize, Vadeem would lay odds the two were in cahoots.

She wouldn't shake him again.

Vadeem followed her as she plodded down the street, thankful he had both Grazovich and Moore now in pocket. Grazovich, true to form, had headed straight for the Intourist hotel, found a room on the second floor, and ordered a bottle of Absolut. A couple of purple five-hundred ruble notes in the clerk's pocket and Vadeem would know if Grazovich did anything but drink himself into a stupor.

Miss Moore stopped, set her backpack down on her suitcase, and stared up the street. No, no taxis. He could read the realization on her face and in her drooping shoulders. She worked a small book out of a side pocket—a traveler's guide, no doubt. A slight wind pulled her hair back from her face as she frowned, flipping pages, worrying her bottom lip as she read. She looked up, as if to gather her bearings, and he turned and memorized the contents of a nearby bread kiosk. A moment later, she was again trolleying her baggage down the street in the direction of the *Avtovoxhal*. He gave her begrudging points for her on-her-feet thinking.

Then again, anyone with the slightest travel savvy—and especially an international fence for combat accessories—would know that taxis loved to pick up fares at the local bus station.

Vadeem zipped back to his *Zhiguli*, a loaner from the local FSB setup, and followed her, just to keep her in his sights as she adeptly scored a cab at the depot. He stayed on her taillights all the way back to Pskov and hung out at the ATM machine, fighting his awakened suspicions while she checked in at the local Intourist hotel. Lodging options were few in Pskov, but it slammed a few more nails in her coffin that she chose Grazovich's hotel.

She finally loaded her gear into a rickety elevator and headed upstairs.

He approached his newly acquainted desk clerk informant. "Which one is she in?"

"Three–O–Two." The desk clerk offered a conspiratorial smile, as if she'd joined the police force.

"Thank you." Vadeem took a seat across the lobby, behind a full hibiscus, and crossed his arms over his chest, wondering if his little tourist was staying put for the night.

She appeared thirty minutes later, face scrubbed, and looking sharp in a pair of khakis and a pink, wide-collared blouse. She'd obviously emptied half her backpack. It sagged like a deflated ball off her shoulder. He fell in thirty paces behind her when she stepped out onto the street.

The wind reaped her perfume and sent it streaming back at him. Oh my, did she smell good. Floral, maybe roses or lavender. Something simple. He paused on the steps, watching her go, debating the wisdom of leaving Grazovich unguarded.

Except, what was she doing wandering around Pskov?

He stuck his hands in his jacket pockets and followed her trail.

He found her just around the corner, sitting in an outside bistro, backpack at her heels, and nibbling at a fingernail while studying a menu. One leg was crossed over the other, and her tennis shoe moved to the pop rock they were piping over the boom box on the cashier's table. At first glance, no one would guess she had just spent the day on the lam and wading knee deep into a terrorist's agenda.

A half block past the bistro, he bought an ice cream from a vendor and ate it while he watched her pick at a potato salad.

She had her cover down to an art form. Presently, she looked about as forlorn as he felt every Saturday night in the bleak months of winter—restless, frustrated. But he suspected the brain behind those woeful eyes held a knowledge of the inner workings of a howitzer or a SCUD missile. Vadeem threw his cone into the trash, tired of this charade.

He skidded to a halt, stunned, as Ivan Grazovich approached the café like a man on a mission. He wore a smile. Vadeem bristled. Somehow the fact that his gut instincts had played true felt like a knife in his chest.

Okay, so he'd hoped in the tiniest corner of his heart to be wrong. He edged near a building, folded his arms on his chest, and waited in the shadows, craning his ear.

"Miss Moore!"

Vadeem grimaced as the young lady actually looked happy to see the international thug.

Grazovich sat down. Miss Moore smiled, a pitiful one, but still, the smuggler was on the receiving end, and it seemed as if the world had tilted toward evil.

Vadeem clenched his jaw as she shook her head, those pretty, deceptive eyes tearing up. She pulled up something from under her shirt, a brass key on a shoelace. Grazovich touched her arm. She looked grateful. The smuggler ordered a Pepsi.

Vadeem fought a sneer, knowing the man had already consumed half a bottle of vodka.

Then she laughed, and the sound of it speared Vadeem's
bones. He felt sick and wanted to hit something, hard, when
the grin that followed looked genuine. Vadeem considered his
options. Could he arrest the team yet, or did he have to wait
until they actually committed the crime?

He'd already amassed enough evidence to satisfy his
suspicions.

The pair stood, and Grazovich picked up her bill. Vadeem
followed them like a hungry dog as they strolled back to the
hotel, she with an obviously lighter step.

They said good-bye for a long time, while Vadeem was
stuck examining a display of *Matroshka* dolls in the lobby gift
shop. Grazovich left first, taking the elevator.

Vadeem turned to follow.

Miss Moore walked into the gift shop, nearly smack
into him.

"Excuse me!"

Vadeem blinked, suddenly at a loss for words. Those eyes
were honey to his reflexes. He turned away, his head down, his
adrenaline spiking. "No, excuse. . .me," he stuttered. He picked
up a porcelain Gel vase, examining it. Although he'd traded the
militia jacket for his brown leather coat and wore a pair of sun-
glasses on his head, one lingering look from her, and his surveillance gig would combust on the spot.

She said nothing and moved past him. The perfume stayed.

While she examined a scarf, he made a quick exit, scooting
out into the lobby and hiding behind his favorite hibiscus. The
desk clerk gave him a look. He frowned at her and shook his
head. The last thing he needed was an untimely update from his
cohort in crime.

He was back at the ATM machine when Miss Moore exited the shop and headed up the elevator.

He took the stairs.

She was collecting her key from the floor monitor when he reached the landing. He backed down a step and flattened himself against the wall. He just wanted to get a layout of where she was, what side of the hotel, what room. He'd find a perch in the grocery store across the street and make sure she was tucked in before he trained his binoculars on Grazovich's room for the night.

He was on the landing when he heard a scream. Fifteen strides later, he stood in her doorway, his pulse roaring.

She was on her knees, holding a green sweatshirt in one hand and a wool sock in the other. Her body shook.

He heard feet thumping down the hall behind him. She turned, looked at him, and went white.

"Calm down. I'm not going to hurt you."

She put down the sock and held the sweatshirt to her chest, her eyes wide. Recognition washed over her face. "Get away!"

What game was she playing? She'd spoken perfect Russian before, had been rather stubborn about it, to boot. *"Nyet.* What happened here?" Either she was an extremely messy unpacker or someone had done the honors for her. He averted his eyes from a slip draped over the television set and a pair of pink silky pajamas that had landed on the desk lamp. Instead he took a survey of the toiletries bag that had been emptied onto her bed. "Thorough, huh?" He picked up a gooey bottle of shampoo with two fingers, wondering what the thief was looking for *inside* the bottle.

She looked at him, half-horror, half-confusion, her knuckles white against her sweatshirt. "What are you doing here?" Her Russian, although stuttered, had returned.

He crouched before her, a little shocked at her fraying composure. "Did you think I wouldn't find you?"

She opened her mouth, closed it. Clenched her jaw. He looked away when tears edged her eyes.

"Any idea who did this?" He tried to keep his tone dark, dangerous, refusing to allow her sobs to reach past his disgust. The woman obviously wasn't above playing games with a man's emotions.

"No." Her pitiful tone found soft soil and twisted. He had to admit, everything about her smacked of authenticity.

Except, of course, her rather telling relationship with an international smuggler.

"You know you're under arrest, right? It'll only help your case to tell me everything."

All bravado dropped from her expression, and she looked like she might just wail, right there. "My case?" She backed away from him. "I don't know what you think I did, but I did *not* run away today. Someone let me go. And," her voice shook and she wrestled it back into submission, "I have no idea, none, *nyeto*, who did this. *Panimaish?*"

Her Russian vernacular, slightly sarcastic and sassy, seemed completely out of sync with the fierce tremble of her hands. Still, it chipped another crack into his suspicions.

"My name's Vadeem. I'd like to help you." Now why did he say that? He felt like an idiot, holding his hand out to her like he wanted to make friends. Still, the damage was done, and all he could do was muscle up a smile.

She looked from his hand to his eyes, studying his face with unmasked disbelief. She'd obviously had her share of scrapes for the day. Her eyes looked battered and fatigued. Still, if he'd learned one thing about her, she wasn't going to shatter in front of him. "Kat Moore, and I still don't know anything." She slipped her hand into his. It felt warm and just strong enough for him to know she fought her fears.

"Glad to meet—"

The window behind her exploded.

A million spikes sprayed them as Vadeem threw himself forward. He caught Miss Moore in his embrace and landed on the palms of his hands. They fell back onto the rug. She screamed, her hands clawing into his chest as he held her down. His arms covered their heads, his face next to hers, as he listened to the gunfire of a semi-automatic Makarov chip cement from the wall above the bed.

CHAPTER FOUR

K at leaned her head on the dirty glass pane in the interrogation room. Hard as she tried, she couldn't shake off the tremor that buzzed like a low hum under her skin. Two stories below, moonlight strafed the street in a long pale strip, and the trees jutted spiny arms into the sky, black skeletons silhouetted in ghostly light. She heard the low murmur of voices outside the door. Hopefully one of them was the soldier who had pinned her to the ground and saved her life.

So, maybe he wasn't the menacing thug she'd pegged him to be.

She put a hand to her face and remembered the rub of his whiskers, recalled his warm breath as he whispered comfort to a stranger and protected her with his own body. She blinked against the burning in her eyes. Nope, after the bullets stopped flying, she'd dubbed him a bona fide hero.

As if on cue, the man, Captain Vadeem something, stalked into the room. He still looked like a walking menace with his sculpted physique and battle-etched face. He tossed a file on the metal table, then turned his chair backwards and sat down, straddling it and leaning over the top.

She didn't miss the way her heartbeat revved into NASCAR speed. Why, she wasn't at all sure—whether because of his grim look or the way his blue eyes seemed to peer through her down to her soul.

"How are you doing, Miss Moore?" His voice didn't sound at all like he'd nearly been shredded by a battery of gunfire.

She could only shrug. It seemed particularly ironic that she both began and ended this day in the custody of the Russian militia. She'd stopped asking God to rescue her and moved on to asking why she needed to be rescued so often.

The captain indicated for her to sit. "Can I ask you a few questions?"

He deserved to ask her anything after his heroic stunt earlier in the evening. When he looked at her with worry in his brow, she could hardly say no. Still, their relationship had her on edge—just what, exactly, should she feel about someone who scared the breath out of her one second and felt like an angel from heaven the next?

She sat down, feeling hollow, thankful that she'd pulled on the green sweatshirt before leaving the hotel. An igloo in Siberia was bound to be warmer than the barren cement interrogation room in the cop house. The smell of coffee drifted in from the dingy hallway and knotted her stomach.

The captain flicked open the brown file folder and flipped through it, as if searching for something. Kat pinned her hands together between her knees, hoping the file wasn't about her. He stopped searching, and his fingers drummed on the sheaf of papers for a moment while his gaze swept over her. She swallowed a lump forming in her throat.

"Do you have any idea why someone would ransack your room or shoot at you?"

She gave a small shake of her head.

"Hmm."

She watched his hands, strong and sleek, unearth a color photograph. She remembered those hands guiding her as she slithered across her hotel room floor to the hallway. Those hands took hers and helped her to her feet, even held her around the waist when she discovered her legs had turned to oatmeal.

"Have you ever seen this man?" He handed her a photo and was polite enough not to comment when it shook in her grip.

She frowned. The man in the photograph looked Slavic by birth, with narrow planes to his face, and hard eyes. His tawny brown hair, pulled back, gave him a fierceness that was only accentuated by the thin scar along his right cheekbone. He looked vaguely familiar, but. . . "No."

"His name is Ivan Grazovich. He's Abkhazian, a military general and antiquities smuggler, among other things."

She felt a tight burn, right in the center of her chest. "Do you think he was the one shooting at me?" She searched the captain's face. He'd make a superb poker player if he had ambitions in that realm. He merely drilled her with a blank look. Then, as if satisfied with her confusion, he leaned back and blew out a breath. She felt tension release its death-hold clutch.

"By the time we found the shooter's perch, he was long gone. We're combing it for evidence."

"I don't understand. You think this man has been following me?" She shook her head. "Why?"

The captain took the picture and stared at it for a long moment. She saw something dark flicker through his eyes, and it sent a cold streak down her spine. "I'm not sure. Do you know anything about Bazooka rocket launchers or SAMs?"

Her eyes widened.

He smiled, and suddenly her stomach curled in delight. Was it her imagination, or had the midnight hours turned the Beast into someone kind and friendly? The shadows gentled his hard angles, and in the soft dawn of the night, he seemed even. . . attractive?

So maybe there was more to the rumored jet-lag-induced

dementia than she gave credence.

He tucked the picture into the folder. "We're not even sure you were the intended target tonight. Perhaps he was after me—"

"But what about my hotel room?"

He held up a hand. "We just need to consider all the possibilities if we're going to unravel this mess." He closed the file and folded his hands atop it. "Please, would you tell me why you are in Russia and what you were doing today at the monastery?"

Her heart stopped hard, right against her ribs, and for the first time since her arrival, she wanted to chuck this entire adventure and race back to New York and the ho-hum safety of Matthew's arms.

"Have you been following me?" Her voice sounded as pinched as her courage.

He nodded, his face turning hard. "And you better be thankful I did, or you'd be on your way to the morgue right now."

That thought turned her cold. He'd been following her because he thought a killer was on her trail. Sixteen hours in Russia and already someone wanted her dead.

What was she doing here? Maybe all Matthew's angry prophecies were accurate. Silence became her betrayer as her eyes filled, and she hiccuped a sob that echoed off the walls.

Her dementia had latched on with a vengeance. Through blurry eyes, she saw Captain I-Am-Your-Nightmare Vadeem grimace, as if he'd been walloped hard. He looked away, rubbed his whiskered face with one of those powerful hands. Swallowed.

The big bad bodyguard actually looked. . .afraid?

"I'm. . .ah, *sorry*, Miss Moore. I shouldn't have been so. . . blunt." There was that tenderness again, the same warmth she'd heard in his voice seconds before she'd been tackled, and the kindness in it threatened to unravel her on the spot. She wrapped her arms around her waist and held in a vicious tremor as tears dropped off her chin.

She heard his chair scuff back, then felt his hand on her shoulder. Slowly, he knelt in front of her, then pulled her into his arms. She leaned awkwardly against him, the soft leather of his jacket cold against her cheek, her tears puddling on the smooth fabric. He said nothing, but rubbed a hand along her back. His five-o'clock shadow rubbed against her forehead, and he smelled of soap and leather and, most of all, safety. She closed her eyes and lost herself in the tender comfort of a stranger.

"Please, Miss Moore. Tell me what happened today at the monastery. Then I can get you on a plane for home and the nightmare can be over."

***

"I was aiming for Spasonov." Ilyitch didn't have to be in the room with Grazovich to feel his gunmetal gray eyes boring into him. His icy silence over the phone was enough to raze every open nerve.

"You nearly killed her." Grazovich's voice seemed strained, probably from choking up lies for the *Americanka* while he let him do his dirty work. Dirty Abkhazian. The former military general in what had been the Soviet republic of Georgia had turned thief. He was bent on financing Abkhazia's revolution by unearthing Mother Russia's secrets. The Georgians probably lost the war with their breakaway region on purpose, hoping to rid themselves of this wart to the north. Ilyitch had been out of his brain ten years ago to hook up with the Abkhazian terror forces. Brainless and desperate for cash.

Circumstances hadn't changed much over the course of the past decade.

"Did you at least take the key?" Grazovich had the consonant slur of a man who'd spent the better part of the evening investigating the inside of his Absolut bottle. The drinking had gotten worse since the Georgians had nabbed the general's brother. Torture must be knowing your flesh and blood sat in a rat-infested hole in Georgia, waiting for execution.

"I thought you wanted her to keep it," Ilyitch ground out. "You said, 'Let her lead us to the map first.' " He added just enough lilt to betray his lightly veiled disgust. *It's a fable*, he wanted to scream. But he kept that editorial to himself, remembering the icy clamp of leg irons against his flesh.

"Things have changed," Grazovich growled, affected by Ilyitch's mocking. "She didn't get the book. We'll have to find it ourselves. Get the key. She's wearing it around her neck."

Ilyitch let out a curse. "I could have snatched it this morn—"

"Get the key," Grazovich bit out. "My boy will do the rest."

Your boy's done enough all ready.

"What if 'your boy' is wrong?" Ilyitch kept his voice low, despite the fact no one would dare sneak up on him. He kept a safe distance from—and one eye on—a convention of FSB agents amassing in the hotel lobby. One turned and glanced in his direction. He turned away and leaned against the building, awash in shadow. "Let me grab her. She'll tell us what we want to know." The fact that Grazovich had her close enough to snatch—twice—and hadn't made Ilyitch want to put his fist through the cement wall. What games was the general playing? Miss Ekaterina Moore held the key to their plans—in more ways than one.

The thief on the other end remained silent. Frustration pushed into Ilyitch's tone. "You could have ended this in her hotel room instead of playing noble." He couldn't help but dig in the knife after seeing the way Grazovich had let her waltz up to her room—alone. "Were you thinking you'd romance it out of her?"

"You nearly killed her," the Abkhazian retorted. "We need

her alive and full of answers."

"Ah, a romantic. Perhaps that's why you love digging up Russia's soul."

"Russia has no soul. She sold it to the highest bidder years ago."

"Now you're a philosopher."

Grazovich lowered his voice and added a growl. "Get the key. Call me when you have it."

"It won't do us any good without the map."

"Just get the key, or you'll be wishing we had left you to rot."

Kat pulled the woolen hotel blanket over her shoulder and tried again to curve her body around three very pronounced peas in the mattress of her century-old hotel bed. The springs squealed when she moved, splicing her thoughts with the effectiveness of a blade. It had to be some further cruel jet-lag trickery that kept her mind from collapsing into sleep when her body felt as if she'd run a marathon. Her brain kept circling around two thoughts: she wasn't leaving, despite Captain Vadeem's posted guard and assertions to the contrary, and God had somehow vanished over the past twenty-four hours. Where was the Almighty when she needed Him? Certainly, throughout her life, she'd never needed Him more than now.

She tugged on her blanket. It slid up over her toes, and cool air nipped at them. She couldn't continue to stare at the pale walls. Sitting up, she clicked on the bedside lamp. A dusty glow fanned out over the red blanket. Kat reached for her backpack, hauling up dust balls from the floor under her bed as she plopped it on her lap. She found her pocket Bible inside and flipped to the bookmark. It opened to Psalms, and the words made her cringe.

"The Lord is a refuge for the oppressed, a stronghold in times of trouble. Those who know your name will trust in you, for you, Lord, have never forsaken those who seek you."

"Oh God, where are you now? Have I not sought You? Have I not trusted You?" Kat rubbed her face with her hands. Sleep tugged at her, but the ache inside would not subside. Just when she needed her faith the most, it seemed to crumble in her grip.

Would she be one of those spiritually poor who turned away from God when life smote them? Would her earthly pain eclipse her heavenly joy? God seemed much closer yesterday morning when life was in her grip. She closed the Bible. She had few choices here. Either God would come through or not. But in the end, she could only hang onto hope, or despair would run her over.

As if sparked by her determination to hold onto her unseen God, Scripture filled her mind. "Therefore put on the full armor of God, so that when the day of evil comes, you may be able to stand your ground, and after you have done everything, to stand."

When morning came, she wanted the entire Russian militia, and whoever had decided to stalk her with bullets, to see her standing.

The darkness would not overcome. Not when her brain had the power to pray.

She bowed her head. "Show me You haven't abandoned me, oh God. Help my faith to grow, and give me strength to stand."

She found herself curled with her Bible as she opened her eyes to sunshine streaming through filmy orange curtains and across the wooden floor. Rubbing the sleep from her eyes with her fingertips, she sat up. The cold floor on her bare feet jolted her to full consciousness. Outside, the city still slept. She peeked out the window. Dawn glinted on street signs and across car hoods and turned the windows in the building across the street to fiery gold.

Footsteps in the hallway creaked the wooden planks as someone padded up to the door. Kat tiptoed close and strained to hear voices. She knew Captain Vadeem had posted at least one guard out there, a result of her adamant declaration, articulated in two languages, that she wasn't leaving Russia.

After all his protection and convincing hug, he'd turned out to be just like every other Russian male she'd met yesterday. . . cold and rude when he wanted his way. And to think she'd practically cut out her heart and flopped it on the table for him to walk over. Why did she have to tell him her story? "I wanted to find my past." The sad look in his eyes now made her cringe. At the time, she'd read it as empathy. *Poor American girl, searching for her family in Russia.* Her throat felt raw, remembering the warm feelings she'd cultivated toward the man when she'd finally stopped sobbing. He'd let her spill her secrets right into the middle of the room, even pulling up a chair, leaning forward with his elbows on his knees, and listening. She'd revealed everything, from the mysterious secrets of Grandfather Neumann and the hope that lit when she intercepted the key, to the wretched news about Brother Timofea.

And when she finished, he made a grim face, patted her hand, and informed her that she was leaving Russia in the morning.

Her empty stomach twisted, remembering the tone in his voice.

"Will this bed need to be changed today?" The voice of the hall monitor filtered into her room. Kat pressed her ear gently against the paper-thin door.

"Yes," came the terse reply of the guard, obviously on edge

and fatigued by the midnight watch. She tried not to smile at that. "When does the café open, by the way?"

"It's open now."

Kat wondered what food would do to her flopping stomach. She knocked on the door, then opened it a crack.

The guard looked worse than he sounded. His eyes, draped in weariness, held no patience. She attacked with a smile. "Can someone get me a cup of cocoa?"

He shook his head. "I'm not allowed to leave you, *Zhenshina.*" His eyes narrowed, as if she'd committed a felony. She closed the door and leaned against it, a plan forming.

Ten minutes later, fully dressed in a pair of khaki pants and a white polo shirt, hair combed, teeth brushed, and looking as presentable as she could, she again cracked open the door. "I'm dressed. Let's go." She stepped out into the hall and ignored his glare. "I want breakfast, and it's my understanding that I'm not a prisoner. So, protect me or not, I'm going downstairs."

She threw her backpack over her shoulder and headed down the hall, her pace a challenge for her stiff muscles. Ignoring the elevator, she took the stairs. She heard his heavy breaths behind her, but didn't look back.

She found the café tucked into a small room off the lobby. Every plastic chair was empty. Thankful she'd remembered to convert money when she'd returned to the hotel the night before, she perched on a bar stool and ordered a hot chocolate. The hotel staff had seemed less than eager to accommodate her last night, and she couldn't blame them after her presence had put one of their rooms out of commission.

By the cool demeanor of the skinny waitress, news traveled quickly. The woman plopped the cocoa down and turned away as if Kat might have a contagious airborne disease.

Kat closed her eyes and sipped the cocoa slowly, the warmth

seeping into her still-weary bones and the caffeine jump-starting her heart. She just might live through this day.

The cop sat at a table behind her, his angry gaze drilling through the back of her neck. She ordered him a coffee and sent it to his table. He didn't touch it, perhaps zealous about his on-duty status.

Letting the coffee sit until it had cooled, Kat then rose and sauntered over to his seat. She had to enjoy his shocked look when she leaned one hand on the table. "Tell Captain Vadeem you did a good job last night."

Then she tipped the table, just enough to spill the coffee down his trousers. Whirling, she ran from the café, his fury echoing in her ears. She slammed out of the hotel doors, and suddenly the only sound was her own thundering heartbeat and the slap of her feet on the sidewalk. She hadn't won awards on her college track team for nothing. The scent of freedom filled her nose, and she ran nowhere and safely out of the grip of the Russian militia.

❦

"She says she's here looking for relatives." Vadeem rubbed his thumb and forefinger into his weary eyes, seeing only spikes of light against blankness as he pressed the cell phone to his ear. Ryslan's voice crackled on the other end, sounding a million kilometers away instead of across town at FSB HQ, where he'd spent an obscene portion of the night pushing paperwork. From Vadeem's position, he gathered that neither man was in a cheery mood. Vadeem's brain felt filled with wool, and every joint ached from sleeping on the fraying armchair down the hall from Grazovich's room. Thankfully, Pskov's FSB branch had decided to cooperate with their Moscow big brothers and set up surveillance on Grazovich so Vadeem could get some shut-eye. He didn't want to know where, or if, Ryslan had finally bedded down.

Despite the relative comfort of the hotel lobby, Vadeem had spent the better part of the wee hours contemplating Ekaterina Moore and her mysterious key, not to mention her amber brown eyes, the touch of her disheveled silky hair against his cheek, and the smell of her skin as she sobbed into his shoulder.

There he went again, entangling himself in her memory. He'd do well to remember that she was probably an arms dealer with a stellar ability to deceive. Physically shaking himself, he tried to focus on Ryslan's words. "Her parents are dead, but her visa application says she's part Russian."

"She said her grandfather is some sort of World War II hero," Vadeem said. "And she says she came looking for an old monk who sent her a key. Maybe they're related?"

"A key?" Ryslan's voice perked up. "What kind of key?"

"Some old relic. She's wearing it around her neck." Vadeem stalked to the hallway, peeked down at Grazovich's room. No movement told him the guy was still in his vodka stupor. "I'll tell ya, Ryslan, she looked me right in the eye, with tears, and told me that she just wanted to find her ancestors." He rubbed a tense muscle in the back of his neck, quickly giving up. "She's got her story cold."

"What if she's telling the truth? What if she is related to the old monk?"

"Yeah, and I'm related to the last czar." Vadeem nodded at a woman in a rumpled cocktail dress emerging from a room across the hall.

"Well, your highness, think on this. What if her *dadushka* hooked up with Timofea during the war? We had Americans running all over our borders. Or better yet, what if he found himself a nice little peasant girl and brought home a *Russki* souvenir."

"I thought the Americans stopped at Berlin."

"Not the partisans. There have always been rumors American OSS ran supplies in and organized missions throughout Estonia and Belorussia. Maybe he hooked up with Timofea through the partisan network. After all, no one can be trusted in war. . .not even a monk!" Ryslan laughed, and in the early morning, it sounded more like a snort.

Vadeem cringed. "So that could be a link to her past." Although after what she'd told him, the link had obviously been severed. The woman had him convinced, however briefly, that she'd come to visit the old monk. Her tears had certainly felt real—damp and hot. "What do you think about the key? Does it mean anything?"

"Nothing about a key in her file. What's up with Grazovich?"

"Sleeping like a baby in his room." Vadeem paced back to the floor lobby, trying to work life back into his muscles.

"Did he contact her again?"

"Yes, although I didn't get much of the conversation. I've never met anyone with her *tvordost*. She didn't even blink when I showed her the picture."

"He looks a lot different now. A plastic surgeon is a terrorist's best friend. You think she's on the level?"

Hearing his partner suggest it aloud fertilized all Vadeem's gut instincts. He did wonder, think, well okay, maybe just a teensy bit, that Miss Ekaterina Moore might be exactly who she played herself to be.

A naive, gutsy, in-trouble tourist.

"I don't know."

Ryslan said nothing, but in the silence, Vadeem heard his own voice, calling himself a fool. If this *Americanka* had nothing to do with the general's smuggling plot, then the real fence was out there—without even a hint of FSB surveillance. Vadeem wanted to bang his head against the wall.

"You'd better keep her in your sights, just to make sure," Ryslan said quietly, fatigue weighing his tone. "I'll watch the general."

"I'm putting her on a plane today." Vadeem tried not to remember her pitiful pleading, her tears, the way she hit him in the chest when he'd turned off what little part of his heart he could still feel and stood his ground. Yes, she'd chipped away at his gut instincts with her sob story. So much so, he spent the night wondering how a woman with such honest, honey-brown eyes could lie like a serpent and wishing, in the darkest corner of his soul, that he was wrong.

The sooner he got her out of Russia—and his mind—the sooner he could tail Grazovich with a vengeance. "If she's his contact, the general will start getting jumpy."

"Are you sure that's the best thing?" Ryslan asked. "If you're right, she could lead us right to our source."

Or down a rabbit trail that would cost him precious weeks of investigation. Besides. . . "Someone tried to mow her down last night in her hotel room. She's not staying in Russia."

He heard Ryslan swallow. "Just don't blow this, Vadeem. Remember your priorities." He clicked off the line.

Vadeem pocketed his cell phone, thankful the call had at least roused him early enough to get a cup of coffee before he had to wake poor Miss Moore.

"Captain Spasonov!"

The tone put to his name notched his pulse up a beat. He didn't like the hue of the sergeant's pallor nor the beads of sweat trickling down his wide face.

Vadeem's stomach clenched, and he instinctively knew before the agent said it.

"She's gone. The American has escaped."

V adeem leaned against the gate of the monastery cemetery, watching Ekaterina Moore trace her finger across
the lettering on a simple gravestone. How long had he
been watching her? He'd memorized the taut set of her jaw as
she lifted her face occasionally into the morning sun, the red
lines etched down her cheeks, her shoulders slightly slumped,
her long legs pulled up to her chest and locked with a firm arm.

If she was an arms dealer, she had her alibi down to a sci-
ence. The wind from the Velikaya River, not far off, teased the
hair around her face, now turned bronze by the remnant hues
of dawn.

She looked so bereft, his fury had disintegrated long ago.
She wore a face that said her hopes had turned to ashes. He had
a look of his own, just like it, tucked deep into his past. Perhaps
that was why he felt his suspicions dissolving like badly set
holidyetz—Russian meat gelatin.

It didn't help that he understood exactly what she was
searching for. Identity. Family. A connection. He'd listened to
her story last night with more than a healthy dose of empathy
and hated himself for having to be the bad guy. And the way
she'd leaned forward and let herself cry in his arms. . .well, it
made him feel something he'd long forgotten.

Needed.

But he couldn't sacrifice Miss Moore to soothe the demons

from his past. Grazovich obviously wanted something, and Vadeem couldn't chance letting her get in the smuggler's sights. She'd be flying back to New York by tomorrow morning.

Then Ekaterina Moore, suspected arms dealer, likely tourist, would be out of the equation.

He waited until she looked toward the rocky cliffs that formed a natural fence between the river and monastery grounds. Then he edged out into the cemetery. He kept his hands in his pockets, but every muscle bunched, ready to spring should she see him and try to flee.

A meadowlark called Vadeem's presence, but Miss Moore didn't budge. He drew closer, and his shadow betrayed him. She stiffened.

"I thought I'd find you here," Vadeem said and was surprised to hear compassion in his voice.

She hung her head. "I realized I had nowhere to go. Except here."

"And home."

She said nothing, but she winced, obviously wounded. He crouched beside her and gently drew her gaze to his. Pain edged her eyes.

"Maybe Brother Timofea just wanted you to see the place where he lived," he said in an unfamiliar tone.

"He knew he was dying." She looked so pitiful, it drew him right in. He felt her pain spear his heart before he could block it. "The monk told me Brother Timofea's dying wish was that I get the package. From the postmark, however, it looks like it took a year to send it. Why? And why was it so important to him that I have an old key?"

"There were no clues in his cell?"

Her hazel eyes darkened. "They told me they cleaned it out long ago. No. Nothing remains except this grave."

A breeze rode in from the river, bringing with it the fresh, wet smell. Vadeem sat beside her in the grass and read the cement gravestone. "1898–2001. That's a long time to live."

"Especially if you're carrying around a secret." She worried her lower lip, and it gave her a pensive look. "Do you think he was trying to pass it on to someone else, maybe in absolution?"

"Why you?"

She shook her head. Bags hung in half moons under her eyes, and her face was drawn. "Maybe I'm a relative?"

"To a monk?" He smiled. Her pitiful half-smile drove the spears in farther.

There was only one way out of this, and he knew it.

"I'll tell you what, Miss Moore. The train for Moscow doesn't leave until this afternoon. We have at least two hours before we need to head back to Pskov. You promise not to go running off again, and we'll see what we can find out from these brothers between now and then."

The real smile seemed like a blast of pure sunshine, washing over his wounds. Her eyes lit up, and something jumped to life deep inside his chest. She nodded. "Maybe you should call me Kat."

Two hours with her would pass like a blink.

He placed a call to the Three-Letter Boys watching Grazovich. The man had dressed, paced his room, and received a phone call. They were working on a tap, but so far, they didn't have a glimmer of a lead on the identity of his contact. "Don't let him out of your sight." Vadeem closed the phone and turned his full, and willing, attention on the American with a knack for trouble, telling himself he was only doing his job.

Right. He'd never been good at fooling himself, but he would cling to that rationale like a dying man as he followed her fragrance across the cemetery and through the front gates.

He'd never been inside a monastery before. Not that he'd spent much time availing himself of the opportunity, but when he entered the enclave, his senses awoke and sat at attention. From the manicured lawn, the sound of magpies and sparrows, the smell of spring reaped from the budding lilac, jasmine, and cherry blossoms, to the clean, pure whitewash on the buildings, the compound whispered *haven*. Vadeem rubbed his chest, feeling a pinch deep inside.

Kat seemed to know where she was going. A spring in her step, something new that he wanted to think he'd added, made her seem a carefree tourist bouncing through the campus. He followed her to an office building. Inside, the austere white walls, the planked floor, and the smell of polish whisked him back in time to the painful halls of his childhood.

Institutions were all the same.

He clenched his jaw. This was no haven.

A tall monk dressed in the traditional garb of brown tunic and somber expression met them at a reception desk. "Can I help you?"

Vadeem flipped open his identification. The monk met it with a stoic face that had Vadeem wondering how often they had the FSB darken their doors. "We'd like to see the director."

Efficient as he was stern, the monk had Vadeem and Kat seated inside the rather humble office of Father Lashov within moments. Father Lashov stared out the window at the limestone formations, his hands tucked into the sleeves of his tunic as he mulled over their situation.

"I don't know how I can help you." He turned, and he had the wise eyes Vadeem would associate with a religious man.

Or a seasoned agent. Vadeem tried not to shift under the man's scrutiny. What was it about men of the cloth that caused panic to climb up his spine? He felt like regurgitating every last secret he'd swallowed over the past twenty years. He gulped the gathering lump in his throat and eked out an FSBish tone.

"Miss Moore just wants answers to her questions. I know Brother Timofea is dead, but can you lead us to anyone who might know why he'd want to send a key to Miss Moore in America?"

Kat sat forward, and he felt freshly punched at the raw anticipation on her face. She had poured so much hope into this trip, into these two hours. He was going to make dead sure she got any information they had.

"I suppose you could talk to Brother Papov. He attended Brother Timofea until his last breath."

"Yes!" Kat was out of her seat, and Vadeem put a hand on her arm.

She looked at him, delight brightening her expression. Oh my, if he could get that kind of smile to appear. . .

"Sounds good. How do we find him?"

"Our cloister is what they call a 'working' monastery," the old monk explained as he led them out of the compound into the fields beyond. "We keep cows, horses, sheep, pigs, chickens, and raise our own crops." The sun gleamed through an azure, cirrus-scattered sky and turned the potato sprouts emerald green. Monks moved like ants over the field, working under the sun, their heads covered with straw hats. "We try to have as little contact with the outside as possible."

He turned to his assistant, a tall monk who walked beside Father Lashov like a bodyguard. The father whispered something to him, and the man strode over to another brother, lean and small and in his mid-twenties. The younger man came up to them without a smile, but curiosity ringed his brown eyes. Then his gaze settled on Kat.

He flinched.

The saintly kid knew something. Vadeem watched him hide it, but fear streaked into the young monk's eyes, now shifted away and down. The young monk rocked from heel to toe, listening to Father Lashov's explanation of their presence, nodding as if agreeing to help. He even shook Vadeem's hand, his grip loose and weak.

But the young brother never let his gaze travel back to Kat.

"Where can we talk?" Vadeem asked, hoping to get out of the sun, away from the sight of so many monks wielding rudimentary farm implements. He wasn't sure how loyal they were. . . . Didn't monks have some sort of nonaggression code?

"Perhaps the chapel." Father Lashov led the way beyond the white fence, past the field toward the limestone cliffs. "The monastery is quite old," he said like a tour guide to his little ensemble. "Dating back to the first century, the first cells were in these limestone cliffs. We had our cells, a kitchen, a threshing room, and barns. The cliffs even hosted our first chapel. Perhaps you will find it a soothing place to ask your questions." He flicked a gaze at Vadeem, no menace in his eyes. "Brother Timofea often spent his later years in this place of worship. Perhaps it will hold peace for you, as well."

He stopped before a small grotto, the walls carved out of limestone, gleaming whitewash over gray stone. The tiny cave spoke of orderliness. Two wooden candleholders guarded the inside entrance, homemade judging from their rough-hewn form, but perfect accessories in the irregular chapel. At the far end of the room, the cross of Christ loomed center stage, a carved figure of the Savior hanging in gnarled agony. Vadeem tried to ignore it. Behind the crucifix, pockets dug from the surface held over a dozen tiny, lit candles, flickering golden light along the shadows of the cave. The walls smelled damp, and dust rose from the floor. An icon of St. Nickolas hung on the wall, his mournful golden face and oval eyes gliding over Vadeem, as if scrutinizing his soul when Vadeem stepped into the grotto. He looked away, tensing.

The priest moved forward and lit a candle in a stand near the cross. The brothers gazed in silence as the smoke spiraled heavenward. Vadeem fought the urge but found his gaze forced to the cross, gleaming in the candlelight. The thorn-ringed head of Jesus, glinting from polish, seemed to liven as flame flickered across the carved face.

Vadeem froze. Memory assaulted him like a tidal wave. Behind his eyes, he watched as the reflection turned to fire, then engulfed the cross, its tongue licking at the wooden Savior. He heard screaming, then his name. His breath clogged in his chest as his throat tightened. He braced a hand on the grotto wall, the world cutting into angles.

The father started to lecture in his garbled voice about the history of the chapel, how it was used as a hideout for the partisans in World War II, something about artifacts left behind, hidden in the walls, but the voice spiraled out, as if in a tunnel. Vadeem's heartbeat filled his ears. He could smell the smoke, feel the heat as it beaded on his skin. *Save the Bible!* Then a hand gripped his arm—

"Captain, are you okay?" Kat looked at him, her eyes probing.

He backpedaled out, bumping into one of the candleholders, sending it thumping to the ground. His shoulder skimmed the doorway as he stumbled through the entrance.

The fresh air hit him like a slap. He filled his lungs with the freedom of outdoors, hands on his knees, gulping for breath like a man drowning.

What was he thinking, walking back inside a chapel—a church? Twenty plus years and he still couldn't face it.

"Are you okay?" Kat's worried voice made him bristle. He

straightened and fought for composure. The sweet concern in her eyes made something twist inside his chest. He nodded, his voice trapped in the past.

Some things would never be okay.

***

"Brother Timofea was like a father to me. I had the privilege of serving him the last five years of his life." The young monk Papov sat in the grass, legs crossed, his spine board-straight and hands tucked into the sleeves of his robe. If Kat hadn't known better, she would have felt like she was sitting in her office, listening to a potential young father outline his qualifications, nerves pinching his voice thin. The young monk never looked up, never met her eyes.

It sent a chill through her bones.

"What about the key?" she urged.

Beside her, Captain Vadeem proved little help. Despite the sun adding color to his angular face, he still seemed spooked. Sitting in the grass, he appeared a sullen contrast to the bright chirp of sparrows, the wind combing the willows to the south, the late morning sun winking and turning the ground into a lush emerald carpet.

The sweet spring air hinted at a glorious day, especially if she could wheedle some answers out of the skinny monk, but all the captain could do was pick at the grass, as if searching for the ends to his fraying composure, oblivious to the fact she was trying to have the most important conversation in her life.

"I only saw the key once. When I helped him package it."

"How did he get my address? How did he know me?"

"He had a picture of you."

Kat wrestled with her racing heartbeat. "Of me? How?"

"It was in his Bible."

"Do you still have it?" This news had stirred Captain Vadeem out of his stupor.

Papov shot a look at Spasonov. "I'm not sure. Perhaps. I gathered his things and gave them to the father. I don't know."

"Did he have any other pictures?" Kat asked. "Anything else that might tie me to him?"

"One other picture. A black-and-white of a woman. I think she was American. Her name was Russian, however. I remember it, because he said it sometimes in prayer. Nadezhda."

"Hope," Kat whispered. She fingered the shoelace that held the key around her neck. "That was my mother's name."

She felt the captain's eyes on her, burning into her. "How would he know your mother?"

"She was Russian, or at least her mother was Russian. I think my grandfather met my grandmother here, during the war."

"Perhaps Timofea was related to your grandmother."

Papov shook his head. "Brother Timofea had no family. He had a few horror stories. Some relatives died in the Red Army massacre in 1918, others at the hands of the Nazis. But I'm pretty sure he was the sole survivor. He once told me about it."

Kat leaned back on her hands, her palms digging into the dirt. She lifted her face to the bloom of the sun. "I never met my grandmother. She died when my mother was a baby."

"I'm sorry." This from Captain Vadeem. She met his blue eyes and saw genuine sympathy, the kind that knows pain. It found a soft place in her heart, right next to the memory of him saving her life.

"It's okay," she said, fighting free of the thought. "My mother was raised by a loving father. He never remarried, but we know he loved Grandmother. Her name was Magda."

"So Brother Timofea somehow knew Miss Moore's mother." Captain Vadeem seemed to be recovering, his voice gaining strength, energy outlining his blue eyes. He seemed worlds apart from the shell-shocked soldier who'd looked like he'd seen death materialize from the chapel walls.

Or like a child who'd just watched his world crumble.

It ripped a hole in her heart. She knew too many children whose worlds had shattered. It hurt to see the experience relived on an adult. What secrets did Captain Vadeem Spasonov have hidden behind those bone-piercing blue eyes?

He turned them on her, and for a second, they rattled her right off her footing.

She'd better get a grip on her goals. She'd come to Russia to unearth her past, not to drown in the rugged magnetism of a Russian cop, even if he did have dark, curly hair that begged to be smoothed and arms that still made her tremble when she thought of them locked around her. . . .

She forced her voice out of heart-struck paralysis and stared pointedly at the young monk. "Brother Timofea never mentioned the key or me? Just one day decided to send me a letter?" Her voice was harsh, but her time ticked down.

"He was a strong man. His quiet presence always gave me strength to face my fears. But he was aged, and after awhile, his old bones wouldn't allow him to kneel to pray. He told me that God asked him to fulfill the promise."

"Fulfill the promise? What promise?"

"An old promise. Something from his youth. He began to see people who were long gone, perhaps memories dredged up by a mind sorting out time and place. One day we had a conversation, only he spoke not to me, but someone else. 'Oksana,' he said, 'He has promised, and He is faithful. He will repay the years the locusts have eaten.'"

Papov paused, his voice low and choppy. "Even in senility, he had more faith than I have in my youth."

Kat blinked at him. "But you're a monk. Your life is devoted to God."

He sighed. "I have few moments to truly test my faith. It is not faith honed from the scrapes and blows of life in this world, but rather something I cling to in the hope it will shelter me from that which might destroy me." His wretchedness scraped across Kat's heart. She winced and shot a look at the monastery, the white walls that sheltered the brothers from the brutal world. Surely, this monk wasn't recanting his vows to a pair of strangers?

"Isn't that what faith is, though? A shelter in the storm of life?" Kat resisted the urge to reach out and pat the monk's hand like she might to reassure a young parent that the child he'd waited for so long would join their family soon.

"I believe faith must be more," Papov replied. "Perhaps it is not something to hide behind, but to give us vision. Help us see clearly. The faith of Brother Timofea was true faith. He saw the Master's hand in everything. He had discovered something. . . more about God." His voice pinched into the tight tenor of grief. "I still miss him."

Kat glanced at Captain Vadeem and saw the planes of his face harden, his gaze turn dark and hone in on the monk. "Faith does not give vision, Brother. It betrays and destroys and crushes."

His words punched the breath out of Kat. She stared, shocked dumb, at the captain as he pounced to his feet. "Come, Kat. It's time to go. Your visit in Russia is over."

CHAPTER SIX

No!" Kat's plaintive voice stabbed at him. "I'm not ready!"

Vadeem forced himself to ignore her protests and stalked through the cemetery toward the road. She'd better be on his tail. He wasn't above turning around, slapping her in handcuffs, and hauling her bodily to the train station.

Faith, indeed. Oh, yes, he knew all about faith. How it deceived and hurt. How it killed. He balled his fists and made a deliberate effort to slow his rocketing heartbeat.

"Please, Captain. I need to know more. How did Brother Timofea know my family? How did he know me?"

He heard the unspoken plea in the echo of her words. *Who am I? Where do I fit into this puzzle of life? To whom do I belong?* He kept walking, furious at the burning in his eyes, at the tempest of emotions this little two-hour excursion had whipped up. He was dangerously close to reliving every nightmare he'd been dodging for twenty years, and he had no one to thank but a feisty runaway with a knack for choosing the wrong friend. "Let's go," he growled, not caring that he sounded like some remnant from the Cold War. "Train's leaving."

"No!"

He winced. *Don't make me cart you out of here like a two year old.* He turned and wrung out a polite tone. "Yes. I'm sorry, Kat, but you're leaving Russia today. And if I have to throw you over my shoulder and haul you to the train kicking and screaming, I'm prepared to do that."

"Over my dead body." She stood in the middle of the cemetery, hands on her hips. The wind teased her hair around her face. Her eyes shimmered with fire.

Vadeem sucked in a breath, feeling like he'd been punched in the chest. American to the bone, she actually *glared* at him, like he was her hired farmhand who'd just ditched her with a ripe-for-harvest crop in the field.

"I don't think we'll have to go that far." He strode over, picked up her backpack, and shoved it into her arms. "But rules are rules."

He bent down, grabbed her around the knees, and threw her over his shoulder.

***

Ilyitch stepped off the train and turned up his collar against the crisp Moscow wind. The train belched, and smoke clogged the already polluted sky. Ilyitch lit a cigarette, then crossed the street where a shiny *Moscovitz* waited. He threw the bag in first, then climbed into the backseat.

The driver didn't even turn around. Ilyitch let a smile tweak his cheek as he watched Moscow hustle by. Twelve hours in Pskov had turned his stomach raw. Wooden huts, sunken by time and the shifting earth, ringed the town like a barricade of slums. Only six hours by car from Moscow, the city—the grand Pskov where Czar Nikolai had abdicated the throne—made Ilyitch burn with shame. With her outhouses, central water pumps, and coal smoke spiraling from hovels built in the Lenin era, Pskov embodied the sudden halt of progress. Thankfully, Moscow had marched on. As had Ilyitch. Capitalism wasn't just for the West. Wasn't it Gorbachev who said, "Sell anything, sell it all!"?

He'd taken the old boss at his word.

The car ground to a halt, snared in traffic. Ilyitch considered hoofing it, but he didn't need to ignite any suspicions. He sat back in the seat, cracked the window, and flicked out the cigarette. Spasonov would be boarding the train by now. By tonight, Ekaterina Moore would be back in the city. His city.

A city he'd just as gladly kiss good-bye as decrepit Pskov. No more drizzly Moscow days where the cold dug into his bones. No more traffic, no more press of crowds. No more apartments the size of an American bathroom.

He'd get the key. Get Grazovich's hidden treasure. And get out of Russia.

Kat folded her hands across her chest and tried to figure out where her life had begun to unravel. Twenty-four hours earlier, she had teetered on the edge of her past. Today she was drowning in confusion and fury. No thanks to her not-in-this-lifetime former hero, who had her under virtual arrest on the commuter train. She crossed her arms over her chest and glared at him.

He had tilted his head back, his eyes all but closed as if he were exhausted. Served him right. She was no lightweight, and he didn't have to carry her halfway back to the hotel or hold her hand like a flighty preschooler all the way to the train. She had comprehended his meaning about 2.3 seconds after he picked her up like a sack of grain.

She was going home. Quest over. Door to the past slammed shut.

Tears burned her eyes, and she gnawed her lower lip to keep it from trembling. She could claw his eyes out for stealing from her the only dream she'd ever had. A thousand descriptive words rose unbidden, and she forced them back, deep inside, fighting instead to accept her future. *God*, she moaned, *don't send me home without answers.*

Fulfill the promise. What did Timofea mean? The question made her cry aloud.

She clamped her hand over her mouth, horrified.

Captain Spasonov roused, opened his eyes, and looked at her.

She blinked back her tears and stared down at her new hiking boots, now scuffed and dirty, feeling mortified.

"I'm sorry, Kat. But you have to trust me." He spoke quietly, an unwelcome balm on her razed emotions. "I'm only trying to keep you safe."

"You can't possibly know what you're destroying." Her tone made the tears spill in a hot flow down her face.

To make it worse, he scooted over to face her, his knees bumping hers. He handed her a handkerchief, and when she refused it, he dabbed the tears from her cheeks himself. She flinched and pulled away.

Hurt flickered across his face, as if her feelings actually *meant* something to him. She wanted to slap him.

He sighed. "Tell me what is so important that you'd risk your life."

"Is that what I'm doing?" She forced her chin to remain steady and met his eyes. They seemed genuinely concerned for her.

"I believe Grazovich wants something from you. If he didn't, he wouldn't have spoken to you or pressed his luck at customs, much less have tried to pass off as coincidence your reunion on the train."

"I still can't believe you think that nice professor is a terrorist." She swallowed hard, seeing Spasonov's face harden. Anger streaked through his expression. She winced. Then she remembered Taynov's eyes. Old, battle-weary eyes. *Maybe.*

"It doesn't matter what you believe. What matters is what I know. And I don't want you hurt."

His gentle words hit her in a soft place. Her heart lodged in her throat, and she struggled to speak. "You don't?" she squeaked.

He smiled, and an unfamiliar tenderness gathered around his eyes. "Absolutely not." Then he ran a finger down the side of her face and scooped up a tear.

The kind gesture made her freeze. He must have read her body language, for he immediately withdrew his hand. "Are you hungry?" He tried to hide his embarrassment, but she saw it creep into his face.

She sat up, wiped her eyes. "Maybe. Thank you, Captain." Perhaps he wasn't such a hard-hearted creep after all. He did have blue eyes that looked like the ocean at dusk, eyes that were deep and mysterious, hiding a multitude of secrets—maybe even treasures.

"Call me Vadeem." He smiled and seemed nearly boyish, charm and innocence wrapped together in a heartwarming package. "What would you like?"

She rubbed her arms, feeling goose bumps. "Maybe some M&M's?"

He laughed. "For lunch? C'mon, Kat. You need to eat better than that. I bet I can scrounge up some fruit juice from the food cart, maybe some peanuts."

"M&M's. Plain. I don't do peanuts with my chocolate."

He smiled, her first glimpse into a true friendship, and shook his head. "You Americans. You don't know how to eat right. You live on carbs and chocolate—"

"And soda, don't forget that." She only half-hated the fact she'd warmed to his teasing.

"America has turned Russia into a land of junk food." He signaled to a woman pushing a cart down the aisle. "I need to teach you how to eat, I can see." He pointed to two cartons of apple juice, a banana, and a bag of plain M&M's. Kat reached for the bag, but he snatched it back, burying it in his lap while he paid the vendor.

"Not until you have some real food." He opened the apple juice and handed it over. Kat made a face but liked the way he waggled his eyebrows at her. She drank the liquid down.

"Now some potassium." When he held out the banana, she snatched the M&M's from his lap. He frowned.

"Gimme the banana. I'll show you how Americans eat fruit." She opened the bag of candy. Vadeem eyed her with suspicion as he handed over the fruit. Kat peeled the banana, then carefully put one M&M in the center. "Chocolate has protein, you know. It's made from beans." Then she bit off the banana, taking the candy with it.

Vadeem's blue eyes widened. "That can't taste good."

"Try it." She handed over the fruit and the bag of candy.

Vadeem had strong hands, fingers that were clean. He tore off a piece of banana and made his own treat. She laughed at the grimace he made as he swallowed it down.

"Oh, it's been putrefied!" He gulped down a healthy swig of apple juice. "How do you stay all trim and leggy with this kind of diet?"

His compliment left her speechless.

His smile dimmed and he held up a hand. "No, don't answer that."

Kat wrinkled her nose at him, hoping to reclaim the light moment, desperately needing it after the last twenty-four hours. "I supplement with Diet Coke. It cancels out the calories due to fruit."

His deep melodic laughter filled the train, turning heads. Kat let it absorb her and soothe her fraying nerves.

"I've met a true junk-food junkie," he said, shaking his head.

"What? Do I look like a potato chip?"

He studied her with a smirk and tease in his eyes, then shook his head. "Not in the least."

Her heart thumped hard against her chest as his gaze held hers, reached out, and drew her in.

"I would never mistake you for a Pringle."

Oh, her heart fell down to her knees. She forced herself to breathe and found a smile. "No, just an M&M, huh?"

He shrugged. "Maybe. Hard and crusty on the outside, sweet on the inside?"

She fought another smile. The last thing she wanted to do was truly enjoy this man's company. He stood between her and her past. . .and she had serious plans to ditch him the second they got off the train. She couldn't afford to leave behind a piece of her heart—

What was she thinking? She'd known the man for less than twenty-four hours.

It seemed like a decade.

Kat shifted on the hard bench seat, suddenly weary to her bones. The smell of diesel churned up from the wheels and drifted through the open windows of the train. She sat facing the rear of the car, watching wooded scenery stretch out as they traveled east. The low sun sent streams of golden-orange light through the windows, across the bench seats.

Vadeem finished off his juice. "Done with that?" He gestured to her crumpled box. Kat nodded mutely and handed him the trash. He took both cartons in one hand and stood up, in search of the garbage can.

Kat took the chance and really looked at the man who had protected her from bullets, helped her dig for answers at the monastery, dragged her like a sack of potatoes to the train, and finally made her laugh. The wind ruffled his chocolate brown hair, which curled deliciously at the nape of his neck. He had good balance in the swaying train; his presence filled the compartment like someone who knew how to walk into a room, grasp the situation, and take immediate command. He tossed the juice cartons in the trash, turned, and started back. A five-o'clock shadow had begun to accrue on his face, adding a hint of rogue to his already powerful persona. Dressed in a black leather jacket, a black shirt, and dark pants, he reminded her of a gangster, something out of an "Escape from New York" movie.

He sat down, his feet planted, his powerful hands on his knees, as if ready to pounce. She knew from firsthand experience that he could—and would—spring to action like a panther. The memory of his chest, rock hard and tense as he protected her from bullets, shuddered through her mind. He didn't have the build of a man who spent off-hours at the gym, but of one who worked hard, his muscles lean and solid. She wondered what he did in his time off. Biked maybe, or even swam.

Captain Vadeem Spasonov emanated strength and confidence. He wore it in his stride, in his hands, in his eyes that didn't back down despite her tears.

Then why had he nearly crumbled at the monastery? Something had turned him inside out and left him ragged. Something roamed around his memory like a lion, waiting to devour.

Perhaps it already had.

She put out a hand and touched him on the knee. He startled. "Vadeem, what happened at the monastery? You looked like you'd seen a ghost."

His eyes widened, and the raw look that entered his face swiped the breath clean out of her chest. "I–I can't talk about it." He drew in a deep breath and looked away. She could have sworn she heard a door slam. "I won't."

Oh, how she suddenly longed to do what he'd done to her—throw him over her shoulder and muscle him into telling her what he was running from. Instead, she sat back, took a breath, and settled into her role as an adoption coordinator. "So, where did you grow up?" She kept her voice light, not wanting him to know she was digging. She added a smile to her question, sweet and concerned.

He instantly relaxed. For the briefest moment, she wondered if his walls-up response had been her imagination. But she saw the way he played with his fists when he spoke, cracking the knuckles one by painful one. "There isn't much to tell. My parents died when I was eight. I grew up in an orphanage."

"Ouch," she said. "I'm sorry." She squirmed under the thought of him without someone who loved him, someone like her grandfather. How had he survived? She knew what loss was all about, had buried her own parents. But at least Grandfather Neumann never let her feel the full brunt of that pain. "How did they die?"

He looked away, his face taut.

Kat backpedaled, found a new course. "How did you get to be a police officer?"

He drew a deep breath, as if exorcizing some nightmare, then he leaned forward, hands clasped, elbows across his knees, and looked up at her. "You're pretty curious."

"I want to know the man who risked his life for me."

A definite blush crept into his face, and it made her smile. She didn't soften the compliment any with a giggle, just let it sink into the budding relationship.

He looked away, and she thought she'd lost him when he suddenly replied, "Actually I'm not a cop. I'm part of a counterterrorist unit in the Russian secret service, part of the FSB."

She wanted to stop him there, wrap her brain around that information and the questions that rose like an inferno, but Vadeem continued, as if she met spies every day. "I guess it started when I went into the military right after high school. Most kids from the orphanage don't have the chance to go to college. But that was okay. I liked military life. It wasn't so different from what I'd grown up with."

She tried to imagine him spit poor, owning nothing but the clothes on his back, lining up for bowls of food with big eyes like the children she'd seen on the adoption tapes their field workers sent in. She ached for what he'd been forced to overcome. No wonder he was such a health-food fanatic.

"The military and I got along well enough that I was promoted and asked to join the Red Berets."

"Red Berets?" Kat echoed.

"They are similar to your army's Green Berets. We were the elite, trained for special operations."

Her eyes widened at the image of him dressed in fatigues, holding an AK-47, black grease smeared across his rugged face. No wonder he carried himself like a soldier. She had no doubt he'd been one of the best. "Did you see any action?"

He shook his head, his smile crooked, his eyes etched in secrets when they caught hers.

Okay, so maybe she didn't need to know that. "So how did you get into the FSB?"

"This I can answer." He leaned back, settling both arms across the seat back, visibly relaxed. The gesture made her smile. "I was in special ops for ten years. It was good work, but I just felt like it was time to. . .get out." He ducked his head. "I thought I might want to find someone to, uh, maybe, settle down with. And you can't do that when you travel all over the planet 280 days of the year."

Settle down. Was he. . .her heart wobbled on the edge of a surprisingly painful fall. "And, did you?" she squeaked, horrified at her tone.

Those eyes saw right through her question. He looked at her, a grin that looked downright dangerous tugging at his face. "Not yet. I'm still looking for the right girl."

"Oh." A lump the size of Niagara Falls lodged in her throat. She fought to swallow it down, aware that her face had turned hot and that he was now openly grinning at her obvious discomfort. Where was her wit when she needed it? Her mind went blank.

"And what about you, Kat Moore? Have you found the right man to settle down with back in New York? Do you have anyone who waits for you there, who makes you laugh, who calls you *maya doragaya?*"

His soft endearment sent warmth in a wave to her toes. But she blinked at him, afraid of what she saw written in his eyes. "I," she swallowed hard, "thought we were talking about you."

A shadow crossed his face, his expression wary. "I'm sorry," he whispered. "I guess we were."

"It's okay," she murmured, but something heavy settled on her chest. She hadn't traveled to Russia to find anything but her past. But she'd seen, very clearly, her future traced in the gaze of the FSB cop, and something about it sent a tingle of fear up her spine.

She liked it way too much.

CHAPTER SEVEN

The Moscow sky glittered like a cache of diamonds poured out on velvet, a perfect canopy of romance as Vadeem walked Kat to the Hotel Rossia. He carried her suitcase, rather than dragging it behind him. Kat had balled her fists at her sides, her jaw tight. Anger rimmed her eyes.

So much for romance. Not that any cop in his right mind would consider it after Kat's dash-and-dodge at the train station.

The sneaky vixen had tried to ditch him. As they'd climbed down from the train, he conveniently wrestling with her suitcase, she'd started wheeling through the crowd like an American football player. It felt like a knife in the gut. Especially after he'd actually begun to trust her, well, at least cultivated the *desire* to trust her. Especially when she dug up his past, then acted as if she cared. Her soft words, her tender expression—they unearthed his long buried feelings and made him feel. . .safe.

His throat grew raw just thinking about it. A guy with his past should have an ironclad heart. Instead he'd let Kat's laughter and the counterfeit honesty in her eyes creep under his guard. He'd even started flirting with her. Flirting! More than that, he'd spent about a hundred kilometers cataloguing ideas on how to ease her pain over sending her packing. A fancy dinner had been at the top of the list.

Her fifty-meter dash put a foot through those budding hopes. He'd caught up to her halfway through the train station, and their seedling friendship died an ugly death. Even with an accent, the words "bully" and "creep" stung. When he'd reminded her that she could easily be wearing handcuffs, she gave him a look that might melt nuclear waste.

Oh yeah, she'd yanked up by the roots all tendrils of trust.

Life would improve about three thousand percent when he shoved her on an airplane for America.

Despite the June air, Vadeem shivered. Beside him, Miss Catch-Me-If-You-Can didn't acknowledge his presence. Or the fact that he hauled her bag through Moscow like an underpaid porter.

Egoistaya Americanka.

He wasn't going to give in to her tears, either, although he felt nearly pummeled by her sobs—Plan B on her list of crafty escape methods. But he wouldn't consider pulling her into his arms—to lift his weapon or perhaps worse. And gauging from her white-faced response to the Russian endearment he'd murmured on the train, even if she wasn't an international con artist, and that was a big *if,* she'd obviously rather suffer alone than let a Russian cop soothe her pain.

If only for a moment under the soft canopy of the train lights, he actually thought he'd met the one person who could understand his demons. *"You can't possibly know what you are destroying,"* she'd said. Oh yes, he knew. Better than she could imagine. He knew all about the longing to belong. To have a family. He understood how it felt to stare at the ceiling, conjuring up parents. Conjuring up love. Pain coiled around his chest and squeezed as he glanced at her, stomping along, her frustration audible in occasional gut-wrenching sighs. Oh, he knew exactly what he was making her give up. . .*destroying*, as she put it. If she was, truly, simply an American on a personal mission, he understood exactly why she'd tried to ditch him, twice. If he wasn't tied up thwarting an international thug, he might even help her shake the truth out of the skinny monk.

Who was Timofea, indeed? And what exactly did Kat's key unlock?

More than that, if she was innocent, what did Ivan Grazovich want with a beautiful *Americanka* from New York State?

Some questions would have to remain unanswered.

The last thing Vadeem needed right now was a distraction with caramel-colored hair and eyes that dug a hole through a man's walls. It pained him more than he wanted to admit that when he'd called her "my dear one," somewhere deep inside he wanted to mean it.

Down, Boy. Vadeem drew in a calming breath. He kept his eyes ahead, off her profile, off the way she walked beside him, resolute, waves of anger rolling off her shoulders.

For the first time in two days, he wished his instincts were dead wrong.

The din of evening traffic had settled to a low murmur. The clang of trolley cars occasionally dented the air and mingled with the rumble of late-night buses. The smell of baking bread wafted out of a nearby factory and found a hole in his stomach. It groaned, and he grimaced. She must be starved as well.

"Would you like to stop and get something to eat?"

She shook her head.

So she wouldn't look at him now. He clenched his jaw.

Red Square loomed ahead. The walls of the Kremlin, a fortress from the past, rose shadowed and jagged against the navy sky. On the other side of the square, Hotel *Rossia* sparkled like a casino. He'd called ahead and reserved a deluxe room. He was still debating whether he should post a guard.

"Do you think I can trust you to stay put until morning?"

She pursed her lips.

Yes, definitely a guard. Maybe two.

They stopped at the streetlight. Ahead stood Lenin's museum, dark and foreboding with its grandiose czarist architecture. The brick building cast a bulky shadow across the street, through puddles of streetlights. Vadeem took Kat's arm. She tensed, but he pulled her across the street into the envelope of shadow, toward the hotel.

He stepped onto the sidewalk and released his grip.

He heard a crack as pain exploded in his head. Hitting the ground, knees first, he caught himself on his palms. He felt like the top of his head had come off. The world swirled in darkness and light.

Somewhere distant he heard screaming.

The next blow drove his chin into the cement. Darkness crashed. Swallowed. Took him deep, flooding him with memory. And nightmare.

The wind howled like a spirit, moaning, clawing at the house as snow piled against the door. Vadick felt no fear. The two-room shack radiated warmth—in love and in temperature. Fumes and heat crept out like watchmen from the coal furnace in the center of the room to every corner of the house, playing sentry against the frigid Siberian blizzard.

"Borscht tonight, Mama?" Vadick slid onto a bench, his woolen valenki boots now touching the floor. He'd grown three centimeters just this fall and was proud to see the chip on the door that marked his progress edging closer to Max's tally.

"Shee, Vasha. Meat is for Sundays." Mama ladled out four bowls and set them on the rough-hewn table. The smell curled off the top like fingers, clawing at his empty stomach. "Go, wash for dinner."

Vadick crawled off the bench and ran to the bucket sitting by the door. He grabbed a chip of soap and scrubbed his fingers. The chilly water sent a thousand icicles through his arms as he plunged them in to his elbows.

The outside door thumped, then voices—Papa and Maxim, back from the store to purchase fresh bread to accompany the cabbage soup. Vadick slid onto his seat and had his spoon in hand when the two swept in. Frost spiked Papa's brown mustache and beard, and he made a show of slobbering a kiss on Mama. Vadick smiled as something warm barreled to the center of his chest.

Vadick's older brother, Maxim, didn't even elbow him as he slid onto the stool and reached for his bowl, blue eyes alive with hunger. Mama sliced the bread and piled it in the center. "And what did you learn at school today?"

Vadick scowled, then remembered. He had learned something today. . .something about brotherhood. He dug in his pocket and handed his mother a note. "They sent this home."

"Not now, Sveta. Let us thank the Lord." Papa's hand on Mama's arm made her slip the note into her apron. Vadick's heart fell. He needed an answer by tomorrow.

But prayer came first. He knew that well. Eight years of habit made him stand, clasp his hands, bow his head. Papa prayed for them until the soup cooled.

Vadick's parents warned him never to ask questions about God or of a spiritual nature or to discuss their family's personal religious practices at school. But he never understood why nobody prayed in class. Why, in fact, his teachers never mentioned God. Father Lenin, yes. Once he'd made the mistake of asking Papa if Father Lenin and God were one in the same.

He'd earned a whippin' and never asked again.

The soup warmed his insides and filled him better than any fried peroshke or blini, although he'd happily stuff himself to the ears with any of Mama's baked goods.

"The Bible, Maxim." Papa slid his bowl away, his blue eyes trailing Max as the elder brother went to the sofa, opened the cushion, and dug out the family treasure. He carried it like a piece of Babushka Anna's china, tiptoeing to the table. The book had been in the family for three generations. Gold embossed words had faded off the top, and the corners of the leather cover peeled. Two pages were missing, one in James and the other in Hebrews. His father had painstakingly copied the Hebrews passage from someone else's Scripture and tucked it into the back page. Once, he'd read it aloud. Vadick remembered something about Esau, but nothing else except the memory of shivering at Mama's crying.

"Tonight we'll read in John, chapter nine."

Vadick listened, then asked, "Papa, why was the man born blind?"

Papa's blue eyes always entranced him, drew him in, and finally rendered him powerless to escape. "That's the point of the story, Vasha. There was no reason except that God be glorified in the healing."

"But then that man suffered for no reason."

"Not for no reason. The reason is clear. What confuses you is why God allowed it."

"Yes. Why would God allow His child to suffer?"

Papa laid down the Bible, steepled his meaty fingers, elbows propped on the table. "That is part of the mystery of faith. God allows suffering. It is a part of the believer's life. When we suffer, we turn to God. Through it, our

*faith grows. It is hard to understand, Child, but God
plans for us to suffer. It's not ours to ask why. It's only ours
to trust, to hold onto our Lord for strength."*

*"But what if it is too hard to trust?" Vadick saw his
mother's face blanch white, but Papa smiled. "You will
suffer in this life. It's your choice to suffer trusting in God's
plan or to turn away and walk alone." He closed the Bible
and rubbed his hand on it. "When your time comes, you
will choose,* Moy Lapichka. *If you choose God, you will
find He will give you the light and comfort you need to
walk the path of pain."*

*Vadick swallowed a lump of horror, not wishing for
any of his father's words to be realized. Desperate to
change the subject, he looked at Mama. "The note? Please,
read it. Say, yes, please!"*

*Mama smiled, tiny wrinkles lining up and curling
around her blue eyes. She dug the note out of the pocket of
her apron and opened it.*

*The color drained from her face. "No. Oh, no." Her
brow furrowed and a troubled gaze settled on Vasha.*

*Something inside him tore open, bringing a wave
of pain.*

*"What is it?" Papa took the note and read it. "They
want Vadick to join the Pioneers."*

*Dread cinched Vadick's chest. "Please?" he asked feebly,
bewildered at their ghastly expressions.*

"Oh, Lord, please help us."

"Lord, please, help us!"
Vadeem spiraled away from the echo of the past into the
moaning of a voice, this time in English. "Please, don't let
him die."

"I'm not dead." He heard his voice. It thundered inside his head. Forcing his eyes open, he found himself swallowed whole by Kat's horrified gaze. Her worried expression went straight to his soul. Then her face spun at retching angles. He clenched his eyes shut. "Give me a minute here. My head feels like it's scattered all over the street."

She answered only in sobs.

Slowly he became aware of her. . .holding him. Her hand clutched the back of his head, probably to keep his gray matter from draining completely onto the sidewalk. Her other hand, she rested on his chest, over his heart. It radiated warmth through his muscles down to his toes. Her hair spilled onto his face, and her perfume—it spiraled to the urge inside which had him longing for sweet oblivion and yanked him back to the living.

Except, he was in her arms. Did he have to wake up?

She hiccupped a sob, then begged, "Please."

Perhaps it was the pleading in her voice. Or the way she held him, her hands warm against his throbbing pain. Or maybe it was simply that she was still here when she could have sprinted into the night.

She wasn't in cahoots with General Grazovich. For some insane reason, he wanted to break out into tears.

He opened his eyes. "I'm okay."

Her concerned expression left him breathless. When was the last time he'd seen a look like that. . .for him? "What happened?"

Her face crumpled.

He sat up, aware of the world spinning, feeling like he'd left a part of his skull behind on the pavement. He braced his hand on the ground and cupped her chin, suddenly panicked. "Are you hurt? What happened?"

He blinked, sorting through the final moments. They'd

been walking, his head exploded. . . . "Did you get a look at who did this?"

She shook her head. "He hit you, and then. . .and then. . ." She looked away, her chin trembling. For the first time he saw the angry red line around her neck, a rip in the sleeve of her blouse.

He felt sick, as if he was going to empty his stomach right there on the street, right beside his brains. He scanned her quickly, terrified at what he might find. Her hair was a tousled rat's nest, her eyes swollen. A vicious red scrape ran down her chin. He went cold when he glanced down and saw her blouse lacked two buttons. *Oh no, please, no.*

"Do we need to take you to a doctor?" he asked in a voice that betrayed his darkest fears.

She shook her head. Her entire body trembled. Bewildered, Vadeem did the only thing he could think of. He wrapped his arms around her and pulled her to his chest. She sank against him willingly, clutching his leather jacket, digging her fingers right through it to his soul. Her wretched sobs peeled away his heart in jagged chunks until he, too, wanted to weep. He smoothed her hair, feeling completely undone.

What had happened while he lay sprawled on the sidewalk like a side of meat?

"I need to get you to headquarters. Figure out what is going on, tuck you away someplace safe. Did they get your bag?"

She shook her head but didn't pull away.

Wow. Yes, he could sit here on the sidewalk, the cold digging into his backside, his head screaming, her hands clinging to him like he was her lifeline, all night if he had to. He could stay here for a year. He tightened his grip and pressed his cheek against her head. "Shh," he soothed.

It took a moment for him to realize she was speaking. He

felt movement against the hollow of his neck, felt her lips moving. For a wild moment, he thought she might be. . .no, she was speaking, mumbling. He pulled away and cupped her face in his hands. She met his eyes with the most desolate expression.

Her words stabbed his soul.

"He took my key."

CHAPTER EIGHT

K at curled her hands around the warm cup of cocoa, inhaling the aroma, profoundly grateful for something to focus on while the Twilight Zone shifted around her. She could now describe the layout and general procedures of the FSB stations in two different towns in Russia, as well as the one inside Sheremetova Airport. She should write her own chapter and send it in to Lonely Planet Travel Guide, "How to Conduct Yourself in an FSB Interrogation."

It helped that Vadeem hadn't left her alone. Not once. Not during the ride over, not for the last hour as an FSB doctor gave her a cursory exam, not even when a parade of agents filtered through the office she supposed was Vadeem's, eyeing her as if she were a stolen icon.

If Kat harbored any doubts about Vadeem's connections or abilities as he lay bleeding on the sidewalk while a goliath thug wrestled the key off her neck, they were obliterated when Vadeem called one of his FSB chums on his cell phone and, within moments, an unmarked black sedan screamed up to the curb. She conjured up a plethora of Cold War era images as the car whisked her through Moscow toward the infamous Lubyanka Square and KGB Headquarters.

Because, she realized, that's exactly what organization Captain Vadeem Spasonov was with. New initials didn't hide old identities. FSB—the acronym spelled out meant *Federalnaya*

Slyuzhba Bez-Opostnosti—Federal Safety Service. It wasn't a gargantuan leap from the old, traditional moniker, KGB, *Kommunisticki Gosyudarstvani Bez-Opostnosti*—The Safety of the Communist Government. Even though Captain Spasonov had ceased his menacing posture, that is, if she ignored the fury that crossed his face moments after she'd revealed the thug's crime, his boys in the brotherhood definitely had KGB aura. Take the skinny agent with the crew-cut, coal black hair and darting hazel eyes. He scurried in like a beetle in answer to Vadeem's barked commands and scrutinized Kat like she was a prime cut of beef bleeding secrets all over their floor. She had no doubt he was the type to turn on the bright lights and wear a tread around an unlucky suspect.

As if in contrast, the one who now huddled with Spasonov in the corner of the sparse office looked like a DC Comics villain, all stubby hair and etched glower, muscles that had to be chiseled from pumped iron, a stance that screamed, "Make my day." Even his gun tucked in his arm holster seemed a toy under his timber-sized arms, now clamped over his massive chest. He would produce equally effective results, maybe better, by using those burly hands digging into his biceps to take down a suspect.

They were a cookie-cut bunch, she thought. Tall, dark, and scary, like the hulk to the FSB agent who'd freed her from Vadeem's custody only yesterday morning. A situation she couldn't seem to shake.

Kat shivered and took a sip of the hot cocoa Vadeem had managed to conjure up. It was just barely keeping her composure glued.

Night blackened the windows, but the overhead light glared down on two metal desks that had been shoved into opposite corners of the shoebox-size office. A coat tree divided the room, and beside it, a wooden straight-back chair mirrored the one in which she now sat. Her backside ached, and fatigue pushed against her eyes like weights. She shivered again, feeling cold, raw, and hollow, tasting despair as it rose in her clinching chest.

The key was gone.

She had a multitude of reasons to be grateful she'd only earned a scrape on her chin, but that didn't stop frustration from burning her eyes. She swiped at her tears, determined not to dissolve into a fresh mass of blubbering, although the now somewhat-common act of unloading her sorrows into Vadeem's capable chest, sheltered inside his protective arms, battled her feeble stoicism. The last thing she needed was to encourage him in his mission to pack her up and send her home. Thankfully, he'd abandoned that crusade in favor of justice and retribution.

Poor Vadeem. He looked like he'd been run over by a truck. He held an ice pack to his head while he talked, obviously not heeding the advice of the resident medic to run down to the hospital and get a CAT scan. Kat stared at her hands, still stained with his blood, dried now and cracking in the creases of her palm. She'd have to toss her formerly white blouse and her khakis—well, maybe she could use them for paint pants.

She gulped a breath as she teetered on the edge of shattering. She'd made the mistake of checking out her appearance in the pocket mirror of her backpack and now tried not to conjure up the sight of the face that had stared back, chunks of mascara clinging to her eyelashes, eyes streaked red, a bruise circling an ugly scrape across her jaw. She wasn't sure how she'd added that last feature. Probably when her attacker shoved her up against the building, face first. She could still feel his grip crunching her neck muscles, the icy scrape of his ring finger chafing her skin. The memory of the thief's hot breath on her neck as he growled in her ear sent a prickle down her spine.

She'd never forget the man's voice. Never. Low and animal-like, in control and purposely driving fear through her body. If it weren't for her desperation, she would have collapsed. But the brute wanted her key, and that knowledge kept her upright. Tensed. Furious. The key had brought her to Russia and tangled her into this mess, but it also could unlock answers and perhaps bring peace.

He would take it from her over her dead body.

No wonder she was sore. Her hand went to her neck, felt the raw burn from where the thug had yanked on it, again and again, hoping it would snap.

New shoelaces don't snap. It had to go over her head. He'd nearly ripped off her ears, had surely taken a chunk of her hair in his fist with it.

And still she'd lit out after him as if she were Wonder Woman, completely abandoning her common sense along with the man who had saved her life only twenty-four hours earlier.

Thankfully, she'd stumbled to a halt, guilt hitting her like a fist, in time to run back and pull Vadeem into her lap. She was mortified to think she had nearly deserted him on the sidewalk.

As if he knew her secret, Vadeem suddenly turned and looked over at her.

The look in his blue eyes said everything his unfaltering presence confirmed. Guilt. The guy was beating himself up for being comatose while some mugger roughed her up. The FSB captain had left a huge swatch of pride on the sidewalk.

To seal her suspicions, Vadeem stepped over, peeled off his leather jacket, and draped it over her shoulders. He squatted before her, his hand on her knee. "Ryslan is going to put out a search for the thief. We'll find your key." He reached up and tucked her hair behind her ear, all the time drawing her in with those compelling blue eyes that played havoc with her focus.

"I'm sorry this happened."

So was she. But more than that, she wanted to know why. What was God up to? Had He completely forgotten that she existed? Forsaken her to tromp about Russia on her own?

No, not on her own. With the Russian KGB. There was a particular irony in that. She let a small smile tug at her mouth. "Vadeem, I have to believe God was watching out for us. I'm okay. But I think you should get your head looked at."

He ran a finger lightly over her bruise. "I'm sorry you got hurt." His voice was tender, his touch gentle. And that guilty look speared right to her heart and made her want to weep.

"It wasn't your fault," she whispered.

She saw it again, the flicker of longing in his eyes. In a terrifying, wonderful, exhilarating instant, she remembered herself in his arms, felt his hands in her hair. She again smelled leather, strength, and masculinity, a byproduct of having her nose buried in his chest. Then her mouth turned dry, recalling the horrified look in his eyes when he ran his gaze over her, wondering how terribly she'd been hurt.

She chewed her bottom lip, struggling for words, anything to run from that incredibly delicious memory before he, too, saw longing in her expression. "When you say we'll find my key. . .does that mean I'm staying in Russia?"

His gaze clouded, and he looked away from her. She felt as if he'd ripped out her heart.

"No?" Her voice quivered.

"I have to do my job. I can't do that and protect you at the same time." He glanced at Ryslan, the comic book villain, obviously his partner in crime, who was seated at a black metal desk shoved up against the wall. Ryslan turned away, as if not wanting to be a part of this conversation.

Something ugly, along the lines of sarcasm or argument,

pushed into her throat, tasting bitter. He sounded just like Matthew. *Don't get in over your head, Honey. Make sure you're home early, Sweetheart. You don't want to go to Russia. You'll just get into trouble, Darling.* Protective. . .no, bossy. Dictatorial. Bullying.

Ignoring a whisper of reason inside, she pounced to her feet. The jacket fell to the floor. "Someone's already taken the one thing that will give me any answers. What could you *possibly* have to protect me from now?"

Vadeem's eyes turned dark.

"Just let me go," she ground out, fury gathering steam. "I'll walk out of here, and you'll never see me again."

He clenched his jaw. "I'll see you again. You seem to have a knack for ending up in police custody."

She just barely restrained the urge to slap him. So he thought she went hunting for trouble. Did she put out an ad, requesting Russia's most wanted to track her down? Her eyes filled. She balled her fists at her sides, furious that he made her feel so helpless as he controlled all her options. She made a hideous whimpering sound and wanted to die on the spot.

His anger dropped from his face like glacial ice. "Please, don't cry." His voice was low but wretched enough for her to know he meant it. She clenched her jaw, furious that tears crested and coursed down her cheeks, furious that he'd won. He reached for her, as if to comfort her, but she jerked away, trying to exorcize every tender feeling she'd cultivated toward him.

He'd protected her from bullets, and she had his blood smeared all over her hands. She'd told him everything. . . . He knew what this little jaunt to Russia meant to her. Didn't that bond them into some sort of uncanny relationship?

Kat swiped at the tears and, conjuring up bravery, lifted her chin. It would help if he would wipe that guilty, concerned expression off his face, the one that told her, yes, he remembered every second of their relationship. It did nothing but fertilize all her budding emotions. "Don't make me leave. Not yet. I need to know more." Her voice betrayed her and made her want to wince.

He moved closer, his gaze holding hers, his hand moving up to trace the scrape on her chin. He flicked a glance at his partner, then back. He was so close she could smell the day's lingering cologne. "And what will you do, Kat? The key's gone. Timofea is dead. You've run out of leads."

"I still have you." Where did that idiotic statement come from? She cringed, shocked that it had escaped from her mouth. But she was thinking it. The minute she saw herself in his eyes, she'd begun to wonder. *Vadeem could help her*. Didn't the KGB keep a file on every citizen in the country? Yes, Captain Vadeem Spasonov of the FSB could help her. He could dig around for her, find out who Timofea was, maybe even find her grandmother Magda's history. She had family in Russia. She knew it deep in her bones. And Vadeem held the key to unlock that past. "God sent me you," she repeated and tightened her gaze on him. She didn't want to think about the way she'd just opened up her chest for him to rip out her heart, along with her dreams. *Please, Vadeem, don't betray me!* "You can help me."

His eyes widened, and something desperate filled them. She'd hit a soft spot and, as she watched, his past roared up and consumed him whole. In his gaze she saw fear, a painful, vulnerable, childlike fear that made her lips part and her mouth go dry. Then he blinked, and it was gone. In its place, the cold glitter of resolve. She felt as if a door had slammed on her face.

"No," he said quietly. "I can't."

Vadeem paced the hotel corridor, feeling dead on his feet. But he'd seen Kat's intentions in her eyes, and he couldn't let her run.

She'd slammed the door in his face when he told her he'd be watching her. All night. Camped outside in the hallway. He didn't like what that information did to her beautiful face, how it crumbled as her hopes shattered.

He steeled his heart to it. He had to. He had a job to do, and right now Grazovich could be lurking down the hall, waiting to finish her off.

Of course, the thief would have to be a phantom to do it, because according to Vadeem's last phone call, Grazovich had spent the day exploring Pskov like a tourist and was at this moment passed out in his bed, cradling a liter of Absolut in one arm and a café waitress in the other.

So, who had mugged them?

Vadeem rubbed his head. He probably needed a stitch or two, but head wounds always bled worse than they were. He'd sucked down the two aspirins Kat had fished out of that backpack of hers, which seemed to contain everything.

Everything but answers.

She'd nearly wrung him out with her heart-wrenching plea. *"I have you."* Oh, did he wish that. Over the past twelve hours, Kat's smile had awakened a part of him he'd thought dead. Or perhaps he'd only wished dead. Why did she have to cradle him in her arms, drown him with a look of authentic concern? It resurrected all the dangerous emotions he thought he'd successfully executed so long ago.

He'd do well to veer a wide course around the enticing Kat Moore package. Twenty-four hours in her presence had him contemplating a career change. Personal bodyguard. Escorting her through Russia like a tour guide and helping her dig up answers didn't sound like such a terrible job choice. It didn't help that she'd struck truth with her plea. He *did* have the resources to unlock her past. A few keystrokes and he could access files that still rang fear in the hearts of the general population.

"God sent me you." He didn't even want to think about that statement. God. Back in his life. Fiddling with his circumstances. Sending him a beautiful, kind woman—like some sort of taunt? No, thank you. God had mixed up a potent brew in Kat Moore, and Vadeem had been sucked right in by her beautiful eyes thick with need, her hand gripping his jacket, the same hand that had felt his heart beat. She even smelled good after her harrowing encounter. Her perfume lingered on his jacket and jumbled his concentration. Her ragged plea nearly forced a husky yes out of his mouth.

But he had dredged up a negative reply and felt like a snake for doing it.

She needed him. How long had it been since he'd heard that from someone? He didn't want to dare guess. She. Needed. Him.

No, she needed his position. His connections. Somehow, he hung onto that reality until the cop in him caught up. God hadn't sent him to Kat or vice versa. Kat simply knew how to go straight for a man's jugular.

That thought had given him the strength to lock her in her hotel room despite her tears.

That thought had him camped out in the hallway, his eyes glued to her door, hoping she was feeling as rotten as he was, wishing they could instead be enjoying their last night dividing the spoils of a bag of M&M's.

Vadeem leaned his head against the wall, slid down onto his heels, and stared at the ceiling. Paint, nearly an inch thick, ran in cracks up the Stalin-era hotel walls. A mud brown carpet tunneled the length of the hall, and on the far end, he could just make out the night clerk sitting at her desk, her head braced on her hand, tapping her pen against the notebook she kept to record the guests' activities. She'd be writing a big fat nothing for Kat Moore tonight.

Not that an impulse to take Kat out on the town and show her a taste of midnight Moscow didn't tug at him while he escorted her to the Hotel *Rossia*. St. Basil's Cathedral sparkled like a Christmas tree with brilliant gold, red, and green cupolas pushing against the magenta backdrop of the heavens. Beyond that flowed the Volga, her dimples sparkling as she rippled south under the stars. They could walk along the Kremlin wall, ponder a moment at the eternal flame where the fire would flicker in Kat's eyes and turn her hair bronze. Maybe she'd tell him about her life in America and how she happened to have Russian ancestry and speak his language. Perhaps he'd shed a few of his own stories, tame them down, of course, and omit most of the last twelve years, but he'd had some scrapes in the orphanage that might push laughter through those expressive, sometimes pouty, lips.

Then they'd cross the street to the new underground mall, where he could treat her to some rigatoni at Sergio's or sit and listen to streams of Chopin as they rolled off the grand piano in the mezzanine. Better yet, maybe the Bolshoi would have a performance of *Swan Lake* in season. . . .

There he went, thinking like a tour guide again.

The only tour he was going to give her was a very nonscenic drive to Sheremetova 2 Airport.

And he could bet there'd be no laughter on *that* excursion.

Sometimes he hated his job. He rubbed a finger and thumb into his eyes, seeing stars but hoping the pain might keep him awake long enough to detect if Kat Moore had any more escape attempts on her evening agenda.

Oh, this was perfect. Why hadn't he thought of it sooner?

Ilyitch sat down at his computer, punched in two passwords, and in an instant, he was in. What was her full name? Ekaterina Hope Moore. He typed it in carefully, mouthing the letters.

A copy of her passport popped up on the screen. He read through it and her visa, as well as the visa application notes, grimacing. This girl had the life of a librarian. Adoption coordinator? Ah, the selling of children. Sure, everyone's a capitalist. Why hadn't he thought of that?

He typed in the name of her mother, listed on the birth certificate. Hope Moore. Nothing in the state computers. A big blank. Hope Neumann Moore. Again, zero. He backed up to the younger Moore's passport information. Contact: Edward Neumann, grandfather.

He typed in the name.

Score. Edward Neumann's file loaded for three minutes. Ilyitch considered getting a cup of tea while he read the file, obviously scanned into the system not long ago from some extremely ancient and secure vault. He was shocked it had been so easy to access.

They probably thought the spy was dead.

And they certainly didn't count on his granddaughter returning to the scene of the crime.

But how was the girl linked to Anton Klassen?

He scrolled down, too absorbed to cut away for a cup of tea, not needing the caffeine rush anyway. This treasure hunt just got interesting.

He tapped the screen over the name of the Pskov monastery where it appeared in Neumann's file. "So that's how Timofea knew the girl." He'd have to see what Grazovich's monk had dug up.

Hopefully it matched this ancient KGB file.

Then, there it was, the answer, written in digital black and white. He ran a thumb under the name. Marina Antonova Shubina, maiden name, Klassen.

He moved the file into the recycle basket, sat back, and wove his fingers together, cupping his hands behind his head. He couldn't let Kat Moore leave Russia. She'd just become their link to a tidy, larger than he could count, fortune.

⌘

Kat paced the room. Devious leech that he was, Captain Vadeem Spasonov was out there. She knew it. He had a heart of stone in his chest. He was kicking her out of Russia in the morning despite her pleas. Despite their bond. Despite the fact that he knew she would never find out who she was or what family she might have in Russia.

She'd seen the icy glaze in his eyes. He cared about nothing except tracking down this Grazovich fellow, something she just *knew*, deep in her bones, had nothing to do with either her or that incredibly kind and helpful angel-man, Professor Taynov. But steel-hearted Vadeem had closed off her pleas with an in-your-face *nyet*.

She'd have to find a way around the pit bull out in the hall.

She buried her face in her hands. "Oh Lord, now what?" Perhaps the Almighty had forgotten she was floundering down here like a dazed tuna, but she needed Him now more than air. She had the strangest feeling, however, that when she felt the farthest from God, He was closest. "Please, Lord. What do I do now? This can't be the end, can it? You didn't tell Timofea to send me that key just so that it could end up in the hands of a thief, did you?"

Fulfill the promise.

Brother Papov's solemn voice pulsed in her thoughts.

What promise?

Grandfather would know about Timofea. Didn't the father-monk say that the monastery had once been a partisan headquarters? She rubbed her face with her hands. And Grandfather had worked with partisans. A distant memory flooded back. Crystallized. It was right after her parents' accident when she went to live on the Neumann family farm in Schenectady, New York.

"I have to write a report, Grandfather, on the war." Kat had approached him on the porch, where he sat, staring at the sunset. Grandfather always loved the sunset, and for a long moment, he didn't acknowledge her presence. Just stood there, hands tucked into his pockets, watching the sun bleed out over the western sky.

The expression on his face told her now was not the time. It was Magda's time, perhaps. The woman Grandfather loved. The grandmother who wasn't buried in the family plot.

Kat remembered how she'd made to move away, back inside the farmhouse.

"What war, Kat?"

"Why, World War II, Grandfather. Your war."

He'd turned, and she'd seen something of the past flicker in his eyes. "It wasn't my war. I simply assisted the partisans as they fought for their freedom."

"Partisans?" He'd piqued her interest. She'd read about the resistance in France, Belgium, and Denmark. "Were you in the French Resistance?" Later, the thought consumed her and she spent hours at the Schenectady library, digging up history.

But he'd laughed at her question. "No, I couldn't speak French to save my life. I speak Polish. And Russian. I helped the partisans in what you'd call the Eastern Bloc countries."

"Is that where you met Magda?"

In the years hence, she never forgot his expression. He'd looked at her with passion simmering in his eyes, not angry, but alive, so alive it made her skin prickle.

Then, in a flash, it was gone. Doused. He returned to the sunset, merely a whimper on the horizon.

Kat had tiptoed back into the house.

Fulfill the promise.

It was time for Grandfather to fulfill a few promises. Enough dodging the past and kicking her out of the family secrets. She wanted to know how he knew Timofea and why someone had ripped out a chunk of her hair to get a key that looked like it opened a crypt. She wanted to know who Magda was and why Grandfather never talked about her. She wanted to know about the Medal of Honor and the ancient yellow picture still safe, thank the Lord, in her Bible. Most of all, she wanted a glimpse behind his secrets.

She checked her watch. Moscow, three A.M. Friday. It would be six P.M. Wednesday in Schenectady. He would just be finishing dinner. She sat down on the ancient squeaky bed and pulled the telephone on her lap. *Grandfather, please understand.*

The operator gave her a line outside the country, and she dialed the number on the rotary phone, her finger nearly missing the holes from the tremor of her hand. He wasn't going to like this.

But if anyone could get her out of this mess, Grandfather could. He had secrets tucked away. Powerful secrets. Such as a clandestine relationship with an organization that took him on trips outside Upstate New York for agonizingly long periods of time. Trips that never produced souvenirs or postcards. Trips where he simply vanished one day, then reappeared three weeks or two months later, whistling as he pitched hay on the Neumann family farm. Mama always stayed behind in the tender and watchful care of Grape-Granny Neumann, the family matriarch, and Kat's great-grandmother.

Kat had grown up thinking such disappearances were a part of Grandfather's mystique. It wasn't until she was eight that she realized perhaps, someday, he would never return.

She'd never forget Grape-Granny walking them down a long hallway, gripping Kat's hand in a vise. Grape-Granny had a wide, farmer's face, tanned and deeply lined, and serious brown eyes that rarely sparkled, unlike Grandfather's. She wore a white head scarf—Kat had never seen it off her head, even years later when her body lay in a casket. But this day, Grape-Granny's face jerked and twitched, emotion pulsing against her stoicism. The old woman patted Kat's hand now and again in unusual sentimentality as they clipped down the hall in their Sunday best. Kat saw metal hospital beds, white cotton sheets, heard the clink of carts as nurses rolled them down the halls. Even twenty-five years later, Kat's nose pricked against the pungent mix of antiseptic, cotton, and iodine, ripe in her memory.

Grape-Granny pushed open the door, and Kat stood paralyzed, transfixed in horror at a hideously beaten patient with tubes in his mouth, his arms, his chest. His leg elevated, wired to an assembly of lines above the metal bed. Next to his head, a machine that looked like Kat's slinky moved up and down, wheezing. And there was Mama, also, holding this stranger's hand. "Come here, Kat. Your grandfather needs to hear your voice."

Her grandfather? She pushed against that thought, knowing that a childish wail would follow her acceptance of the gruesome reality lying in the hospital bed.

So she'd spoken to the stranger. She'd talked to the frail person swallowed by bandages, his chest rising and falling with the hiss of the slinky machine. She told him about the farm, about the apple blossoms in the orchard turning to fruit, about the new litter of kittens in the barn. And when she returned to the farm, she'd prayed that Jesus would heal this broken man who they said was her grandfather.

Then, just as suddenly as he'd left, Grandfather reappeared. Thinner, perhaps. But looking nothing like the fractured person she'd seen at that New York hospital. And now Grandfather smiled more. He threw her in the air. And when Kat's parents died five years later, he took her home to the Schenectady farm, away from the cramped city apartment where she'd spent the dreary winters.

He never left again.

The secrets, however, stayed. As Kat grew older, they germinated and blossomed into suspicion, even supposition. Grandfather had lived a life she hardly dared to guess, and he could help her now by activating the power of some of those secrets.

The phone clicked, and she could almost hear the call travel on a giant cable under the ocean into New York harbor, up the coast, inland, and north until it connected with the family farmhouse, sitting in the middle of a New York cornfield, some five thousand miles away. "Hello?"

"Grandfather?"

A gasp, then, "Kat?"

She started to sob. "Grandfather."

"Oh Kat, my dear Kat. What have you discovered?"

CHAPTER NINE

The jangle of keys sliced through the darkness. Vadeem instantly opened his eyes and glued his gaze on a hotel patron in the process of locking his room door. The man cruised by him in long strides, not sparing a glance at Vadeem— the rumpled FSB agent slouched on the floor. Vadeem sat up and smoothed his leather coat, forcing the cobwebs from his mind. The early morning sun, already high above the Moscow skyline, pushed through the haze of lace curtains from the window at the end of the hall and sent a streak of amber down the brown carpet. Dust and fuzz he hadn't noticed the night before filmed Vadeem's pant legs and pricked his nose. The sound of traffic gathered on the street below.

Kat's door remained closed. Victory.

Vadeem felt as if he'd gone ten rounds with Ryslan. Muscles bunched in his neck. His calves screamed, tense and sore. His head wound burned when he brushed it against the wall. He grimaced at how out of shape he was. He checked his watch—eight A.M. He'd had forty minutes of shut-eye. That should be more than enough—had been enough a few years back. Vadeem pushed to his feet and stretched, feeling frowzy. Maybe he could get Ryslan down here to keep tabs on Kat while he dashed home for a shower.

He scrubbed his face with two hands. No, she was smart, and Ryslan didn't know her like Vadeem did. Ryslan would probably cuff her to keep Kat from ditching him. . .and Vadeem couldn't do that to her. He'd already felt like a snake. Being shackled to Ryslan until she got to the airport would mortify her.

His gaze traveled down to the desk clerk. New shift, obviously. He'd missed the shift change. A blond sat at the desk. Pushing fifty, with ample presence, she looked about as friendly as the ward nurses at Orphanage Number 213. He watched her as two well-suited gentlemen approached the desk. She pinched her face, shook her head. They pulled out their passports.

No, not passports. Identification, judging by the way the woman's eyes widened and her fake smile appeared. Vadeem stiffened.

They turned and walked down the hall with the bearing of. . . Americans. Pressed black suits, dark ties, faces stern, confident. Two peas in a pod. *CIA.* Vadeem grimaced. *What now?* He sucked a breath and took a step toward Kat's door. Certainly, they weren't here for. . .

They were reading room numbers, but they paused when their gazes settled on him. Up close, Mr. Rough and Mr. Tough were cut from the same cloth. Tall, with wide shoulders and dark thorny eyes. He hadn't forgotten the few times he'd trained with, or against, American military. They'd earned his respect, even if their arrogance ate at him. He offered a diplomatic smile.

"We're looking for Ekaterina Moore."

His smile dimmed. What had she done? He looked pointedly at her door, and as if in response to some unseen cue, it opened.

She stood in the doorway, looking every bit like the dream he'd had only moments earlier. Her eyes glowed with anticipation. A smile played on her lips. Dressed crisp and clean in a pair of black jeans and an orange cotton sweater, she'd slicked her hair back in a ponytail and wore just enough makeup for his heart to hurt. She flicked a gaze toward him, and his heart sank.

"Good morning," he said. "These men are here for you?" He said it like a question, hoping it was some sort of mistake. *Please Kat, don't run to your embassy. Take my advice. Get out of Russia.*

She nodded. He felt slapped. He backed away, resisting the urge to hold up his hands in surrender. Instead, he locked his jaw and held out his hand. "Good luck, Kat."

She took it and held it a moment, saying nothing. But he felt in her grasp everything that had passed between them— from the moment he'd tackled her, protecting her from the bullets in Pskov, to his mortifying reaction in the chapel, to the compassion in her eyes as she held his bleeding head on the dark street. He tightened his grip and couldn't stop himself. "Please, don't do this. I don't want to see you hurt."

She yanked her hand away. "My visa says I am here as a tourist. To my understanding, I haven't broken any laws." Her eyes glittered. Bold. Hard. She stepped away from him and turned to the black-suited soldiers. "Thank you for coming for me."

Rough and Tough didn't even glance at him as they turned and bracketed her with their protection. They walked down the hall, away from the FSB. Away from him.

Vadeem felt freshly punched when she didn't even turn and look back.

<hr />

Ilyitch stood on the street corner, waiting for the Canadian Bagel Company to fill his order. *Ah, capitalism. It brings out the best in a man,* he thought as he dangled a key from his thick index finger.

Well, most men. The key's metal winked gold as it caught the morning sunlight. He swung the shoestring fast, and it spiraled around his finger. "I got it," Ilyitch muttered into the cell phone he held propped to his ear with his shoulder. "And she's got a secret."

Grazovich coughed, his voice harsh and filled with gravel, the aftereffects of a full night. "I've always told you that your position would be an asset to our situation."

Ilyitch fought the urge to throw the phone against the wall. Grazovich leaped on every chance to bury his face in the past. Ilyitch ground out his voice. "Her grandfather was a spook. Control agent."

"CIA?" Now he'd gotten Grazovich's attention.

"Ran a ring of operatives in the sixties. KGB burned him and his entire ring in 1968. He got away, but we unearthed his assets here. They were executed."

He enjoyed the long pause on the other end. "The thing is. . .he came back. In 1970, he showed up in Pskov. KGB picked him up, had him against the ropes when a couple of sleepers, undercover agents, came to life and whisked him out of the country."

"They get anything out of him?"

"Name and rank. The basics."

"Hmm." Grazovich's antenna had gone up. Ilyitch pictured the general smoothing back his graying hair, pacing the floor as he held the cell phone to his ear.

"There's more," *and this is going to cost you.* "He was OSS. Ran a partisan op out of Pskov during the Patriotic War."

"Well, isn't that coincidental?" Grazovich paused long enough to light a cigarette on the other side. Ilyitch heard the scrape as the lighter flared to life. "What would bring an agent back to a country where his cover's been blown?"

The answer buzzed in the silence between them as Ilyitch

smiled. "I think your cousin is right on the money, General." Big money. Four million dollars of big money. Ilyitch's finger began to turn purple from the pressure of the key's string. "I should have taken the girl. She knows something. Maybe even went into the family business."

"Find the book. It's got our answers."

Ilyitch spat on the ground and earned a glare from a woman sashaying by in a short black leather skirt and skimpy vest. He ignored her. "What if there isn't a book? Pumping the girl for her information would be faster."

"And messier. The FSB is all over her like a hound to a fox. The last thing we need to do is raise a few heads."

"Tell your little monk that I'm starting to lose patience."

"He says he doesn't know."

"I told you he was an idiot. Let's get the girl and pry it out of her."

"Okay, calm down. Follow her. See if she's got the book. If not, bring her to me." The line clicked off.

Ilyitch snapped the cell phone shut. Morning rush hour in Moscow had traffic snarled, horns on high, motors spitting out exhaust. Pedestrians pushed past him on their trek to the sub-way. Ilyitch leaned against the building, suddenly feeling old. After five years of running this game, his nerves were starting to raze. No, his nerves had been annihilated ten years ago in a renegade prison camp on the Georgian-Abkhazian border. He'd barely slept a night through since. If it weren't for the filthy General Grazovich and his brother, he'd be rotting in a three-meter community cell.

Two million dollars was a good retirement sum for a man who had bartered his soul for a solid meal and a ratty cot. He turned and walked into the Bagel Company. Capitalism had its perks, in more ways than one.

Kat had just taken a giant leap back to reality. A reality, at least, that didn't knock her to her knees. The smell of brewed coffee, a plate of doughnuts in the middle of an oak coffee table, CNN on the television in the corner, and a fresh copy of *People* magazine on the end table, all told her she was back in the land of the living. Someone with taste had decorated the reception area in the normal colors of navy blue and cranberry. Not a hint of orange or lime green in the entire building. Kat sat back in the navy corduroy armchair, tucked her feet up, and blew on the cup of instant hot cocoa she'd been grateful to find in the well-stocked embassy cafeteria. Across from her on the plaid sofa, a young couple sat clasping hands, looking infinitely distressed. She knew how they felt.

She didn't want to ponder her grandfather's powerful connections, but the events of the morning crushed any doubts she'd entertained about his previous profession. Ten minutes on the phone last night with Grandfather Neumann, a man who spent his days beating old Bart Gunderson at chess, and the next morning the CIA—working on the other side of the world—show up at her hotel.

She never thought she'd be so happy to see the US embassy. Forty-eight hours outside America seemed like a century here in the former Soviet Union.

Kat, what have you discovered? Kat watched the television screen, saw the female reporter's lips move, but she heard last night's conversation in her head.

"Oh, Grandfather!" Kat had fought the tremor in her voice. "The key was stolen."

"Stolen. How?" The connection crackled. Kat kept it short, not wanting to frighten the man. Regardless of what he'd seen in the past, she was his granddaughter, the granddaughter he'd given it all up for, and she knew he'd race to conclusions that might strain his grandfatherly heart.

"I'm okay. It was. . .stolen. I went to the Pechory monastery." She opted not to tell him about the shooting in Pskov or her near miss at the airport. More important wasn't what had happened to her since her arrival in Russia, but what would happen twelve hours from now if Mr. Russian Cop still sat outside her door.

"I met the monk who took care of Timofea. He said the old monk had a picture of me."

Silence.

"And of mom."

She'd heard him breathe in and out heavily.

"Please, Grandfather. There is a Russian FSB agent who wants to kick me out of Russia. He thinks some sort of international smuggler is after me."

"Are you okay?" He'd sounded more calm, more cold than she'd ever remembered.

"Yes, I'm fine. There's been some sort of mistaken identity here. I'll be fine, but. . ." Her voice turned plaintive. If anything, her stoic grandfather, raised from tough farm stock, would respond to her need for the truth. "I need to know who Magda was. I want more. I feel as if half of me lies buried in Russia, and I don't know why. Can't you do this for me?" She paused and threw in her last card. "For Magda?"

He groaned, and she imagined him scrubbing a hand down his face, his green eyes filled with sadness as he conjured up the image of his deceased wife. Her heart twisted. Maybe it was too much for him. Guilt stabbed at her. Maybe she should just return home and savor her memories with the only family she had left.

"I met Timofea during the war."

She'd waited, her heart in her throat.

"He was my contact. We worked together for awhile."

"You were in Russia helping the partisans."

"Yes."

It teetered on the edge of her tongue to ask him. Were you with the CIA? Were you a spy?

No, some secrets were too deep. "Do you know anything about a promise someone made Timofea?"

"No, my *lapichka*. I have no idea why Timofea sent you that key."

She believed him. It was the same voice that read her the Bible, told her the truth about boys, and whispered promises to care for her as she stood out in the rain sobbing over her mother's newly dug grave. Her heart sank.

"Do you want to stay in Russia?" The sorrow in his voice felt like a leaden weight on her heart. "I suppose it is time you discovered your ancestry. I don't know, truly, if you will find what you are looking for. It was such a long time ago." His voice fell, became old. "I tried. . .once. . ."

She tensed. Grandfather returned to Russia? When?

"Where are you?"

"I'm staying at the Hotel *Rossia,* room 312."

"The one off Red Square?"

She was struck dumb.

"You promise to come home to me?" She could almost see him pacing, see the worry lurking in his wrinkled face.

She made a squeaky sound that she hoped sounded affirmative. Her throat closed.

"Sit tight. And I'd say a prayer if I were you."

Say a prayer. Unfortunately, it felt like her prayers didn't travel past the cracked white plaster ceiling. *Please, Lord, help me find the answers. Help me find my past.* Despite her pleading, she couldn't escape the feeling that the doors of heaven had slammed shut over the past two days.

Yet she refused to forsake the joy that could be hers. The words of David reverberated through her head. "You, Lord, have never forsaken those who seek You." Plenty of times, David had felt abandoned by God. The prophets, Elijah, Jeremiah, even Jonah grieved the loss of God.

Why couldn't she?

He was out there, and a drowning person has only one choice—grab the lifeline or go under.

She dug through her backpack and found her Bible, opened it to Psalm 9, and continued reading David's song. "Sing praises to the Lord. . .he does not ignore the cry of the afflicted."

Faith wasn't only about clinging to the unseen God. It was about praising Him while she did it, while she waited for rescue.

She spent the night praising Him for the salvation yet to come.

"Miss Moore?" The door to the reception room opened, and a small woman with black hair down to her waist, dressed in navy pants and a sleeveless sweater, motioned her out into the hall. Kat set the cocoa down next to the doughnuts and stood to meet her.

"I'm Alicia Renquist," the woman said as they left the room. "I've been requested to help you in any way we can."

"Thank you." Kat followed her down the carpeted, paneled hallway to a conference room. A large oak table filled the room. A spray of freesia with lilies in the center sent out a rich fragrance. Miss Renquist pulled out a padded, leather, rolling chair for Kat, then settled herself in the next one, turning it to face her.

"I came to Russia to find my past," Kat said, not sure what this woman knew. "I'm part Russian, and I think I have family here. My grandmother was from here. I was thinking we could start there?"

"What was her name?"

"Magda Neumann. I think her maiden name was Klassen." She dug into her backpack, pulled out the Bible, and produced the picture. "I was given this picture. It's the only clue I have." She handed it over to Miss Renquist.

The woman stared at it, turned it over, and read the back. "It says Klassen on the tombstone. Do you think it was a relative?"

Kat nodded. "Perhaps one of these two women was Magda Klassen."

Miss Renquist handed her back the picture. "I'll request a search from the FSB database and see if they'd be willing to help."

Kat forced a smile, but her hope tripped. Sure, the FSB would be begging to help after she'd snubbed Captain Spasonov this morning.

He'd looked rough standing there in the hall next to the two crisply attired American CIA agents, his brown curly hair mussed and sticking straight up on one side, gray bags hanging under his eyes. The guy needed a decent night's sleep and most likely medical attention. Instead, he'd spent the night crouched outside her door.

Obviously, he knew her better than she wanted to admit. She'd had every intention of bolting the second he settled her in the hotel room, and he must have read it in her eyes or by the way she too easily acquiesced to his plans to drive her to the airport the next morning.

He'd abandoned a good night's sleep to keep her safe. He might be stomping on her dreams, but he did it with good intentions.

There'd been hurt in his eyes when he'd said good-bye at

the hotel. Hurt, a touch of anger, and plenty of worry. She pushed away the feel of his hand, warm in hers, sending tingles racing up her arm. She'd never forget the fear etched in his tired eyes when he took her hand. He'd meant his words, "I don't want you to get hurt."

Then she had to smart off to him.

She winced. Two days with the guy, and she felt as though she'd betrayed her best friend. Ragged emotions and adrenaline had her clinging to Vadeem Spasonov like a buoy.

She'd certainly cut the ties of friendship with her in-your-face exit this morning. She swallowed the bitter taste of regret.

"Thank you," she said to Alicia Renquist. "I appreciate any help the embassy could give me in locating my family."

Miss Renquist patted her hand. "It may take a few days. We were wondering, actually, if you might be able to help us."

"Help whom?"

"Your country."

After the save by the black suits this morning, she was Uncle Sam's best friend. "How?"

Miss Renquist had long, red, manicured nails, and she tapped them on the table. "We have a situation."

Kat knew all about "situations." She'd had a few herself over the past forty-eight hours. "I'm not sure I follow you. How can I help?"

"You're an international adoption specialist?"

Kat sat back and frowned. "Yes."

Miss Renquist stood and pushed in her chair. Kat watched her walk over to the window and stare out, rubbing her hands on thin arms. She wondered how long this American had lived in Moscow.

"The couple you saw in the other room. He's the son of Senator Watson from Ohio. He and his wife are here to adopt a baby." She turned and rubbed her forehead. "They've run into a snag."

"Do they have their paperwork from the States?"

"Yes, translated and in triplicate."

"Well, what is the problem then?"

"The agency representative they were working with in Russia just landed in the hospital with appendicitis."

Kat made a face. "Here, in Moscow? Ouch." No wonder Miss Renquist looked wrung out. "It can't be that hard to find another agent."

"You'd be surprised. Russia isn't entirely pro-adoption, and very few regions even consent to international adoptions. Thankfully, the orphanage in which the Watsons' child lives has been a forerunner, and because of your agency's reputation, I believe they would agree to work with you. It takes a special touch to work with these orphanage directors. It wasn't so long ago that Russia believed we abducted their children and did medical experiments on them."

Kat flinched. But she, too, had heard the tales of propaganda designed to keep Russia's orphans safely inside the Motherland.

"I'm afraid we need your expertise," Renquist continued. "This is their second trip in-country. If it doesn't happen this time. . ."

The woman didn't have to finish for Kat to grasp her meaning. The distressed woman in the lobby was one unfortunate step shy of losing the child she'd longed for.

"But I've never worked in the field before. I don't really know what I'm doing."

"You speak Russian. They have their paperwork, and your agency has the legal standing. Just travel with the Watsons to the orphanage, meet with the director, go with them to court for the adoption finalization, and bring the baby back to Moscow. We'll process the baby's immigrant visa here. We've already cleared the paperwork, so it'll be a three-day job at most, and I think, from looking at your file, you can handle it."

She had a file at the embassy? Kat chewed her bottom lip.

"In the meantime, we'll hunt up your Magda for you."

Kat fingered the picture, drawn to the faces, wondering if one of them could be Grandfather's lost love. "Where am I going?"

***

Vadeem slammed his fist into the punching bag, feeling his frustration scream through his tense muscles. *Bam!* For Mr. Rough. *Bam!* For Mr. Tough. *Bam!* For Ekaterina Moore and the way she could chew up a man and spit him out without a second glance. *Bam! Bam!* And two for Grazovich, the man he should be chasing instead of figuring out how he was going to storm into the American embassy, escape the Marine posted at the front desk, dodge the staff in the foyer, and wrestle a kicking and screaming Kat Moore under the steel gate before it crashed down on his head—and his career. *Bam!*

"You planning on coming in to work today?" Ryslan leaned against the doorframe, nursing a bottle of lemonade.

Bam! "What are you doing here?" Vadeem didn't ask his partner how he got in.

"Where's the girl?" Ryslan looked crisp this morning, dressed in black suit pants and a matching leather jacket. He was all angled planes and ferocity. Rough and Tough would have thought twice about whisking Kat away under Ryslan's nose.

Bam!

"She's at the embassy." Vadeem jogged in place for a moment, then lowered his hands. Ryslan picked at the paper label on the lemonade bottle.

"Is she leaving?"

Vadeem worked off his gloves and dropped them on the floor. "I don't know." He picked up a towel, scrubbed it across his face, and draped it over his shoulders. "And I don't care." He flopped down on his sofa, a utilitarian black vinyl piece he'd picked up second-hand. The cool fabric sent a chill down his bare back. "They picked her up like she was the First Lady, and I haven't seen her since."

"Hmm." Ryslan paced across the room and stared out the window. "What's Grazovich up to?"

"Sleeping off last night's party." Vadeem noticed an odor rising off the sofa. If he didn't get a shower soon, he was going to alienate even himself. He pushed himself up, feeling his muscles starting to bunch after the abrupt halt in his workout. He stretched from side to side. "Any leads on the weapons contact?"

"We have a guy watching Bartyk in St. Pete, and our man on Fitzkov in Novosibersk hasn't moved. Then again, he could be buying from a legitimate dealer. You can order Russian weapons off the Internet these days." Ryslan grimaced. "Don't you just love capitalism?"

Vadeem winced. Just because Russia was broke didn't mean they had to parcel off their future. It burned him to see his country surrendering to despair. "Doesn't it bother you even a little that Grazovich risked his neck to pull her out of customs police, just so she could sightsee around Pskov?" Vadeem shoved a hand through his hair and grimaced as it came back slimy. Shower. Now.

"What about that key? Did you ever find out what it unlocks?" Ryslan turned and finished off his lemonade.

"She doesn't even know. Probably the deluded musings of an old man." But from the description of the young monk, Timofea hadn't sounded deluded. *Fulfill the promise.* It seemed eerily sane, in a cryptic sort of way.

"And you're just going to let her go? I don't know, Vadeem. I got a gut feeling on this."

Vadeem had more than that. Gut, heart, and soul feelings. He put a hand to his chest, remembering those amber brown eyes that drilled into him and left him gasping. That sweet smile, so hard earned, but delicate and warm when he draped his coat over her shoulders and when he'd said good-bye. Such a smile could entrance a man. . . .

Vadeem slammed his fist again into the bag. Yes, that's exactly what she'd done. Entranced him. And he'd nearly fallen face first into her little trap. The key gone, gullible Vadeem will simply rifle through top-secret files, totally abandon his common sense, his focus, his *job,* and help her uncover her family secrets.

Bam!

"I need a shower," Vadeem said. "I'll be in later."

"You want me to assign another agent to tag along after her?"

"No, forget her. I'm going back to Pskov to keep my eye on Grazovich. Whatever he wanted with her, he's obviously lost interest."

Ryslan saluted him with the empty bottle. "So be it, Comrade. Miss Moore is officially on her own."

CHAPTER TEN

Kat gripped the armrests with white knuckles. Flying on a 757 was one thing. Safe, like sitting in a giant movie theater where they served drinks and dinner, then eight hours and two movies later, she exited into a surreal foreign world, a continuation of the movie she'd entered on the plane.

But this little puddle jumper, an AN-2 biplane that looked like something out of an Indiana Jones movie, went far beyond the surreal. The reality of flying meant her stomach lodged in her throat, her heartbeat charged into overdrive, and her ears filled with the high-pitched whine of the engine. And she'd never before had the privilege of flying with a goat strapped in the seat behind her. The odor of a few dozen layers of barnyard filth had long since numbed her sense of smell. She just prayed the odor had not also latched itself irrevocably onto her attire.

They were going down. She could tell by the ache in her head. *Please, let us be landing and not crashing.* Across the aisle, Sveta and John Watson looked worse for the wear. Sveta had her fingers curled around her husband's grip, her other hand white as it grasped the armrest. Her head lolled back against the headrest, her face pale and framed by blond hair that had lost its life. She had beautiful brown eyes, Kat remembered, and the gratefulness in Sveta's small voice told Kat she'd made the right decision. God worked in mysterious ways. That's what Mrs. Watson had said, and Kat wholeheartedly agreed. She liked the petite woman and her husband, John—Mr. Senator's son. He seemed a kind fellow, perhaps shell-shocked and fighting impatience, but he, too, had given Kat a warm handshake. "I don't know what we would have done if you hadn't come along."

That comment had sealed her decision.

No one, however, had warned her about the mode of transportation they would take to the city of Yfa, in a republic of the Commonwealth of Independent States—the new Russian Federation—that few people outside the region had ever heard of before, Bashkortostan. The orphanage was located thirty miles farther in a village called Blagoveshensk. As her ears began to pop, the suggestion of traveling by rail for two days didn't ring horror in her like it had when Alicia Renquist had mentioned it four hours earlier. The train stayed safely on the ground. On a train, food didn't rise off the plate when the transportation hit an air pocket. And on a train, she didn't feel like curling in a ball and hiding under the seat.

"There it is," she breathed to herself. They cleared the whitewash of a cloud, and the city sprawled beneath them like litter. Gray houses ringed the outside of the city, set on a circular grid that spiraled toward pale high-rises in the center. On the other side of the Belaya River, a muddy snake that slithered north and south, Kat made out the airport. Her confidence took a final nosedive. It appeared little more than a weed-jutted runway with a two-story, windowed garrison at the end. Kat instinctively dug her feet into the floorboards of the plane.

Her lunch nearly emptied on the seat as the AN-2 landed, bounced, and finally slammed to a halt.

"Wasn't that fun?" John Watson's attempt at a joke. Kat gave him a wry smile.

An hour later, after a bone-jarring drive to Orphanage

Number 87, she was still trying to find her usual good humor as she employed her sweet-talking wiles on the sentry barring them from the orphanage entrance.

Kat had tried to recover her composure in the backseat of an ancient *Lada*, an exact replica of a 1972 Volkswagen Rabbit her grandfather once owned. The attempt to smooth out her attire and frayed coiffeur in a car without shock absorbers and crammed with suitcases and gifts had shredded her already ravaged nerves. Now, the orphanage guard, dressed in a worn white medical jacket and doing a linebacker move in front of the orphanage door, had about three seconds before Kat completely unraveled. "But I believe the director is expecting us," Kat explained to the elderly woman who wore an expression the color of stone.

"I was under the impression the paperwork was completed. . . ." Kat wrestled out another smile and fought her rising tone. Maybe she should rethink her desire to do field work when she returned to New York. Then again, she'd never before heard of a field worker being barred entrance to an orphanage. Maybe it was her disheveled and slightly unsettled demeanor?

Or maybe there were details to this assignment that had been carefully omitted. She tried to muster her fading confidence. "Please, we would appreciate just five minutes to speak with the director."

The woman eyed them as if all three had serious cases of smallpox and harbored intentions to infect her precious community. She wasn't a big woman, but her flashing brown eyes, sharp jaw, and work-worn hands clamped on her hips had Kat at an emotional disadvantage.

Lord? Kat thought and looked heavenward.

"Ludmilla Petrovna, what's the problem?"

Kat's glance settled on an elegant, middle-aged woman with sandy brown hair and intelligent hazel eyes. She came down the stairs, curled an arm around the sentry at the door, and gave Kat a smile that seemed reasonable, even welcoming. "Can I help you?"

Kat nearly collapsed with relief. "My name is Ekaterina Moore," she explained in Russian. "And this couple here"—she gestured to the two stricken foreigners beside her—"are John and Sveta Watson. They're here to adopt a child."

The smile warmed. "Thank you, Ludmilla. I think I can handle this."

The older woman scraped a warning look over the foreigners as she turned.

"You'll have to forgive her. She loves these children like her own. My name is Olga Shasliva." She extended a hand. Her grip was firm, but gentle in Kat's. "I'm the director here. I've been expecting you." She cast a look at the Watsons, and it reflected a tenderness appropriate for their frazzled state. "So nice to see you again, Mr. and Mrs. Watson," she said in Russian. "Gleb has grown, and I am hopeful the adoption will proceed as expected."

Kat interpreted, and relief emanated from the Watsons. John pumped Director Shasliva's hand a moment too long, but the woman seemed to understand. "We all know how difficult it must have been for you to leave without Gleb on your last trip."

Tears pricked Kat's eyes. She couldn't imagine the agony of leaving a child behind after looking into his needy eyes and feeling him wrap around your heart. No wonder Sveta appeared to teeter on an emotional tightrope.

Director Shasliva led the way into the building. "We'll stop by Gleb's room on the way to the office."

Kat followed Olga and the Watsons down a long hall decorated with the cheerful drawings of butterflies, rainbows, and flowers. The place was surprisingly clean. Perhaps a bit lackluster, with dull blue paint on the walls and orange-and-brown linoleum that looked like it had been laid in Stalin's era, complete with peeling edges, but generally clean. Kat could smell bleach, and farther down the hall, the enticing aroma of soup, perhaps the famous Russian borscht, beckoned from a noisy room. "How many children do you have?"

"Right now, ninety-seven."

"Ninety-seven children? In this small building?" It looked no bigger than the middle school she had attended in upstate New York.

"We are divided by ages. This section is for the preschool children." She stopped at a door with a giant paper daisy tacked the length of it. "Please don't go in yet," she said quietly, her face suddenly solemn. "The other children will see you, and it will be difficult for them."

Kat couldn't help but wince. Of course. They were taking one. Ninety-six would be left behind. "Which one is he?"

Olga pointed to a small tot, all blond spiky hair and pudgy legs, chasing a ball. He fell, giggled, and climbed back to his feet, wobbling like a top. "That's Gleb."

Kat watched Sveta as she spied her son again after months of separation. Surely, she was calculating his growth, grieving over lost moments and small achievements. Still, a glow washed over her face, wonder, then a smile. Tears filled her eyes. Kat couldn't breathe for the magic of the moment.

Yes, this is what she'd always dreamed about, what she longed to be a part of. Uniting families. Perhaps that's why her own search had consumed her thoughts for so many years.

"I'll ask the teacher to bring Gleb to my office. You may

meet him there, and we'll get the paperwork started," Olga explained.

John had to pull Sveta from the door. Kat lingered also, counting heads. She estimated over twenty toddlers playing, laughing, waddling around the room under the watchful care of three thin women in medical jackets. She noticed the lines on the faces of the older women and the worry in the younger woman's eyes as she watched the visitors retreat.

Tears pricked Kat's eyes. This wasn't easy for anyone. She could imagine the bittersweet joy of seeing a child you've loved and cared for since birth—even if he wasn't your own flesh—get carried off to another land. Heart-wrenching happiness.

John and Sveta settled on the sofa in Olga's office, Sveta with a dazed, unearthly glow around her. John looked equally undone. Kat patted their clasped hands as she took the straight-backed chair. "The Watsons tell me a court date has been set for tomorrow morning at nine for the adoption finalization proceedings. Have there been any changes to the schedule since they received this word?"

Olga sat at her desk, serious. The warmth lingered in her eyes, but she'd become the institutional mother of ninety-plus children, and responsibility hued her expression. "No, all the paperwork is in order, and we've not been notified of any changes to the court docket. We'll plan to meet outside the judge's chambers tomorrow morning at eight forty-five. Thankfully, our region was one of the first to open our doors to adoption, and our local administration is favorable. I don't foresee any problems." She pulled out a file and began rifling through papers, checking each one.

"Actually, the previous director made my job that much easier by pushing for adoption during the early days of Glasnost. This was her dream for decades." She looked up. "All of Gleb's medical records appear to be in order. Since the Watsons have already passed initial approval, the court appearance should serve as a mere formality to satisfy the legal adoption requirements. There's nothing to be concerned about at this point. I believe they'll find the judge to be quite cooperative. Tomorrow afternoon, we'll need to arrange for Gleb's new passport, and hopefully, he'll be ready to travel to Moscow with his new mama and papa within a day or two, depending on what flight arrangements we can make."

Olga addressed the Watsons. As Kat interpreted, the director handed her a sheaf of papers.

"When the time comes for you to get Gleb, please bring a change of clothes for him. We'll take him out of the class and change his clothes, and he will leave the orphanage immediately, without returning to his group, to begin his new life as your son." Olga's voice turned hard. "No looking back for any of us. Okay?"

Kat interpreted, forcing words through her thickening throat. No looking back. Was this what she was doing? Looking back into a past her grandfather wanted forgotten? Was she about to unlock secrets that might bring pain pouring down on the man who had given her a future? Perhaps she should hop a plane for New York, just as Vadeem hoped. Despite her prayers, she couldn't help but feel as if God had closed His ears. But her job wasn't to evaluate His response, or lack thereof.

Her only job was to trust and obey. To pray and wait for rescue.

The sudden image of her former stalker-rescuer, the one God had sent to save her life, sent stinging tears into her eyes. Maybe she should look harder for God's intervention.

A knock sounded at the door. It opened, and in a moment, a teacher appeared with chubby, round-faced Gleb in her arms. He held the ball, his big brown eyes saucer-wide, rippling more than just a little fear. His pink flannel shirt missed two buttons, and he had dug his feet around the waist of his nurse, his brown cotton tights bagging at his ankles. "Meet your mama," the teacher said softly, and Kat saw the woman's forced smile.

"Natalia," Olga said to the teacher, "could you take the Watsons down to the music room with their son?"

Sveta was already on her feet. She reached for the child, eager. Gleb pulled back, his face crumpling. Kat started to intervene, yearning for this moment to be beautiful.

"Nyet," Olga said, stopping Kat. "Let them go alone. They need to learn to trust each other." She shooed the Watsons off down the hall with Natalia.

Kat ached with happiness. Mother and child. "Lord, help them," she said in English.

"Are you a believer?" Olga said, shock on her handsome face.

Kat nodded. Warmth for this well-groomed woman washed over her. She didn't know what she'd expected—probably some large-busted matron with bushy gray eyebrows and steely eyes. Director Shasliva was a pleasant departure from the stereotype with her olive green suit jacket and matching skirt. She conveyed confidence and pride in her establishment.

"You?" Kat countered, hoping.

A smile creased Olga's face. "Since I was a child. In fact, I grew up in an orphanage. If it hadn't been for Babushka Antonina, I may have never found the Lord."

"Was she your director?"

"More like my grandmother. She had beautiful blond hair and these brown eyes that could part my soul and find my sins. But she loved me, and I adored her."

Kat could picture the woman through Olga's eyes—rounded body, strong hands, a way with her love that made every child feel special. "I never knew my grandmother." Kat took a deep breath.

"In fact, that is the real reason I came to Russia. To find my family."

Olga's forehead creased into a frown. "You have relatives in Russia?"

"I think so. My grandfather worked in the OSS with the partisans. I think my grandmother was Russian. Her name was Magda. . .I think her last name might have been Klassen."

"Russia is a big place." Olga shook her head. "And there aren't many partisans left. I remember them being honored every year in a parade." She steepled her fingers on her desk, her eyes suddenly alight. "You know, I think our itinerant pastor's mother was a partisan. I remember reading an article about her not long ago. She happened to be a lawyer, and she pioneered the laws that opened the doors to international adoptions."

A Russian pastor. This trip certainly had some hidden blessings.

"They live about an hour from here, but I'll call him and see if you can meet them for dinner. I'll drive you out. From what I can remember reading, Marina Dobrana and her husband spent their lives campaigning for adoption, and it was her dream to see every orphanage emptied. She even received a medal for her pioneering work. I'll bet she could give you a few ideas. The partisan network was tightly knit back then. If anyone could point you toward your Magda, Marina Dobrana could."

Vadeem paced his office, glancing now and again at the computer, his jaw clenched. Kat's words kept running through his head. *"You can find out. The FSB has files on everyone."*

Okay, more than just her words were running around in his noggin, but he fought the places his nightmares were taking him and focused only on what he knew. She'd flown out today to Blagoveshensk, to help some rich American couple adopt a child. She was most likely safely checked into a hotel, eating potato soup, not giving him a second thought.

Whereas he couldn't seem to force her out of his brain.

He plopped down at his desk, drumming his fingers, staring at his computer's screen saver. Denis was at his perch out in the hall, checking on the history of Pskov, trying to read a smuggler's mind. Vadeem hoped the kid dug up something. Grazovich hadn't moved in two days, and the surveillance team was starting to get antsy. If Kat was somehow entangled in Grazovich's scheme, he didn't seem panicked about her disappearance. Unless he knew where she was.

Vadeem would be less than an FSB sleuth if he didn't follow his gut and look into her past. Something tied her to Grazovich, something more than coincidence or the smuggler wanting a pretty companion during his tour of Pskov. And the fact that a thug mowed them down and ripped the key—only the key—off Kat's neck, leaving behind both her suitcase and her backpack, screamed volumes.

That key had to open something of value.

Vadeem surrendered to the investigator's urge and keyed his password into the FSB computer. He pulled up her visa application and read it through. Ekaterina Hope Moore. Born in Nyack, New York. Thirty-three years old. Occupation, adoption coordinator.

He rubbed his chin and typed in her mother's name. Nothing. How about that grandfather she mentioned?

He typed in the name from her application, where it was listed as "next of kin."

Nothing. He rubbed his eyes, recalling a conversation only yesterday with his partner. *"She said her grandfather is some sort of World War II hero. Maybe he did some time on the Eastern front."*

If Kat's grandfather had set foot in Russia, the NKVD, the forerunner of the KGB, active during the 1930s and '40s, would have known about it. Which meant it would be in the FSB data bank. The screen blinked "no data."

Vadeem sat back in his chair and wondered what games Miss Ekaterina Moore was playing.

Kat sat at a round wooden table in the kitchen of the log home and knew she'd finally found the Russia she had dreamed about since childhood. A wood stove bullied heat into the room as Kat sat on a rough-hewn bench nursing a cup of *chai*. Golden-fried *peroshke* piled a plate at center stage, spicing the air with the smell of baked apples and sunflower oil. Faded pictures of stoic ancestors peered from the walls, and on the wooden countertop, steam billowed out of a silver samovar and heated the *zavarka*, a spicy tea concentrate simmering in the teapot perched on the top. A very old, wrinkled babushka sat across from Kat, eyes shining and filling Kat's ear with a story that took her to the edge of disbelief.

"Back in the forties, Stalin called up everyone to join the army. Hitler had pushed all the way into Stalingrad, Stalin's namesake. We all knew if the fascists crossed the Volga, they wouldn't stop until they got to the Pacific Ocean."

The old woman's amber eyes sparkled, the lines around her eyes crinkling as she focused on her listeners. Kat glanced at the man next to her. Pyotr Dobran had the look of a work-worn pastor, wearing a slightly stained, short-sleeved dress shirt and black pants. He'd reported that he spent the day visiting sick babushkas, painting the church outhouse, and meeting with the church youth leaders about the summer evangelism camp. Kat was struck by his pensive brown eyes, eyes that seemed to look right through to her soul. His smile, however, won her over. He clasped her hand gently, smiled with welcome, and she knew he'd been rightly called to his profession.

Night pressed against the tiny windows, a full blackness that betrayed the late hour. The fatigue that weighed Kat's jet-lagged body warred with her brain, the only awake portion of her being. After trekking nearly a mile from the bus stop with Olga, who hadn't been able to find gas to fill her *Lada*, and clinging to the promise that Pyotr would drive them back to Yfa, Kat finally felt as if the hard knots in her back were worth the prize. Olga, obviously exhausted, had commandeered a section of sofa and made sounds of slumber in the next room. Kat, however, wouldn't have missed this evening if she had had to prop her eyes open with a couple of those finely crafted teaspoons.

As if also cherishing the moment, Pastor Pyotr sat with his chin in his hands, enraptured with his mother's story, although Kat suspected Pyotr Dobran had grown up feeding on this rich history. His daughter had also joined them, a spunky blond with the name Nadia. The seven-year-old snuggled into his side and played with one of her long blond braids.

Babushka Rina, as she had insisted Kat call her, had all the makings of a farmstead grandmother despite her career as a lawyer, with her head scarf, navy polyester house dress, brown cotton tights, and hands that looked like they could both lift the world and soothe a broken heart. Kat noticed how graceful the babushka's fingers were, even at her advanced age. They reminded Kat of her mother's hands for some reason. . .long fingers made for playing the piano or the violin. She watched them now as Babushka Rina peeled an apple in one long peel for her granddaughter.

"We had a motto back then. 'Nothing beyond the Volga.' It meant there was no land for Hitler to take, and we'd fight until the last man, or woman, fell."

"Women fought in the war?"

"Oh yes, my dear, we had women bombers, women infantry, women snipers. The Russian women fought right beside their men to push Hitler back to Germany."

"Did you fight?"

Her gaze fixed on Kat's with an odd mix of melancholy and pride. "Yes. I was a sniper in the 248th Division. I fought at Stalingrad, among other places."

Kat blinked at that, having a hard time picturing this tall, rounded, but still elegant lady holding a gun to her shoulder. "That must have been difficult."

Silence filled the room. Babushka Rina let it soak up Kat's question. Then she nodded slowly. "Often in this life, we are forced to do things that might, at other times, be unthinkable." She sighed, then handed the peeled apple to her granddaughter. "We won, however. We beat the fascists, and after the war, Pavel and I came east to start a new life." The lines around her eyes crinkled as she smiled. Her face filled with a swirl of youthful memory. "And what a wonderful life it was. Pavel was more than I ever expected."

"Pavel?"

"He was my father." Pyotr reached into his worn wool jacket, which hung on the chair, and pulled out a wallet photo, a small black-and-white photograph. He handed it over. "He was a doctor. Went on to Glory five years ago."

Kat looked at a young man with shining eyes, a shock of dark hair, and a smile that couldn't be anything but kind. He leaned against a tree, hands in his pockets, forever youthful, forever strong. She was instantly sad she hadn't met him. "Pavel. That's Paul in English, right?"

Babushka Rina nodded. "Your Russian is amazingly good, young lady. Where did you learn it?"

"My mother was part Russian and my grandfather, also. He taught me."

Larissa, Pyotr's petite wife, rose from the table and began taking cups and saucers from the sideboard. "Have you been to Russia many times for adoptions?" she asked.

Kat laughed. "Oh no. This is my first actual field adoption. I work for a small international adoption agency in New York. We place babies from all over the world, but our Russian field is just beginning to develop. Thankfully, we were already registered in this territory, and our agency was able to step in to help the Watsons." She cast a smile at Babushka Rina, imagining for a moment the miles of red tape she must have untangled during her adoption campaign. "I hope this is the beginning of many such happy occasions."

"I hope so, too." Babushka Rina's eyes glowed, and Kat had the oddest feeling the older woman was looking beyond her to another place in time. Her voice sounded miles, even decades distant. "I've always had a special place in my heart for adoption."

Then in a blink, Babushka Rina returned and smiled brightly at Kat. "What was your mother's name?"

"Hope. Hope Moore. Well, that was her married name. Her maiden name was Neumann."

Larissa poured a tablespoon of *zavarka* into the bottom of Kat's teacup. She filled it with the boiling water from the samovar and handed it to Kat.

"But Neumann is a German name, isn't it?" Larissa asked. "I thought you said your mother was Russian."

"It is. My grandfather's father was German, but my grandmother was from Russia. My grandfather met her during the war."

Pyotr accepted his tea from his wife. "In Russia?" He shook his head. "Americans didn't fight on Russian soil."

"Yes, they did." Babushka Rina thumbed the handle of her cup, her eyes staring at Kat. Kat couldn't shrug off the intensity of the old woman's gaze. "They came over in the early days, helped organize the partisans."

"Yes," Kat breathed, caught like a deer by the woman's stare. "I think my grandfather was one of those. He said he worked with the partisans."

"Well, isn't that interesting." Larissa sat down next to Babushka Rina, whose eyes never stopped looking at Kat's face, and put an arm around the older woman. "Baba Rina was a partisan for awhile."

Silence filled the room as Kat's heart thumped hard. "Did you ever meet any Americans?" Here it was—the possibility this woman might have met, even worked with, Grandfather. Kat held her breath.

"No." The abrupt response crushed Kat's hopes. Babushka Rina glanced away. "I don't remember that much about the partisans. It was a horrible, dark time. War is awful. It simply tears out your heart, and there's no way to survive but to forget it all. Erase it." Her voice dropped to a harsh whisper. "I shouldn't have brought it up."

The silence felt so sharp, it brought tears to Kat's eyes. She bit the inside of her mouth to fight them back. "I'm sorry," she said in a mustered voice.

No one moved. Then thankfully, Larissa reached across the table and touched Kat's hand. "Why don't you ask your grandmother about your grandfather's activities?"

Kat's grief seemed to clog her chest. "I never met her. She died when my mother was a baby."

The tightness in the room dissolved in a moment. "I'm so sorry," Larissa said. Babushka Rina gave her a pitying smile. "What a shame. What was her name?"

"Magda. He called her Magda."

The old woman's smile froze, and in a blink, she aged to her eighty-some years, perhaps beyond. "Magda?" she repeated, and an unmistakable tremor strummed her voice.

Kat nodded, a strange feeling gripping her heart.

"That's not a Russian name."

Kat's mouth dried. "It's not?"

Babushka Rina shook her head slowly. "That's a Hebrew name. It means 'tower of strength.'"

"Are you sure your grandmother was Russian?" Pyotr asked Kat as he reached for a *peroshke,* obviously unaware that his mother's face had drained of all life.

Kat nodded, her gaze glued on the old woman. Baba Rina broke Kat's stare and sipped her tea. Her sleek, aged hands trembled.

"Could I. . .could I show you something?" Kat asked. Her heart pulsed in her throat as she dragged her backpack into her lap and pulled out her Bible. She took out the ancient picture her grandfather had given her, stared for a moment at the two women in front of the grave, then she handed it to Rina.

Larissa took it because Babushka Rina refused. "Who is this?"

Kat kept her eyes on the old woman, her emotions wanting to leap from her skin. "I don't know. That's why I came to Russia. To find who these women are and why my grandfather has this picture."

Larissa showed the picture to Rina. "Klassen," she said softly.

Babushka Rina stared at it, blinking. Then her eyes filled and she looked down at her tea.

Kat felt her soul burn in panic as she watched the old woman shake her head.

"I'm sorry. I can't help you."

Ilyitch yanked his carry-on from the overhead compartment, cursing the cramped seats, the stuffy, smoke-filled air that wanted to close his throat, and especially the low-hanging thunderheads that made their landing as close to suicide as he'd like to experience.

He slung the bag over his shoulder and nearly flattened the doddering *dadushka*. The old man shuffled at the speed of molasses from the cramped cabin. Ilyitch sucked in a calming breath. Keeping tabs on Ekaterina Moore suddenly felt like taking candy from a child. He smiled despite his frustration.

Yes, things were clicking into place, but before he spent the next ten hours on his feet, chasing down a light brunette with a gift for evasion, he had to know the truth. He had skimmed too close to detection this time. Ilyitch ducked out of the cabin into the fresh, moist air. Twilight slung enough shadow across the tarmac to keep him safely disguised, for now.

He lolled at a snail's pace as the rest of the passengers filed through the locked gates into the terminal. The air smelled of diesel fuel and rippled with the ear-piercing whine of an AN-2 motoring down in post flight. A slight wind kicked up dust and sent grit into his eyes. Ilyitch muttered an oath as they watered. He wiped them and fought a wave of frustration.

Grazovich had better be right. He didn't like to waste time, not with interest rates on his investments plunging in the States. He should thank his dumb luck that the FSB had the answers buried in their files and that he'd found them before Captain Spasonov had the brains to follow Ekaterina Moore's suggestion. Now he just needed to exert a little influence and confirm his suspicions. If Ekaterina Moore had his answers, he'd get them, one way or another.

CHAPTER ELEVEN

Kat stared at the ceiling in her dark hotel room, running over the night's events, believing in her gut that Babushka Rina was lying. The old woman had all but declared it with her eyes—she never again looked Kat straight-on during the rest of the stilted evening.

The old woman knew something. But what? Had she met Kat's grandfather or someone who knew him during the war? Did Baba Rina recognize someone in Kat's faded photograph?

Her skin prickled remembering the way Larissa read the name, Klassen.

It was familiar to her. Kat knew it in her bones.

Her chest felt heavy, thick, and her eyes burned. "I feel as if I'm teetering on the edge of discovery, Lord, but something keeps yanking me back!" She slammed her fist into the ancient bed.

The Watsons were in the next room, probably staring at their own whitewashed ceilings, anticipation pushing sleep into the realm of impossible. Kat sat up and trudged to the window. A lonely streetlight swept back the darkness in a puddle of light. In a nearby doorway, a man slouched in the shadows, probably a drunk dozing off his latest liquid meal.

While she watched, the bum staggered to his feet and walked to the edge of the sidewalk—fairly gracefully, she thought, for a man soused enough to sleep on the street. He stood dimly illuminated by the envelope of lamplight and stared boldly at the hotel.

At her window.

At her.

Kat's heart stopped in her throat.

No, it couldn't be.

In a second, she whirled, ran for the door. She slammed it open and dashed down the hall. Her heart raced her down the stairs, into the lobby. . .

Where she skidded to a halt and blinked.

"*Privyet,* Kat."

⬥

"Let me get one thing perfectly straight with you right now." Kat's eyes sparked in fury. "I am *not* going back with you." With her hands clamping her hips, her face flushed, dressed casually in a pair of black leggings and a baggy T-shirt, she'd never looked more enchanting to him.

He gulped back a smile. "I missed you, too."

Her mouth gaped. He saw her working up a response and held up a hand to save her the trouble. "It's okay, Kat. I'm not here to drag you back to Moscow." Although the thought had crossed his mind more than a thousand times as he winged his way to Yfa, having totally discarded his common sense. Well, perhaps not completely. After what he'd finally dug up in the FSB computer, he knew Kat had landed herself smack in the middle of a century-old mystery, and her connection with Grazovich had suddenly taken on an entirely new meaning.

Vadeem was here to protect her. At least that's what he told himself as he turned to butter before her blazing eyes. He sucked a deep, calming breath. "I'm here to help you."

She harrumphed, raising the attention of two ladies dressed to kill in thigh-high black leather skirts and sequined blouses, smoking cigarettes near the restaurant entrance on the far end of the ancient Intourist lobby.

Vadeem took a step toward her. Kat stiffened, her eyes narrowing. "What you are doing here?"

"I told you, I'm here to help you." Oh, he'd forgotten how good she smelled. "C'mon, let's go have a cup of coffee." He tried a smile.

She eyed him up and down as if she could judge his intentions by his rumpled gray shirt, his black jeans, or the way he burrowed his hands into his jacket pockets. He gave her the courtesy of not moving until trust edged into her eyes. It earned him a smile. "Okay. But I don't drink—"

"Coffee. I know." He pulled out two packets of hot cocoa. "I picked them up in Moscow."

The next smile was genuine and went right to a soft place in his heart. So maybe he'd done the right thing by following his gut instincts instead of his brain.

"Okay," she said, raising an eyebrow. "You've piqued my interest. Why are you here?"

He shot a glance at the decked-out duo near the restaurant, still eavesdropping, then at the desk clerk, who was trying unsuccessfully to bury her attention in a day-old newspaper. "There's an all-night café down the street." A place where he'd spent much of the evening waiting for her to return to the hotel. He was dying to know why she'd sent the Watsons to the hotel alone and where she'd spent the last six-some hours of her evening. He shrugged away the questions and offered her his arm.

She looked at him a long moment. Then quietly, she said, "I need to go upstairs and change clothes." She said it with enough smile to make every emotion he'd successfully buried over the past fifteen hours rise to life with a shout.

"I'll wait." He would have no problem enjoying her company in whatever attire she picked. However, he had to admit when she changed into a lavender shirt and jeans, it did magical things to her face. Softened it. She'd added a touch of makeup while he paced in the hall, confirming in his heart that jumping on a plane that afternoon and racing to Yfa had been, yes indeed, the right thing to do.

Even Ryslan had agreed, once Vadeem tracked him down, that they would need Kat's help if they were going to untangle Grazovich's little scheme. So maybe his brains hadn't taken a vacation.

She trotted through the lobby, hauling her backpack over her shoulder. "I can't believe you found me. How did you know where I was?"

He gave her a look that made her screw up her face in shame. "Kat, the FSB knows your every move." He laughed when she turned ashen. "It's okay. I really wouldn't have followed you if it wasn't important."

Like keeping you alive. He didn't voice the thought, knowing she'd laugh at him, but the truth of it made his chest tighten.

They walked out into the street under a canopy of stars. The night breeze tangled in Kat's hair, laughing at her efforts to comb it back, away from her face. He noticed she shivered slightly. He peeled off his coat. "Here."

She shook her head, but he ignored her protest and slid it over her shoulders. Hopefully her scent would rub off on it like last time.

"Did you really miss me?"

Her question hit a soft spot. He debated, feeling as if he were about to cut out his heart and lay it before her. "Yes."

Was that a giggle?

It bolstered his courage. "In fact, I couldn't stop thinking about you."

Her sudden silence made his heart stall in his chest. Oh no, he'd gone too far, too fast, again. He turned.

Yep, her face was pale. Eyes wide, luminous, fear haunting her expression.

"Sorry," he rasped. "But it's the truth. There's something about you that I can't shake."

She ducked her head, started walking faster. He winced, scrambling for recovery. "So that's why I looked into your background."

That stopped her. It wasn't quite the place he'd wanted to go with this conversation a second ago, but at least she'd stopped.

"Yes, Kat. I looked up your past. I couldn't find anything on your mother or your grandfather. In fact, I couldn't find anything on you at all."

Her face fell.

"But I did find something about Pskov." He had her. Big amber brown eyes alive and simmering with hope. "During the 1917 Bolshevik Revolution, Russia was fighting World War I against Germany. Czar Nikolai, despite the fact that his country was falling to pieces, was at the front, directing his armies. In Russia, up until Peter the Great's time, the czar was also the head of the church. He was considered God's envoy on earth."

Kat nodded, moved closer. The breeze caught her perfume and sent it at him, playing havoc with his concentration.

"Even though Nikolai wasn't officially the patriarch of the church, rumors circulated that the position might be reinstated, and Nikolai, as commander of the army, blessed the troops as their spiritual father. A part of his religious garb was, among other things, a necklace. A diamond, ruby, and sapphire necklace set in gold, called the Crest of St. Basil the Blessed."

"Like the Cathedral in Red Square?"

He nodded. "It's worth millions. Even then, it was priceless.

Dated to A.D. 1500. He had it with him when his train was stopped in Pskov."

She chewed her lower lip. "I don't understand."

He took her arm and began to walk slowly. Her big-eyed stare had his focus disintegrating with the effectiveness of a hot blast. She obviously wasn't ready for his feelings—probably never would be—and he'd better start working overtime to put some distance between his emotions and reality.

Why did she say she missed him? It only opened all sorts of old wounds, sparked hopes he'd never considered entertaining. He fought for a steady, professional voice. "Rebel forces had seized St. Petersburg, and the royal family was under house arrest. Czar Nikolai was returning from the front to be with his family, but the Bolsheviks turned his train back and sent it to Pskov. A couple of Duma representatives met it there and demanded his immediate abdication. He stalled them as long as he could, hoping for aid from his White Army and from his family of royals scattered around Europe."

"No one came."

"No. You see, Russia was fighting a war. The White Army, his army, was at the front. By the time they pulled out, it was all over. The family was dethroned and civil war had started."

"And the crest?"

He stopped in a pool of lamplight, then turned to look at her. "It vanished. Although he'd been guarded, when Czar Nikolai finally surrendered the throne and they stripped him of everything he owned, the crest had disappeared."

"How?" The wind was teasing her hair. He wanted to catch it, tuck it behind her ear, or better yet, entwine his fingers in it, imagining it would feel like silk in his grip.

He tucked his hands into his pockets. "Well, that's where you come in."

Her puzzled look made him smile, wide. Oh, she was so worth calling in a few favors from a certain clingy redhead at the embassy, who, after extracting a promise to hook her up with his partner—who wouldn't mind anyway—called in a favor of her own at the bureau of Social Security in America.

"You know, Kat, ancestors are a funny breed. You just never know when they are going to pop up." He smiled.

She glowered. "Vadeem, you're being a little too cryptic for me." She grabbed his shirt, burying her fist into it. "Spit it out!"

She was so close he could just lean down and kiss her. Gently, as soft as a whisper, but finally he'd touch those lips that could pout and smile and tremble with devastating effectiveness. He swallowed hard, his gaze on hers.

"It's a fact that Czar Nickolas stopped the train on the outskirts of Pskov after abdicating his throne. In the wee hours of the morning, he walked in the woods and, of all things, picked mushrooms. According to an account by one of his personal guards, a lone traveler, later connected to a certain monk with close associations to the czar's family, was spotted near the place where the czar had gone walking. That traveler was Anton Klassen."

She stepped back, releasing her grip on his shirt. He didn't move away, struck by the disappointment coloring her face. "Klassen. Don't you know that name?" he asked.

"No. I mean, it's on the picture. . .but I don't. . ."

He heard her frustration. "Kat, Anton Klassen had a daughter. I couldn't find records on his wife, and the last known Russian address for Anton was reported in 1918. We think the two might have immigrated to America. But the daughter stayed here, raised by a woman from their village."

"So?" Kat shrugged, hands high. Her eyes filled. "I don't know any Anton Klassen. Or his daughter."

"Yes, you do. Marina Klassen. Marina Antonova Klassen, who, according to the birth certificate of foreign birth filed in Schenectady, New York, 1941, was listed as the birth mother of a baby girl born in Pskov, Russia. The name of the child's father is listed as Edward Neumann. They named the infant Nadezhda. Hope. Hope Neumann. Your mother."

"So this Marina Antonova Klassen was my grandmother?"

"Yes."

"But I thought her name was Magda."

"Not according to the record of foreign marriage they have on file at the Department of Social Security. Edward Neumann to Marina Antonova Klassen. November 1938."

To his utter shock, she threw her arms around him.

He hung on tight.

⚜

Oh no, what was she doing? Kat's heart stopped with a thump as she realized she had just leaped into the arms of a Russian FSB agent and was hugging him like a long-lost friend.

If the strength of his arms locked around her were any indication, he didn't mind at all.

She released him slowly, aware suddenly of his smell—fresh soap, cologne, worked leather. "I'm sorry," she whispered as she stepped away from him. Her knees felt like freshly cooked *kasha*. She took another step back and met his gaze.

What she saw turned her mouth dry. He stared back, unfliching, his eyes etched with longing. "Vadeem, Captain. . . I. . ."

"Don't Kat. Don't back away. Don't say you're sorry, just don't. . .move." He turned away and ran a hand through his hair, then cupped the back of his neck, kneading a muscle. "I don't know what is wrong with me, but I can't seem to get out from under your spell. You came into my life like a *Katoosha* rocket, totally knocking me off my feet, and I can't seem to find my footing. You're playing serious havoc with my ability to walk a straight line here, and if you come a step closer I'm liable to kiss you."

Kat blinked at him, shocked still. No, she wouldn't move. She wouldn't even breathe. Kiss her? She swallowed and noticed her pulse strummed in her ears. The image of his expression when he'd seen her in the lobby—surprise and not a little relief—rushed back to her. No, not surprise. Happiness.

He had missed her.

And it had only been fifteen hours.

Worse, she'd missed him. Missed his protective hovering. Missed his gentleness, missed his smile and taut humor.

But she wasn't ready to kiss him. She'd barely said good-bye to Matthew, although that relationship had died months, maybe even a year, ago. Pleasantries, companionship, and mutual dinner dates were all that remained of their college romance. Matthew had been safe, even at times tender, but he didn't make her heart beat. . . .

Not like Vadeem.

What was she thinking? She couldn't kiss him. Ever. Regardless of their cultural differences, which should be blaring like a siren in her head, Vadeem wasn't a Christian. Danger. Back away, no, run while her heart still had a hint of survival.

Vadeem turned back to face her, and his expression was one of reined desire, hurting and wanting and fear rolled into sharp angles, a rugged shadow of whiskers, and blue eyes that seemed to swallow her whole.

He took her breath away. She stepped back, afraid that she might totter toward him. "How can you want to kiss me? You barely know—"

The expression on his face silenced her. "I know you, Kat. I might not know you as well as I'd like. . .but I know you." He ran his hands through his hair, staring at her with eyes that brimmed with raw emotion. "I know that I've never seen a more beautiful woman in my entire life. I know that your hair begs me to touch it, that your eyes can look right into my soul, and I cringe, wondering what they see. I know that you've come halfway across the world to find a part of yourself, and that you've got enough guts to dig until it happens, even if it gets you killed."

"I'm not going to—"

"I know that you're impossibly stubborn and that it only makes me want to shake you or. . .or maybe wrestle you until you listen to me." He drew in a deep breath. "I know that you love chocolate, and that you aren't afraid to be Russian, and oh, I can't tell you how much that makes me like you. I know that you can poke fun at yourself and smile, and that you smell like sunshine and flowers and hope, and that you are incredibly. . . breathtaking. . . ." His voice dropped. "Especially wearing my jacket."

She swallowed her heart back down into her throat.

"I know that we are different and that you can't possibly know anything about me. But Kat, I can't dodge this feeling that you've stepped into my life for keeps." He lowered his hands, deliberately crossing his arms over his chest. His expression turned sweet and vulnerable, kneading all the soft places in her heart. "At least, I hope so."

"You do?"

He reached out and touched her arms. His gentle grip traveled right through his leather jacket and into her bones. "I know that I am probably scaring you with all this. But Kat. . .did you miss me?"

Had she missed his hovering, his bossiness? Had she

missed his domineering protectiveness? Had she missed his tenderness, the smell of him close to her, the feel of his breath on her face, the way his eyes filled with her reflection? She gulped back her confusion.

"Vadeem, I don't know how I feel. I. . ." She chewed her lower lip. His gaze fell to her action.

"And I know you chew your lip when you're scared." He let her go and backed away. "Maybe we should go back to the hotel."

Her eyes widened. "Vadeem, I'm a Christian—"

"Oh, no, Kat. . .I didn't mean. . ." He groaned, cringed, and turned away. "I wouldn't even think of compromising your honor."

Her heart tugged at his embarrassment, despite her own. "It's okay, Vadeem, I understand." She put a hand on his muscled arm and felt him jump.

He turned back, his blue-eyed gaze in hers. "No. I want you to believe me. I'm going to be hovering, as you so delicately put it, until we figure all this out, and I want you to know that you're safe with me. . .in every way." His eyes traveled over her face, looking at her nose, her eyes, stopping at her mouth. "In every way," he repeated softly. Then he gazed into her eyes and stepped back. "I'm going to take good care of you. I promise."

She felt warmth flood her heart, soothing, like hot cocoa on a cold night. If she didn't know it before, the realization that FSB Agent Captain Vadeem Spasonov cared about her honor, as much as her safety, came crashing home with the fragile look on his face. "I believe you."

"Good." One side of his mouth tilted up in a rueful smile. "The last thing I want to do is scare you out of Russia."

His wry smile settled over her like a warm blanket.

"Now that you're here, I'm not sure anything can scare me away."

He crooked out his arm, and she wrapped hers around his elbow.

"Now," she said impishly, "where's that hot chocolate you promised?"

CHAPTER TWELVE

Vadeem had camped out in the hall. The die-hard cop again forsaking sleep and a bed so that he could keep her safe. Kat scrubbed her face with both hands as she sat on the bone-hard wooden floor. Vadeem had jugular tenacity when it came to protecting her. If it weren't for his twinkling blue eyes and cockeyed smile, she'd package the guy in the category of stalker. . .well, endearing stalker. She leaned her forehead against the door. The painted wood felt cool against her skin. Vadeem was out there and she was in here, and only a door separated them. . .a door of eternity.

Vadeem wasn't a Christian. She'd known that since he'd nearly decked the monk at the monastery. But until this moment, this evening, she hadn't given it more than a passing consideration. Shame roared up in her soul. Regardless of their future, she should have begun praying for Vadeem's salvation the moment she'd caught up to him outside the chapel, white faced and looking like he was going to shatter. She ached for him. Never, regardless of how desperate she'd been as a child or even now with her life supposedly in danger, had she felt that bereft of hope.

Kat had God. That meant whatever tragedy befell her, God could pull her through. Even when she felt the Almighty was hiding on the other side of the Cosmos, inherently, she knew He cared. Faith told her that.

Faith was the one thing Vadeem didn't have.

She pressed her palm to the cool wood, fighting the urge to yank the door open, skid to her knees in front of him, and pull him in her arms like she might a potential adoptive mother waiting the results of a judge's decision, whispering, "Have faith."

Instead, Kat folded her hands and looked up to the dark ceiling of her hotel room. "Lord, I don't know what You're doing here, but I like this fella way too much for my own good. Please help me to stay on my feet, not to give my heart away."

Kat knew better than to leap into the arms of an unbeliever. The momentary happiness would slowly be eroded by their differences. She served the living God. Vadeem served himself. As much as he worked to sacrifice himself for others, Vadeem's basic desires would always be for himself. That's what separated Christians from non-Christians. Christians followed Christ. "And please, Lord, help Vadeem see Your truth. Give him faith to turn to You."

Kat closed her eyes, letting the memory of his sincerity seep into her bones. *I'm going to take good care of you. I promise.*

Funny how that same statement coming from Matthew turned her into knots and tightened her jaw. Matthew meant, "Don't do anything foolish. Obey me, and everything will turn out okay."

She'd been obeying and dodging foolishness for three decades. She'd obeyed Matthew through college and beyond, too afraid to step out and follow her dreams, waiting year after year for him to finish school, believing that he knew best for her. She'd obeyed Grandfather, growing up on the farm, happily sheltered inside his singular attention. She had even obeyed when her parents lay dying after a semi mangled their Chevy station wagon. How she longed to replay that moment, to break the rules, run into the hospital, and embrace the parents who'd shown her how to live a life of faith. A life of love. A life of adventure, whether in New York City or on the farm.

She knew they had secrets, and often, years later, Kat longed to have the opportunity to unlock them. To find the source of their faith and passion for truth. Her father had a strength about him, a driving purpose that felt nearly supernatural. Without a doubt, Kat knew he treasured her. That truth resonated and kept her from shattering. But it was her mother's eyes Kat remembered the most. Golden brown and rich with wisdom. She could search Kat's soul with a look and somehow knew how to minister to the hurts inside. Still, they guarded their past, as if it might someday leap out and bite their only child. And, on that hot summer day, her parents' secrets went into the dark loam with their bodies.

"Stay here with Uncle Bert and be a good girl," Grape-Grandma had ordered as she slid out of the pickup truck and slammed the door. "I'll be right back."

Kat stayed, counting the windows in the three-story county hospital, wondering why her great-grandmother had cut short Kat's unpacking to rush them to the hospital, as if the old woman itched to go on her weekly visitation. If only Kat had known her mother lay bleeding from a ruptured spleen, her life leaking out by the second.

Kat remembered her anger as she crossed her arms over her chest and willed Grape-Granny to appear through the glass hospital doors. She'd waved good-bye to Mama and Papa only two short hours ago, looking forward to an entire glorious summer before her, riding through the timothy, and helping Grape-Granny put up pickles and pick peaches and apples from the orchard. Summertime meant freedom and a life gloriously undefined by rules, conformity, and hemlines. Kat fought the urge to prop her feet up on the dashboard, anxious to get her vacation started.

She counted windows, mesmerized at the tint of morning sun turning the glass bronze. This hospital was minute compared to the one in New York City where she'd visited Grandfather. A trickle of sweat streaked down her forehead and pooled at the stiff collar of her polyester dress. It wasn't the first time, nor would it be the last, that she had been stranded in the truck while the old woman visited the infirm.

Kat's stomach lurched as she leaned her head against the hotel wall. Remnants of anger at the hospital regulations that decreed no one under the age of twelve allowed, at her grandfather for being absent, out of town again, at Grape-Granny and her notions of propriety that forced her into a Sunday dress when she would have much rather been in a pair of jeans and riding her mare, Hickory, on the farm. The injustice of Grape-Granny's abrupt morning plans had Kat gritting her teeth, and the drone of Uncle Bert drumming his fingers on the steering wheel only increased her pain. Uncle Bert wasn't what she'd call overly sensitive. A bachelor with his own farm to run, he looked the disheveled part. Grandfather's mutt collie, Butch, had a larger vocabulary than her gloomy uncle Bert.

Grape-Granny finally appeared in the door, and something about the old lady's expression had made fear coil deep in Kat's stomach. She sat up as Grape-Granny approached, wringing a cloth handkerchief, her face solid, but her lip twitching just slightly, as if pain was about to leak out. Kat opened the car door.

"Oh, Kat," was all the woman said.

Her wretched tone told Kat that the world as she knew it had shattered.

How could she step over the line after that? Rather, she'd been grateful for their protective hovering. First Grape-Granny, then Grandfather. They treated her like something made out of milk glass, and Matthew easily took over the job when she met him at Nyack University. She often wondered if her grandfather didn't set up the meeting. It wasn't every day that a medical resident wandered into the Nyack library, especially when he had his own prestigious library at Columbia. But he'd helped her pick up a stack of books she'd dropped, and she should have seen then that he'd made it his mission to keep her safe. . .too safe.

So safe that, after seven years of dating, her world consisted of Matthew, her college roommate, and two colleagues at work. A world that seemed to cinch tighter each year, her dreams becoming smaller and smaller. "You need me, Kat. You won't be okay without me." Poor Matthew. He'd been wrong. This journey to Russia seemed like the most okay thing she'd ever done. She'd helped unite a family, she'd met a woman from the past who'd cracked open the door to her grandfather's war, and she'd met a man who made her feel brave and beautiful.

"I'm going to take care of you," Vadeem had said. For the first time, she liked the idea of a man looking out for her. And Vadeem's sudden appearance gave her the distinct feeling that he had invested in her mystery. Invested enough to do some digging into her past. Invested enough to hop a plane. Invested enough to surrender sleep to make sure she got hers. And that meant he wouldn't hold her back.

Vadeem was a good man. Kat knew it in her bones. She sensed his controlled emotions as they walked back to the hotel, the way his muscles tensed under her arm, and his tenderness as he ran a finger along the bruise on her jaw line, now turning yellow. "See you in the morning," he'd said, as he lowered himself onto the hard wooden floor. He hung his arms over his up-drawn knees. "Go to bed. You'll be fine."

It wasn't herself she worried about. She couldn't let him sleep in the hall. Not another night. Taking care of her didn't mean he had to sacrifice his health. Guilt pushed her to her feet, and she yanked open the door before common sense reined her in.

Vadeem stared at her, his face muscles tight, as if he'd been watching her through the wooden door with Super-Vadeem-man X-ray vision. "What's the matter? Are you okay?"

She shook her head. "I can't let you sleep out here."

He smiled, his blue eyes lighting up and sending fire through her veins. "Well, I can't sleep in there, and I'm not going to put any more distance between us." He pushed to his feet. "Kat, I'm fine. I've gone days without sleeping before." He smiled, and she saw a hint of his classified past on his handsome face. "Trust me. I'm okay out here."

She wasn't buying. She saw weariness bagging under his eyes. The guy had traveled a thousand kilometers with news that could change her life. She wasn't going to let him sit in the hall like a bug. "I have an idea."

What was she up to now? Worry flickered through Vadeem's mind, the briefest suspicion that she was about to make a run for it.

But if that were the case, she would have gone through the window, not be trying to convince him she cared about his stiff neck muscles and lack of sleep. He stretched as he followed her down the hall to the desk clerk, then beyond to the tiny second-floor lobby.

Tall windows framed the night and sent shadows like a blanket across the two fraying armchairs and the brown velour sofa. Kat sat on one end and patted the place next to her.

With that, his heart began drilling through his chest. He sank down next to her, every muscle taut. What was this sudden shower of warmth? The last thing he needed was for her to encourage the emotions he was having a hard time ignoring. He leaned forward, clasped his hands, elbows on his knees, suddenly more awake than he had been in the past twenty-four hours. "Uh, Kat, I think you should. . ."

"I read someplace that soldiers can take naps, a full REM cycle in about twenty minutes. Can you do that?"

Where did that come from? "Well, yeah, but if I'm asleep, how can I watch over you?"

She put her hand on his back. It sent ripples down his spine. He jerked, then hated himself for it. He couldn't sleep if he wanted to.

"Maybe *I'll* watch over *you.*" Her hand moved up to the nape of his neck. "Lie down on the sofa. Stretch out and take your twenty minutes. Take an hour. I'll sit here and keep watch."

He turned, blinked at her, any words locked in his chest. Oh, she was so beautiful with her tousled hair, her eyes searching his, warm and candy sweet. She took her hand away. His gaze trailed to it, remembering how she'd dug that hand into his jacket only twenty-four hours earlier. "I'm supposed to protect you, remember?" He was having a hard time remembering that himself at the moment.

"So, I'll wake you if any terrorists show up." Tease played at the corners of her mouth.

The idea rubbed against his better judgment. No, he shouldn't lie down, bring his legs off the floor, curl up next to her. No, he definitely shouldn't rest his head in her lap and get lost inside her tender expression.

He was never any good at following better judgment.

Only, it would be a miracle if he got one minute of sleep.

She must have seen the turmoil in his eyes, for she patted his chest. "Tell me about your childhood, before the orphanage, Vadeem."

He winced. Why did she have to sour this incredibly sweet moment with that question? A jaunt down memory lane, however, was probably a whole lot safer than the memories he wanted to create.

"I had a big brother. My father was an electrician, my mother a nurse. We had a small home, lived a normal life." His mind drifted back, warmth cascading over him.

"What did you do for fun? Did you have any hobbies? Did you play sports? Were you on any teams?"

He hesitated, feeling the answer as a burning flame in his chest.

"I was a member of the Pioneers."

It was the worst day of his miserable short life. Vadick sat in the back row of the auditorium on the third floor of his school, kicking the legs of the straight-backed chair.

Everybody knew. His best friend Sergei Ishkov's eyes bore a hole through Vadick as Sergei stood in line with the rest of Vadeem's classmates, waiting for his pin. Sergei looked so smart in his red handkerchief, his eight-year-old face glowing with pride.

Vadick ached to have a red scarf. Tears burned the back of his eyes as he looked away. He searched the audience for Ivana Ishkova. She was lost in a cluster of other parents filling the first three rows of auditorium seats. Vadick hung his head, not able to watch as names were called, and his classmates filed forward, one by one, and received their Pioneer pin.

He would run away. That's what he'd do. He'd run as soon as the snow melted and the river broke; he'd take his father's lodka and let the current take him south, to Nevyansk or perhaps even to Ekaterinaburg. That would scare them. Not far enough that they wouldn't find him, but enough for fear to do its duty. His mother would clasp him to her chest and beg forgiveness for keeping him from being a Keeper of the Motherland, a Pioneer member, dedicated to preserving their strong and pure State.

Vadick's chin bobbed as tears burned his throat. He heard Sergei's name called and quickly swiped at his shame, wanting to watch.

The Pioneer leader, Comrade Korillovich, a wide, ruddy man with power in his arms and fire in his brown eyes, bent over, shook Sergei's hand, and handed him the pin.

The pin with Father Lenin's face engraved in the front. The pin they would all wear to school on the days of Pioneer meetings. A pin Vadick would never own. He pounded his hand against his knee.

That's when his legs moved forward. So his mother hadn't signed the permission slip? It was a formality. Hadn't Comrade Korillovich said just that when he asked Vadick why he wasn't joining?

Vadick ran furiously to the front, up the center aisle, dragging with him a hundred piercing, curious stares. He skidded to a halt at the back of the line. His labored breathing drew the attention of his classmates, boys and girls who frowned at him.

He ignored their stares and fixed his gaze on Comrade Korillovich. His heart pounded in his throat. The sides of Korillovich's mouth tilted just slightly, and a hot wave rushed through Vadick. Oh, yes, he'd be a Pioneer.

He still remembered the way the straight pin drew blood in his palm when Comrade Korillovich slapped it into his hand. "You did the right thing, Son. Welcome to the Pioneers."

"Vadeem, are you sleeping?"

Vadeem blinked, and the world of his childhood vanished. Kat's gaze kneaded his with concern.

"You stopped talking, but your eyes were open. I didn't know."

He was horrified to feel moisture filming his eyes. He blinked and it squeezed out, dripping down his cheek like a marble.

She saw it; her face twitched. Then gently, she drew her thumb across his cheek and wiped his tear. Silence drummed between them as he stared at her, feeling her questions in her worried expression. The answers rolled into a lava ball in his chest, and it was all he could do not to let them erupt, spewing horror and pain across their fragile relationship.

He closed his eyes.

She sighed, then said, "Sleep, Vadeem. I'm trusting God to watch over the both of us, and I'm not going anywhere."

She'd been saying that for three days. For the first time, he was glad she meant it. He smiled slightly and buried himself in the sweet envelope of sleep.

"I don't know!" The young monk's face twisted against the knife digging into his neck. True to his Abkhazian blood, he glared back at Ilyitch like a mangy dog in a corner.

"Back off, Ilyitch. I already asked him. He doesn't know." General Grazovich looked considerably less foreboding than he had after Ilyitch's arrival an hour prior. So their uneasy relationship might have spiraled a bit out of control. It set Ilyitch's every nerve on edge trying to get face-to-face with a man hounded by the FSB, and perhaps it did make him a bit trigger happy with his fists, especially when Grazovich accused him of trying to get them both collared. Right, like he ached to return to a Russian prison. He'd tasted enough ten years ago. Did the slimy Abkhazian general think he did this for the game of it? Ilyitch knew better than the general the torture techniques of the FSB.

Grazovich wiped at the trickle of blood that seeped out from the corner of his mouth. "You're making too much noise." Warning edged his tone. Ilyitch tried to ignore it, as well as every voice that rose like a howl from his past to haunt him, to push him toward terror.

Instead, Ilyitch tightened his grip, his meaty hand digging into the windpipe of Brother Papov. "I'm getting tired of these games. You said that if we waited, the girl would bring us the book."

Ilyitch heard a hammer click back and felt the spine-chilling press of metal against his neck.

"Back off."

The Abkhazian general always did have a weakness for his Abkhazian family members.

Ilyitch slammed the monk against the wall, cursed, and let him go. He turned and jerked away from the weapon Grazovich held at his neck. "Your cousin is considerably less help than you led me to believe."

In the moonlight, Ilyitch saw danger gather in the general's eyes. Time flipped back, and he saw General Grazovich and his "troops" as they mowed down the Georgians guarding the makeshift prison, saw what the Abkhazians were capable of, fueled by seventy years of Communist oppression. Ilyitch's Adam's apple scraped his throat as he swallowed. He backed away, hands slightly raised, fighting against turning them into fists.

Suddenly, the general turned his glare at the younger man, his cousin, as if suddenly realizing the web the man had tangled for him. "You specifically said you knew where the crest was hidden. I'm counting on you, Cousin. I'm in no mood to let my brother die."

"I–I'm not sure. I thought it would be in his belongings or at the very least that the girl would have it. Timofea was so desperate to send the key to her." Papov raised his hands, his sleeves falling back to reveal skinny arms. "She has to know where the crest is. Please."

If he didn't know better, Ilyitch would have thought the monk was about to curse. Or cry. He was just thankful the general had turned his predator's gaze away from him.

"Listen, maybe I put too much stock in the legend. Timofea was old and delirious. . . ." Papov's voice pinched on the high edge of panic as his gaze flickered down and caught on the damp weeds pooling around their feet. "I told you everything I know. Really. The old man had been talking about the crest in his sleep, and I assumed. . .well, I'd heard the stories. . .but I was probably. . ."

"What exactly did the old man say?" Ilyitch took a step nearer.

The blood drained from Papov's face. He looked at Grazovich for comfort. "Timofea told me about a man he met, someone who knew about the crest."

Ilyitch grabbed his tunic, shook him just enough to arrest his attention. "Who was this man?"

"He. . .he called him Anton. He told me that Anton had sought refuge at the monastery, and when he left, he left behind the key. . .and a book. I looked for it for nearly a year. I thought for sure. . .the way he talked about the girl. . ."

Ilyitch exchanged a glance with Grazovich, who was nodding, eyes dark. Their relationship had righted, soldier and general. Ilyitch taking orders, just as he had been for a decade. General Grazovich reminding his soldier at every hesitation to whom he owed his freedom, even today.

"She's a smart one. You sure she doesn't have the book?" Ilyitch asked, releasing the monk and wiping his hand on his jeans.

Papov shook his head. His voice turned plaintive. "I—I don't know."

"Are you sure you don't know?" Ilyitch kept his voice low. "Absolutely?"

"I'm sure."

"That's good to know. I'd hate to think I was killing you when you might still be of some use to us."

The monk stared at him a long time, long after Ilyitch buried his *pero* into his lungs.

"That quiet enough for you?" Ilyitch muttered as he wiped his knife on the grass. But when he turned, Grazovich was gone.

CHAPTER THIRTEEN

Vadeem opened his eyes without moving a muscle.

Kat was a horrid watchdog. Terrible. Bottom of the pit. One hundred percent failure.

But he would take beauty over protection any day.

Her chin had bobbed down to her chest, her hair cascading like a waterfall over her face, tempting him to reach up and wrap a finger around a thick, silky end. Her eyes were closed, and this near, so near he could feel her breath, he could see she had a tiny smattering of ginger freckles across her nose and cheeks. He could hardly breathe for the sight of her.

I'll take care of you. Her words came back to him, and he smiled at their accuracy. He'd slept well, too well judging by the dent of pale light creeping in through the windows. Outside, sparrows chirped.

She stirred. He didn't move, hadn't moved except for his eyes, having learned the technique of waking motionless years ago. Now he held his breath, unwilling to disturb her.

He heard a scrape, the thud of feet on the stairs, and his mind tensed. Surely, Grazovich hadn't tracked them here. No. Only Ryslan knew where he'd gone, adding a crude laugh and a promise to keep his eyes on Grazovich.

And as of last night, Grazovich hadn't budged. He was still playing tourist in Pskov, taking up residence by day in a local library and by night in the hotel bar.

Vadeem watched out of the corner of his eye as a man topped the stairs. He stood in the second-floor lobby, scanned the room.

His gaze landed on Kat.

Vadeem shuttered his eyes as the man approached. Solid underneath a thin brown jacket and dark dress pants, he looked mid-forties with sandy brown hair thinned at the temples. Pursing his lips, as if dreading the task before him, he held a package in both hands and crept toward Kat. . . .

Vadeem launched off the sofa like a panther.

He hit the man hard. They slammed into the wood floor. The man grunted and sprawled like a sack of potatoes while Vadeem pinned his neck to the ground.

"Vadeem!" Kat grabbed his arm, yanking. "That's Pyotr. Get off him!"

The man blinked at him, brown eyes filled with confusion.

"Pyotr." Vadeem rolled off his victim, who eyed him warily.

"Pyotr—as in I had dinner with his family last night?"

Vadeem grimaced. He held out a hand as he found his feet. "Sorry, I guess I'm a little—"

"Jumpy? Aggressive? Paranoid?" Kat filled in, her hands on her hips.

Vadeem met her frown. "Cautious."

Pyotr stared at the two, eyebrows high. "Yes, well, I'm glad someone is. After the tale she told us last night of being mugged in Moscow and shot at in Pskov, I'd say a bodyguard is a good thing to have around." He took Vadeem's hand, who hauled him up from the floor. "Glad to meet you, Vadeem. . . ."

"Captain Vadeem Spasonov." Vadeem shook his hand, sizing him up. Despite having the grip of a factory worker, not a hint of vodka dimmed Pyotr's sparkling brown eyes, something rare for a man of Pyotr's age. In fact, Vadeem wondered how he'd been able to take the man down so easily. Pyotr had Viking shoulders and the girth of a man familiar with the rigors of hard work.

"I'm sorry to surprise you so early this morning," Pyotr said, screwing up his broad face in apology. "But my mother asked that I drop this off immediately. I'm on my way to morning prayer service south of here, in Bersk." He held out the package to Kat. "It's a book."

She took it like she was accepting a newborn child. "What kind of book?"

He shook his head. "I don't know. I've never read it nor seen it until last night." He took a deep breath. "My mother was very upset after you left. Something you said unnerved her." He motioned to the sofa, asking Kat to sit.

Kat was chewing her lip as she sat down, eyes wide. Vadeem remained standing, not entirely sure she wasn't out of danger.

"Listen, I have to tell you that my mother is. . .well, she's old. She's lived a long time and seen a tremendous amount of history. She fought, shoulder to shoulder, with the men at Stalingrad, and I'm sure that's never left her. War ages people, you know. I don't really remember my mother young. She and my father had me late in life. I think they believed they would never have children. She wasn't the kind of mother who played games with me, but she is loving, and I know she wouldn't hurt you for the world."

Kat frowned. "What are you saying?"

"She may or may not know the people you were looking for. But she thinks she does, and if it proves to be false, it's not because her intentions aren't authentic." He swallowed and looked away at the window, where dawn pressed through filmy curtains. "She goes in and out of the past these days. She calls me Pavel, my father's name, more often than I want to admit. If it helps, I know that she used to live in the west somewhere, near Moscow. There are many things about her that I don't know, things she's buried that make me wonder. Like how she can speak a little Polish or why she never talks about her parents. The answers to these questions are in the past—one that may or may not have anything to do with you or your search." He scrubbed a hand down his face. "Does this make any sense?"

Kat looked at the pastor, and Vadeem recognized a look of kindness that made him appreciate her even more. "I think so." Her eyes glistened. She gazed down at the package, wrapped in brown paper.

Pyotr cupped a hand around his neck. "I think she believes she is helping you in some way by giving you this. I don't think she'd part with it otherwise."

Kat was moved. Vadeem could tell by the way she nodded, her chin quivering.

"Open it, Kat," he urged.

She looked at him, and the hope in her eyes was so palpable it lodged a lump in his throat. She slid a finger under the wrapper and tore it gently away.

Inside the folds lay a book. Fraying twine bound its leather cover twice around. It smelled of dust and age. Kat looked at Pyotr, then carefully untied the twine.

Curiosity pushed Vadeem closer. "What is it?"

Kat opened the front cover. He saw her swallow, hard. Her face, when she looked up, was raw with emotion. She opened her mouth, and after a long moment, words finally emerged. "It's the diary of Anton Klassen."

⁂

"I'd like to talk to your mother." Kat lifted her chin, her gaze unflinching as she stared at Pyotr. Her tone had turned bolder now that she'd downed a cup of cocoa in the hotel café. At least some feeling had finally returned to her body. Shock had turned her numb, and it wasn't until Vadeem suggested they grab some breakfast that reality brought life to her muscles.

If the information Vadeem had unearthed yesterday proved correct, the past lay right beneath her fingers, contained in a four-inch-by-six-inch book on yellowed, dusty pages of tiny printing. She traced the cover with her finger. "Please, Pyotr, your mother must know something."

"I don't think you should ask her anything else. I'm not sure you would even find answers." Pyotr stirred his coffee with a red stir stick, then let it go and watched it circle round with the momentum. "She's pretty. . .incoherent at times. She has wild stories."

"She didn't seem too incoherent last night."

He smiled, sadness ringing his eyes. "She had a good night."

Kat considered him, his posture seeming slightly defeated, shoulders rounded as he stared into his cup. He smiled ruefully. "I'd like to believe all her wild stories are true."

Kat touched his arm. "Maybe they would make sense to me."

He looked at her, and she couldn't help but notice he had the kindest set of deep brown eyes, congruent with what she expected of a pastor. "You know, maybe they would."

His words lit a flame of hope. "When?"

He checked his watch, then leaned back, rubbing his wrist where the watchband had creased a mark. The sun streamed through gauzy gray curtains, bright light flowing over the wooden café floor like syrup. Vadeem sat across from them, stirring his tea, watching Pyotr as if the pastor might be a spy, ready to pounce if the need should arise.

Not that Vadeem had needed a reason before. She couldn't

believe he'd flattened Pyotr, poor guy. Thankfully, the pastor looked like he could take it, with his sturdy muscles and solid frame.

Still, it made her smile to think Vadeem had pounced, protecting her. Again. It seemed to be developing into a habit over the past few days.

Pyotr scrubbed his hand across his chin. "I have a morning prayer meeting in Bersk, then I need to do some visitation. I'll be back in town for our local prayer meeting tonight. Why don't you meet me here, around six o'clock? We'll go to the meeting, and then I'll drive you out to talk to my mother."

"Prayer meeting?" The idea of worshiping with Russian believers had Kat's heart leaping. "I'd be thrilled." She looked at Vadeem. "What do you—"

"No. Forget it, Kat. You can go. I'll stand outside the door." Vadeem's expression sent icy daggers through her soul. His words from their conversation outside Pskov came up like a wall. *Faith destroys.*

Her faith was all she had. It held her together, built her up, kept her alive, gave her confidence that this crazy quest was worth the costs.

She nodded, not agreeing for one second. "See you tonight, Pyotr."

She'd find a way to get Vadeem inside that church tonight, and she'd start with prayer.

Pyotr stood up and held out his hand to Vadeem. "No hard feelings, okay? I know you're just doing your job."

Vadeem looked like he'd been sucker punched. He blinked at Pyotr, then his head dipped down in a half nod. "Right."

Pyotr turned to Kat, his signature kind grin on his face. "And I'll see you tonight." He clamped his hand on her shoulder. "Kat, whatever happens, remember that God has a plan in all this. He hasn't forgotten you or your family, wherever they are."

Words failed her. She nodded.

Vadeem watched him go, suspicion swishing about his eyes. "Creepy."

Kat frowned. "What do you mean?"

Vadeem leaned forward. "Aren't you feeling the least bit weird about this? Last night I tell you you're related to Anton Klassen, and today his diary shows up in your hands?"

The way he put it, it did sound incredible. But then again, his disbelief discounted God's omniscient ways. The Almighty had a knack for the incredible. Like Phillip's ordained meeting on the road with an Ethiopian searching the Scriptures. Or Saul, before he was Paul, helping to stone the very first martyr, Stephen. Or even Joseph, sent to Egypt years before famine, to become ruler and save the family that had betrayed him. Holy coincidences. "Not weird at all, Vadeem. Maybe planned. Maybe this entire thing has been planned out from the beginning by the Master. I have been praying for His intervention."

"No." Vadeem folded his arms across his chest. "I'm not buying it."

She shrugged. "Are you saying God doesn't orchestrate our lives?" Her heart pinched. "Or are you saying you don't believe in God?"

He smirked. "Calm down, Kat. I believe in God. I know He's out there. I even believe He plans out our lives. I'm just not talking to Him, that's all."

She felt as if she'd dived into the big mysterious ocean that was Vadeem. She stared at him, seeing beyond the soldier, the defiant expression, his solid set jaw now sufficiently covered in dark whiskers, and into the past.

Vadeem and God were at war.

Faith destroys.

Vadeem hadn't won the last battle with faith. He'd crashed and burned. How long ago had that fight been waged?

He sat back, arms crossed over his muscled chest, gaze fixed hard on her.

She ached to know what he was hiding. "It's a pretty dangerous thing not to talk to God. He is, after all, *God.*"

He shook his head, raising his gaze to the ceiling. A couple shuffled into the café and sat down at a table behind him. A muscle pulsed in Vadeem's jaw. He licked his lips as if trying to form words. Finally, "I suppose I can't face Him."

The words made her wince. She leaned across the table and touched his arm. "You know, God doesn't hold us responsible for the things that happen to us. Just for how we react to them."

His voice dropped to a wretched whisper. "That's the problem."

<hr />

Vadeem sat outside the courtroom on the hall bench. He held Anton's diary on his lap, carefully turning the pages, skimming for clues. Inside he could hear the hum of voices. Kat had dressed to perfection today, looking impossibly beautiful in a white sleeveless sweater and black pants. It brought out a tan on her arms and a delicious dotting of freckles on her shoulders.

He'd struggled to let her walk into the courtroom alone, but common sense told him if she'd be safe anywhere, it was in the local halls of justice. And after the way she'd carved out the secrets of his soul, he needed a little breathing space. Not too much, just enough to get his feet back under him.

She was entirely too perceptive for his own good. Where did she dig up those responses that opened his heart with one slash? *He is, after all, God.*

He, better than anyone, knew what *that* meant. He knew

exactly whom he'd messed with twenty-odd years ago and harbored no illusions that the outcome had been anything but the righteous wrath of God.

He felt pretty sure that God wouldn't talk to *him*, even if Vadeem scraped up the courage to face Him.

He breathed deep and long, trying to break free of the impending doom that had coiled around his chest. Perhaps it was the mention of the prayer meeting.

He was a strong man, and it would take a small army to get him inside that church. That—or Kat's tears. But he'd steeled his heart to her plaintive cries before. He could do it again.

Right. He winced. He'd been so good at ignoring her that he was sitting in a dirty hall, a thousand kilometers from Moscow, reading a diary from a man who'd likely been dead for close to a century, while the man he should be chasing was reading library books and plotting his next great heist.

Ekaterina Moore had turned his life inside out.

He stretched out his legs, feeling like he'd aged a year in the past forty-eight hours. He hadn't felt so wasted since basic training.

Vadeem rubbed his eyes and stared at the diary. Who was Anton Klassen? And what was an old babushka in the middle of Russia doing with his diary? Vadeem had skimmed a few pages and read about a man who obviously struggled between two worlds. Anton wrote about a world of war. . .a time Vadeem understood only through the lectures of his teachers. But through Anton's eyes, Vadeem saw a different history.

March 3, 1917

    Chaos rules the land and I sit here, immobilized, in the icy clutches of pure fear. Over and over again, my heart cries out with the cadence of a repetitive prayer—a

*desperate plea for wisdom and divine guidance. How can
I ever hope to fulfill my hastily spoken promises? Where do
I begin? How could he ask me, an ordinary citizen from
the steppes of southern Russia, to accomplish such grave
tasks? O Lord, please, direct my steps. Show me the path
You would have me take. Give me courage to do Your will.
May I prove myself a loyal patriot in these days of uncer-
tainty that lie ahead.*

What tasks, Anton? What are you afraid of? Vadeem kept flipping, searching for any mention of the crest.

March 20, 1917

> *To think, the somber beauty Oksana now bears my
> name. Oh, but what have I done? How will I ever
> explain to Papa without breaking his heart? Even so,
> I shall willingly, and in silence, bear the reproach of my
> father should I, through this commitment, find it possible
> to discharge my patriot vow. If only the Lord will bless
> our union and forgive me for betraying the faith of my
> ancestors.*
>
> *In the taking of a bride, I have brought upon myself
> sure misery when I return home. In truth, misery lurks in
> the shadows even now, for my new wife seems no happier
> with our marital arrangement than I. Her sullen disposi-
> tion appeared to sink to the depths of sadness after the cere-
> mony. Yet despite her solemn countenance, her beauty fills
> my heart, my soul, and at times, I struggle to even breathe.*

Vadeem closed his eyes. He knew what it meant to struggle
to breathe around a woman. He'd been gasping for air ever since
Kat walked into his life. He'd been as dazed as a freshly netted

fish, but eerily happy to perish, if only beside her.

He cringed. Kat Moore was turning him into a poet.

He turned more pages, skimming, noting dates.

November 1917

Untold sorrow fills my soul on this day, which should have been my most joyous ever. No sooner had I found myself adrift in Oksana's sweet love than our world came crashing in. They died as my wife and I looked helplessly on from our secret place. Their screams echo in my heart, torment my every thought, even my soul. What kind of man am I that my brothers should die while I live? How can my faith survive such horror?

Vadeem's breath clogged in his chest. He reread the words, their accuracy like a spear through the soul. He closed the book, unable to swallow, feeling saliva pool in his mouth, bitter. *What kind of man am I that my brothers should die while I live? How can faith survive such horror?*

What had happened to torment Anton Klassen's thoughts?

Vadeem knew all about souls filled with sorrow. And questions of why. He forced himself to swallow, to breathe in and out.

He opened the book, his chest tight at what he might find.

June 1918

Oksana came to me, full with our child. She knows what we must do, but do I have the strength to say yes? I've been entrusted with too great a task. I fear my shoulders are not large enough for it. Even now, as I hold Oksana and the night air blows with the warmth of spring, fear nips at me like a wolf. The Bolsheviks will return. And we have nowhere left to hide.

July 1918

Banya with Timofea. I cleared my soul as we sat as brothers in the Lord. He understands. He is a good friend and will help carry my burdens. He says God will find a way to keep His promise. I know it now to be true. I tucked my past into the darkness, then turned toward the light. I even found a verse upon which to cling. John 11:9. His light has illuminated my dark paths. He has set me free. Now, my prayer is that Timofea will keep his promise in due time. Only God knows the future, and I am trusting in His Word. Peace can be had for those who have faith.

Peace? Vadeem nearly threw the book across the hall, furious. Not a word about the crest, but plenty about suffering and pain. . .and now peace. Vadeem slammed the book shut and clenched his jaw.

"Vadeem, are you okay?"

He flinched, then looked up into Kat's gaze, honey sweet and brimming with concern.

"Yes."

"You look. . .angry."

Vadeem took a breath and pasted on a smile. "How did it go in there?" He looked beyond her to the couple who had just exited the courtroom. They were beaming; tears dripped down the woman's cheeks. "I assume, well?"

Kat smiled, radiant. "They can pick up Gleb tomorrow. Director Shasliva booked them on a late afternoon flight back to Moscow tomorrow." She touched his arm. "Are you sure you're okay?"

He handed her the book. "I couldn't find anything we might use in here."

She took it, her smile dimming. "Are you sure? Maybe you didn't look hard enough."

"I'm sure," he said, a little too stiffly for his own taste. He looked away but saw her frown and feared she'd seen beyond his words to the wound festering in his soul.

CHAPTER FOURTEEN

Vadeem sat in the lobby, hands white, clutching the arms of his chair, looking as if he awaited execution.

Vadeem had to be wrestling demons. Spiritual warfare was the only reason Kat could conjure up that could turn a kind, even gallant man into a sullen tag-along. What had happened to the lion-hearted soldier who had camped outside her door for two nights, dug up her past, and even made her tremble with unspoken emotions?

Kat had to get him inside that church. She'd prayed all day, without ceasing. Even as she made her plea before the Russian judge, her mind, her prayers lingered on Vadeem. She didn't know why, but some inner, unspoken urge pulsed at her to pray, to plead for help like the persistent widow before the judge's door in the eighteenth chapter of the Gospel of Luke.

God, I don't know what is going on, but please help Vadeem find peace. Her heart ached at the agony on his face. He leaned forward and buried his face in his hands, and her spirit groaned.

Had he read something in Anton's book? She'd entertained misgivings about handing it over to him even for the few hours she was in court but had hoped his sleuthing prowess would catch clues her uninformed eyes would pass over. True to character, he'd taken good care of the book and passed it back to her moments after she'd exited the courtroom, almost as if he couldn't wait to get rid of it.

She tugged out the diary and smoothed her hand on the cover. Soft and worn, it wasn't a heavy book, but it held the weighty secrets of a man's past. It told the Klassen heritage, one she suddenly longed to claim as her own.

Kat checked her watch. Pyotr was late. She flipped through the book, but the uneven scrawl in early twentieth-century colloquial Russian would take more scrutiny than she could muster at the moment. She tucked the book into her backpack, hoping for a quiet moment that night to read it.

Perhaps Rina, Pyotr's mother, could also help illuminate the dark past. She prayed Pyotr was wrong and that Baba Rina's stories, while wild, might be just what Kat needed to tame the restlessness in her heart.

"Maybe he's not coming."

Kat looked up, read the look of hope on Vadeem's face, and slowly shook her head. "He'll be here." She hesitated a moment, then surrendered to the urge and touched his arm. "Vadeem, I think you should come with me. God loves you, and He's waiting for you."

"I'm not going, Kat." The tight expression on Vadeem's face left no room for argument.

Kat nodded, her throat tightening. She sat back, crossed her arms, and prayed for a miracle. Only a holy act of God was going to get Vadeem Spasonov in the church.

But God had been abundant with miracles of late. She tucked her backpack over her shoulder.

⁘

Ilyitch sat in the café, cursing his bad luck. Captain Spasonov was on the woman like glue. If Ilyitch didn't watch it, everything he'd spent the last five years building would explode. The last thing he needed was for the FSB captain to look up and see him nursing a beer in the hotel café.

Kat had the book. He watched her zip it into her backpack. Across from her, Spasonov looked wrung out, like he'd been dragged behind a Russian *Kamaz* about a hundred miles. His face was lined, his hair spiking in all directions, his shoulders slumped. He appeared about as capable as a babushka in a fifty-meter dash.

Perfect.

Vadeem leaned against the hood of Pyotr's ancient blue *Zhiguli*, crossed his arms, and shot daggers at Kat.

Tears weren't going to move him. He'd summoned his defenses and planned for her attack.

But her latest tactics left him outflanked and weakening quickly. She wielded her miraculous smile like a weapon against his icy resolve, and he was melting fast. He ground out another no, desperate for her to comprehend what she was asking and understand that it was unthinkable. "I just. . .can't."

Her beautiful smile dimmed. "Don't go anywhere."

Relief whooshed through him with a sigh. No, he was resigned to park here for the next three hours in misery, staring at a small, green, log cabin church, listening to believers sing songs that would unravel time and pain and take him to a place he had tried to forget. Her amber eyes committed him to that much. "Don't worry. I'll be here when you get back."

She turned and headed into the church, waiting as a hunched babushka wrapped in a wool head scarf and brown polyester coat shuffled in before her. The door opened, and for a brief moment, the light from inside pushed out into the twilight, illuminating the worn wooden steps.

His light has illuminated my dark paths. He has set me free. Peace can be had for those who have faith. Vadeem opened the diary Kat had left with him, in hopes, he supposed, that if she couldn't get him inside the church, he might find some spiritual wisdom from her ancestors. She'd practically shoved it in his hands, despite his protests. "There have to be answers in here, Vadeem, and we don't have time for me to decipher every word like an archeologist. Please, do what you can to figure out what secrets Anton buried in here."

He opened to the page where he'd left off. Secrets, indeed. How about finding the secret dark path God's light had illuminated for Kat's deceased relative?

From what had Anton been set free? The burden of the crest? Or something deeper, more hideous?

Like betraying his family. Vadeem, too, had seen a building burn, heard the sounds of anguish echoing into the night. Had Anton been freed from memories and guilt so gut-wrenching it could make a man wake at night, screaming?

Vadeem closed his eyes and pushed back a wave of pain so hot he thought he might gasp.

"Moshchina, could you help me?"

Vadeem opened his eyes.

"You, *Moshchina."* A small woman, her skull outlined by baggy skin and a cherry red head scarf, smiled up at him. She leaned heavily on a smooth, weathered walking stick, scoliosis wrestling her nearly half over. Her backbone jutted from a thin, gray sweater. Her arthritic hand reached out to his arm, grasping his jacket with thin fingers. "Could you help me?"

He ran a tongue over his dry lips, his heart pounding. "Sure, Babushka." Her brown eyes, set deep, lit up like candles inside an earthen pot. "Please help me into that building there. My old bones can't make the steps." She gestured with her head to the church across the street.

Vadeem stared at the building and felt something heavy crash into his chest. He swallowed. *"Ladna."* He shoved the diary into his pocket and angled out his elbow.

They shuffled across the street, toward the church, Vadeem's feet weighing a thousand kilograms each. He helped her up the stairs and breathed considerably easier when she opened the door.

It swung in. He glimpsed Pyotr in front, standing between two endless rows of pew benches crammed with bodies. The familiar smell of body heat, aged wood, and dust rushed back to Vadeem. His head started to spin.

The babushka shuffled in, her hand knotted in his jacket. She seemed to have forgotten him, her eyes on the pastor. Vadeem put a hand on hers, intending to work her grip free before he passed out, or worse, lost the battle with his churning stomach and delivered the borscht he'd had for lunch onto the sanctuary floor.

No one turned around, thankfully. His heart lodged in his throat when she stopped at a back pew and gestured for him to enter. He looked at her, unable to voice his horror.

She pushed him, powered by some mystical babushka force that wielded him helpless. He found himself stumbling into the pew, his feet taking a mind of their own. He tried to turn around, to force his way back, but the babushka shuffled in behind him, blocking him in, sandwiching him between herself and a padded crony in a brown wool shawl and green head scarf. His legs betrayed him again and he sat, hard.

The room spun, and Vadeem focused on Pyotr in a desperate attempt to keep from dropping to the floor. This was some sort of psychological reaction to the fear he'd bottled for twenty-five years. He simply had to clench his teeth and bear it out, just like he'd endured basic training and a hundred life-risking missions.

It didn't help that Kat sat in the front row like a lighthouse, her eyes glued to Pyotr. If she knew Vadeem was sitting in the sanctuary, a mere fifteen rows behind her. . .well, she was liable to jump the pews and drag him to the front.

Pyotr opened his Bible, and the plump babushka beside Vadeem handed hers to him. It smelled of wisdom. He shook his head, but she shoved it into his hands. He gave a half-grunt of thanks.

John 11. The pages crackled as he turned them, not needing to read the words. The story came back to him like a fresh breeze on a hot day. The miracle of Lazarus. He closed his eyes and tried to block out Pyotr's voice as he read: " 'This sickness will not end in death. No, it is for God's glory so that God's Son may be glorified through it.' "

"Vadick, what have you done?" His father stood in the doorway, holding the pin, his face contorted with a pain Vadick had never before seen. Vadick's heart dropped to his knees, and his legs wobbled. He tried to find words, but they locked in his chest, along with his breath. His father shook his head. "Son, you already belong to a brotherhood of believers." His voice seemed mournful, like when Babushka Nina had passed on without the "saving grace of God." Vadick's eyes burned.

"You don't need this." His father dropped the pin and ground it into the dirt with the heel of his boot.

"Papa, no!" Horror drove Vadick to his knees. He scrabbled after the mangled emblem.

His father caught him in his meaty, gentle hands. "The way of the Pioneers ends in death, Boy. Don't be duped."

" 'A man who walks by day will not stumble, for he sees by this world's light. It is when he walks by night that he stumbles, for he has no light.' "

Vadick buried his hand in his pocket, his fingers curled around the mangled pin. His face burned under Sergei's stare. "Where is it?" his friend repeated.

Vadick couldn't bear to voice the truth. He didn't have to. Sergei grabbed his hand and pried open his fingers. Horror was written in his expression. "Father Lenin's face is. . ." Sergei's eyes widened. "You're in big trouble."

Vadick snatched back the pin. "We'll fix it. I'll hammer it back together. Color in Lenin's eyes."

Sergei shook his head, his voice low. "Who did it, Vadick? Your pop?" Only Sergei, his dearest friend, comrade, Pioneer brother, could have read Vadick's wretched expression. Sergei's face darkened and the Pioneer creed flashed through Vadick's mind. "Protect the Motherland. . . ." The pin, ruined in his pocket.

"Don't, Sergei. Don't tell. Please."

" 'Lazarus is dead, and for your sake I am glad I was not there, so that you may believe.' "

Vadick hung his feet over the wooden-edged pew, playing with his wool shopka. The pastor's words droned on, now a blur in the boy's mind. Spring beckoned outside. A fresh and hopeful spring with the smell of apple and lilac blossoms thickening in the air. The kind of spring that made a boy tear off his boots and run through the muddy fields, earth squishing between his toes, oblivious to the switching he'd earned—

The back door to the small house church slammed open. Vadick turned, his mind ripped from springtime whimsies, and his heart froze at the sight of NKVD officials, silver tanagers in their grips. "This church is an unregistered body. Everyone is under arrest."

Vadick tried to become a millimeter small as Comrade Korillovich stepped out from the cluster of black-coated men and stared at him. A smile tweaked the Pioneer leader's cheeks.

Vadick glanced up at his father, who'd gone white, and suddenly he wanted to cry.

" 'I am the resurrection and the life. He who believes in me will live, even though he dies; and whoever lives and believes in me will never die.' "

The mud squished up between his boots, into the knees of his pants as Vadick crouched behind the fence, watching, hiding after he'd snuck out in the confusion of threats and violent arrests.

Papa never looked more fierce. He stood, facing the NKVD officials, his dark eyes challenging, on fire. His gaze moved beyond the soldiers and fixed on Vadick.

Vadick thought he might go up in flames.

Then came a scream, a collective moan, and a torch sailed through the air. It landed atop the church. The roof whooshed into flames.

"No! The Bible!" Mama's voice, high above the crowd, sent terror through Vadick's veins.

"Save the Bible!" Vadick heard his father's voice, or maybe his own. The family Bible left on the rough-hewn pew. The Bible with the copied pages, the three-generation Bible.

Vadick left his senses behind the fence and scrambled toward the burning church. He dashed behind a NKVD guard and dove into the building.

Screams behind him. Heat blistering his face. Save the Bible. Then an arm grabbing him, hauling him out.

" 'When Jesus saw her weeping, and the Jews who had come along with her also weeping, he was deeply moved in spirit and troubled.' "

Vadick sprawled on the ground, eyebrows singed, watching paralyzed as the NKVD guard wrestled Papa to the ground. Knee in his back, the soldier held a gun to Papa's head. "Wreckers die."

Mama's arm tightened around Vadick's chest. Her tears fell on his singed face. "Please God, help us."

A shot parted the crack and hiss of flames.

Vadick closed his eyes and wept.

" 'Jesus wept.' "

Vadeem stared at Pyotr. Grief fisted his chest in a death hold. Fury rolled into a ball in his throat and threatened to close it. It hurt to breathe.

" 'Jesus wept,' " Pyotr repeated. "Our Lord saw Mary's pain, and it moved Him so that He wept for her." He looked up, eyes on the congregation, mercifully moving past Vadeem without hesitation. "And He weeps for you. He knows the trials, the horrors we've all suffered, and He weeps for us."

Vadeem felt tears gather at the back of his eyes, and he ducked his head. The old woman's hand still gathered the folds of his jacket. He wrenched it away, wishing he could dive over her and crawl out of this miserable sanctuary, out of this town, out of this life.

" 'Could not he who opened the eyes of the blind man have kept this man from dying?' "

Vadeem's head snapped up, gaze tight on Pyotr as the pastor read. Vadeem held his breath.

Pyotr smiled. " 'Did I not tell you that if you believed, you would see the glory of God?' " He closed his Bible, reciting the rest from memory. " 'Lazarus, come out!' The dead man came out, his hands and feet wrapped with strips of linen, and a cloth around his face."

Pyotr paused. In the space of sound, Vadeem counted his heartbeats as they slammed against his chest.

"So they might see the glory of God and believe, my friends. Only God can take tragedy and carry us through it, showing Himself glorious. Only He can free us from our pain of suffering, our losses. Only He can take us out of death into life. It is all about believing in the eternal. Believing in the plan of God. Believe. . .and you will see the glory of God. 'A man who walks by day will not stumble, for he sees by this world's light. It is when he walks by night that he stumbles, for he has no light.' Keep your eyes on the light and believe."

Vadeem wove his hands into his hair, surprised to find sweat beaded at his temples. He'd been walking in darkness so long, the light might be more than he could bear.

~·~

Vadeem was still waiting, just like he promised. Kat stepped out of the church, into the night, feeling fresh and clean. Renewed. Fellowship with the body of Christ, regardless of the country or the language, invigorated her spirit. Pyotr's words came back to her. "Believe in the plan of God. Keep your eyes on the light and believe."

The story of Lazarus always moved a place inside her. *Jesus wept.* Seeing the character of God weeping at human pain and sorrow touched her heart in ways she couldn't express. Oh, how she loved a God who didn't hide emotion but let them see His love in the tears on His face.

If only Vadeem could know such a God. If only he might believe that, whatever lay hidden in his past, God wept for him.

The night air was fresh, laden with the fragrance of the poplar and willow. The dark sky to the east sparkled with a smattering of stars peeking out between the camouflage of clouds. Kat hitched her backpack on her shoulder and started toward the car, anxious for Pyotr to finish his duties with the believers inside so she could talk to his mother.

She prayed the old woman would be able to connect Kat, somehow, to Anton Klassen. In her wildest dreams, Baba Rina would know about an ancient key and a monk named Timofea.

Kat stepped onto the sidewalk, paused, and waited for a car to pass. Vadeem hadn't seen her yet. Obviously weary of waiting, he had his head down, a thumb and forefinger pinching his temples, his other hand balled into a fist at his side as he leaned against Pyotr's blue *Zhiguli*. The car passed.

Kat didn't move. She stared at Vadeem in horror as realization washed over her. Vadeem's shoulders shook, his jaw clenched so tightly she could feel the pain knotted in his chest.

Vadeem was crying.

Saliva pooled in Kat's mouth as she watched him drag in a long, ragged breath.

Panic rushed into her limbs; was he hurt?

In an abrupt movement, he whirled, balled his right hand, and slammed it into the hood of the *Zhiguli*. The sound thundered into the night.

Kat jerked. No, definitely not hurt. At least not physically.

Her own eyes burned, watching him struggle.

The last thing he needed right now was her sudden appearance. Prayer, yes, definitely prayer, but walking into his pain would only make it worse.

Kat backed away, turned, and stiff-walked past the church to a small grove of trees beyond the wooden fence line. Leaning against a poplar, she set her backpack down, watching Vadeem out of the corner of her eye. He braced both hands on the car hood, head down, breathing hard.

She lifted her gaze to the heavens and prayed.

A gloved hand clamped over her mouth, crushed her lips to her teeth. "Don't scream, and you might live."

CHAPTER FIFTEEN

V adeem braced himself against the car hood, his teeth clenched, his pulse hammering in his head.

Get ahold of yourself. He had nearly mowed down the startled babushka with his faster-than-lightning escape from the church. He put a hand to his chest, pushing against a burning deep inside. Trotting down memory lane rehashing his nightmares was the last thing he needed to do with his addled brain cells right now. He slammed his fist into the hood of the car. What was he doing here, out in the middle of nowhere, hanging onto the heels of an American like a lonely puppy, when he had a smuggler to catch?

Keep your eyes on the light. Oh yeah, he'd seen the light. Seen it sputter, burn out, and plunge him into darkness. A darkness that got deeper and colder every day he lived in the orphanage, a darkness that eventually became his friend, secreted him from feelings, from pain. Darkness that became comforting in its oblivion.

Unfortunately, Kat was all light and hope, and he could feel that brightness moving into his dark places, sunshine over the frigid tundra. And like heat moving into frozen limbs, it *hurt*. The sooner he got Kat and her precious book back to Moscow, the sooner he could shove her on a plane for the States and resume his stumble through life.

His throat burned. He could strangle Kat for being so breathtaking. For having amber-speckled eyes that reached out to him like a gift. For having laughter and a tenderness to her touch that made him ache. He'd just have to bury it. Bury the memory of waking up to her delicious smile, bury the fragrance she left behind like a souvenir. Bury the feeling of joy that bubbled to the surface when she entered his atmosphere.

Where was she?

Swiping at his eyes, he sucked in a breath and turned, his gaze fixed on the church entrance. The babushka who had nearly wrestled him into church hobbled out through the front doorway, hanging on another young victim. Vadeem crossed his arms over his chest. A car drove past him, kicking up dust. Around him the night was closing in, the sun to the west already gone, leaving only a dent of lavender in its wake. The church fence sent jagged shadows across the road.

Pyotr appeared in the door, looked at Vadeem, and waved like a long-lost friend.

Oh yes, the pastor had definitely seen him in the back row. Vadeem looked away, jaw tight. If the guy even hinted—

"Where's Kat?"

Vadeem looked at him, panic swelling in his chest. "What?"

Pyotr tucked his Bible under his arm and zipped up his jacket. "She left before I did. I thought she would be out here, waiting with you."

Vadeem ran across the road, toward the church. *Kat, if you ditched me—*

He'd wanted to believe they'd established some sort of magical bond of trust last night. He wanted to believe she trusted him. Still, her quest had driven her beyond what he'd call normal behavior. . . . "Kat!" His voice betrayed his frustration. He dashed into the church, ignoring the tightening of his chest. The gloom of dusk filled the sanctuary. A lone parishioner swept the floor and straightened pews. Vadeem stood for a moment with a hand clutched to the back of his neck. Then he whirled and strode out.

Pyotr met him at the door. The tall man looked stricken, his face white. "No one has seen her."

Vadeem stifled a curse and instead pushed past the man of God and stalked out into the street. "Kat!"

A scream rent the night sky and speared right into his soul.

———

Kat had bitten the man right through his leather glove. He cursed, let go.

She screamed.

His hand came back hard against her face, crushing her teeth against her lips. *"Tiha!"* He yanked her head to his chest, sour breath in her ear. "I'm in a very bad mood, and you don't want to make it worse."

Her knees buckled, leaving her heart in her throat. She fought the muzzle of his hand, very aware of his cruel grip on her upper arm, dragging her back, away from the church, into the dark web of trees and vines tangled behind the church property.

Away from Vadeem and any chance of rescue.

Branches tore at her face, her jacket, her backpack as he finally packed her in a headlock and dragged her along, his other hand still clamped over her mouth, clogging her breathing. He'd dressed appropriately in black, at least from his jeans to his squared-off shoes, and his legs were moving fast.

Her heartbeat roared in her ears as she stumbled against his strides, her muscles void of strength. He yanked and hissed at her to keep up. His fingers bore into her face, the pain burning her cheeks as the forest closed around them. After a moment, she heard only his heavy breaths and the sound of her own panic raging in her chest. Wildly, she shook her mouth free, then realized, with dread, he'd released her easily.

They were so far into the claw of forest, no one would hear her if she screamed.

"What do you want?" Her voice rasped tight and high.

"Answers."

He dragged her along, deeper into the forest. The night sky winked out as the tree line tightened above them.

"I don't know anything."

He stopped and threw her down in a snarl of brush. Twigs scraped her face, her wrists. The backpack thudded to the earth.

"Where is the necklace, the crest?"

Her mind blanked. She shook her head. "I don't know what you're talking about."

He towered over her, the biggest man she'd ever seen, dark bulk against a midnight forest. Anger gnarled his face, hooded in shadow, yet vivid in her horrified imaginations. He leaned forward, and the wind washed the smell of alcohol and repugnant body odor across her face. She turned away, gasping.

"The Crest of St. Basil. You know where it is. Tell me."

She shook her head, fear consuming her words, her breath.

He knelt beside her, and she turned cold when he touched her hair. "I know you have the book. You know where it is, and you will tell me."

"I–I haven't read it." Her whisper disintegrated in the torrent of his anger. She braced herself as he bent even closer, his lips next to her ear. "Are you ready to die? I don't think Brother Papov was."

Shock clogged her chest. The image of the young monk, his hands twisting as he talked about his sheltered, safe life, hit her like a slap. *Oh, God! Save me now, if ever!*

Mercifully, the man backed away, began pacing, looking back toward their broken trail as if expecting someone.

Oh, please let him think Vadeem is hot on his tail!

Kat gathered her feet under her.

"Give me the book." The hulk turned, and she bristled. Adrenaline had already flushed into her legs. She sucked in a breath and forced herself to pick up the backpack, the bag that held something more precious than Anton's journal, the one book that might hold the sketchy answer fragments to her piecemeal past. It held her Bible, the only book that held answers without end—and her heirloom picture.

"You want it?" she asked as she pounced to her feet. "Here!" She flung the bag at him, not waiting to see where it landed, and bolted.

The branches whipped her face, bushes tore at her jacket, but darkness was her ally. Terror ignited her muscles. She flew through the dark woods, one step behind her heart.

Crashing and the curses of a man hampered by bulk spurred her to recklessness. She ran without thought. She slammed into trees, tripped, scrubbed her palms, tore her pants. Her mouth bled from the hard slap of a branch. But as distance muffled the threats, she knew she'd won.

Thank the Lord, she'd inherited speed from one of her ancestors.

The clasp of forest eased. She shot toward a gray patch of light. Victory filled her lungs. She burst out of the brush, onto pavement, into freedom.

Brakes squealed. Burning rubber reeked the air. Kat turned into the headlights of an oncoming car and froze.

She left her scream to echo and dove for the ditch, knowing she wouldn't make it.

"You can stop pacing."

Vadeem turned, jabbed a finger in Pyotr's face. "Back off."

Pyotr didn't flinch, obviously accustomed to dealing with people strung tight with stress. Instead, he gripped Vadeem's shoulder. "She's going to be fine."

Vadeem shrugged him off. "She's not going to be fine. Look at her." He didn't have to turn around and point at the pale woman on the rickety wooden hospital bed to know he'd made his point. Kat looked like she'd been through a war and beyond. Swollen lips, one of them cut, a scrape along the other side of her face to match the now yellowing bruise from the Moscow thug, bloodied hands, and a spidering of red welts and scratches up her arms and along her neck. It turned him inside out to look at her. He braced two hands on the wall and shuddered.

But she was alive. Thank heaven, she was alive. And he'd done some thanking today. Need brought him to his knees beside her bed, trembling. He didn't actually address the Almighty, just a general gratefulness to the Being up there who had delivered her safely out of the *Zhiguli's* path. Obviously, she'd hit the ditch, hard. Two hours had passed, and she hadn't roused. But the CAT scan showed no brain swelling. He touched his forehead to the cool wall. "I don't get it. What was she doing out on that road?"

The driver of the car had called the ambulance. It wasn't hard to connect the dots when the ambulance screamed by the church toward the dirt road outside of town. On a hunch, Vadeem had followed it.

He'd nearly cried when he saw them lifting her crumpled body onto the stretcher.

Pyotr sighed and sat down on the bed opposite Kat's. The bed groaned with his bulk. "Maybe the person who attacked her in Moscow came after her—"

"One thousand kilometers away?" Vadeem turned, wincing. Kat moaned and he skidded to his knees beside her bed. "Kat?"

Her chest rose and fell in the rhythm of a deep sleeper. Vadeem curled his fists into the sheets. Despair stretched his voice thin. "What if she doesn't wake up?"

"She's a Christian, Vadeem. She has faith in God, and God is not going to abandon her on either side of heaven."

Vadeem looked up and met Pyotr's gaze. The pastor had his hands folded, elbows on his knees. He leaned forward, earnest. " 'I am the resurrection and the life. He who believes in me will live, even though he dies.' "

Vadeem glared at him, not needing Pyotr's religious rhetoric at the moment. He needed reassurance, not platitudes. He struggled for breath in his constricting chest, unable to find a comeback.

"Vadeem, why did you come into the church tonight?"

He winced. "You saw me."

Pyotr nodded, face expectant.

"I was tricked by a babushka."

"I saw your face," Pyotr said. "You were listening."

Vadeem ran a circle around the back of Kat's hand with his finger. "Yeah, I listened. I've heard it before. The resurrection of Lazarus. My parents were believers."

Pyotr sighed heavily, paused. "What happened, Vadeem? You have the look of a man with secrets."

Vadeem pushed back the hair from Kat's face, then entwined it in his fingers. She looked so vulnerable, it was all he could do not to gather her in his arms. He'd been fighting that urge for the past two hours, and if Pyotr didn't leave soon, he'd do it in front of the pastor, not caring what the man of God thought. In Vadeem's wildest dreams, Kat woke up, nestled in his embrace, touched his face with those beautiful hands of hers, and assured him that she hadn't tried to ditch him, hadn't tried to push him out of her life.

No, in his wildest dreams, Kat simply woke up. He'd unsnarl the truth later.

What was she doing out in that road?

"Have you ever heard of Wreckers, Pyotr?" Vadeem said, not looking at him.

"Of course. Enemies of the state. Wreckers."

"It was a convenient term used to destroy anyone who disagreed."

"Of course." Pyotr's voice was low. "We lived in a dangerous time. No one could trust anyone."

Vadeem touched his forehead to Kat's hand, the feel of it cool against his hot skin. "I was a member of the Pioneers, did you know that?"

Pyotr sighed, deep and sad, like he'd heard this story before. "Most people were. The Communists had a way of making a child want to belong."

Vadeem nodded, afraid of Pyotr's perception. He couldn't look at the pastor as he continued. "I wanted to be a Pioneer more than anything when I was eight years old. I joined up against the wishes and counsel of my parents."

"Because they were believers."

"And they knew the Pioneer party line was atheism and selfishness."

"Yes. But eight years old is hardly an age of reason, Vadeem."

Vadeem shook his head. "I believed in the Motherland, in the Pioneers. I believed what they said. I believed in my comrades. I should have known better."

Pyotr leaned forward, clasping his hands as if in prayer. "Your faith was just misplaced."

Vadeem harrumphed, acknowledging the truth of Pyotr's words. "I've learned the hard way that faith is empty. It's for fools."

"No, faith is a gift from God. It's also a choice. You must put it in the right place. In the New Testament book of 2 Timothy it says, 'If we are faithless, he will remain faithful, for he cannot disown himself.' There is a Friend who sticks closer than a brother, and this Friend is Christ, Vadeem. He'll never betray you."

Regret tasted like acid in Vadeem's mouth. He rubbed his thumb over Kat's limp hand, touching her blue veins through such perfect, translucent skin. His voice came out wretched. "Pyotr, can you leave me alone, please?"

He felt the man's gaze searing through him. He counted time with his heartbeat.

"I'm not going far, Vadeem. Something in my gut tells me you need that Friend, and I'm going to be out in the hall, praying you choose to put your faith in Him."

Vadeem didn't look up as the pastor left the room. The door closed with a whoosh, and suddenly all the emotions he'd piled up erupted in a wretched moan. "Kat, why did you run away?" he whispered. Without thinking, he pressed his lips to her forehead. It was cool, and her skin tasted of sweat.

Come back to me, Katoosha. Please, Kat, open your eyes. Look at me with those beautiful eyes. He stared at her face, willing his words to come true, eerily aware of Pyotr's voice, like a hum, in the hall.

Faith was a choice. Either you bought into the veritable helplessness of man and clung to the unseen Source, or you trod your own path. Alone. Vadeem had no doubt exactly what choice he'd made as he heard his mother's screams and saw his father's blood seep into the thawing soil. Even if he wanted to turn around, run back, and throw himself at the feet of the Almighty, faith in God—or anyone else for that matter—had dwindled to a drip in his life. If he were to admit that he needed a friend, and frankly, only God knew how desperately he longed for one, God would have to slap down some pretty vivid proof that He wasn't going to leave him in the lurch again before Vadeem cast his vote in the Almighty's favor.

Then again, Kat lay there, breathing in and out, prognosis positive. So maybe God might have heard his desperate gasps for help.

But she wasn't awake yet.

Even if Vadeem did possess the slightest urge to glance back over his shoulder at the God of his father, faith wasn't going to rush over him like a flood. Not after twenty-plus years of parched soil.

Perhaps, however, the trickle of faith could start with gratefulness. Yes, he could choose to be thankful.

He shadowed his eyes with his hand. "Thank You, God."

Like the whoosh of oxygen to a dormant fire, his words raked across his heart, and he gasped against the rush of pain consuming his breath, clawing across his chest. His throat began to close as he rasped it out again, "Thank You for saving Kat."

Tears burned his eyes, and he clutched his hand to his head.

Then he wept for the emptiness that roared through his soul.

The top of her head felt like it was coming off. Kat groaned as she clawed her way to consciousness. She ached everywhere, feeling like she'd been mauled, then dragged by a car about a mile. What happened? She scrabbled to the last clear moment. Headlights. Her heart pumping through her chest. Sour breath on her face.

Her backpack, her Bible—the picture! Gone. *Oh Lord, no, please.*

She was suddenly aware of a thumb moving across the

back of her hand. The movement sent a current of warmth through her.

She opened her eyes, blinked in the glare of the room, and heard muffled snuffling, unsteady breathing.

Hand over his eyes, breathing in raggedly, shoulders slightly shaking, Vadeem was. . .crying.

Her breath caught as she stared, horribly, wonderfully mesmerized. This man, who tackled everyone who got near her, who made her feel safe just by being in the room, who'd admitted that he wanted to kiss her and then held himself back, was crying. For her?

If she questioned it before, she didn't now. FSB Captain Vadeem Spasonov had serious feelings for her. And as she watched him suffer, she knew she'd never felt this way about a man. Ever. Matthew had never stirred such feelings of anger or delight. He'd never made her want to hide inside his embrace or hold him, desperately, back.

Vadeem's name stalled on her lips just as he looked up. A tortured look ringed his eyes, and he didn't even try to hide it, but let his pain pulse between them, spilling out everything. . . . Fear. Worry. Love? She found his name in the back of her throat and whispered it. "Vadeem."

"Oh, Kat, I thought—" He looked away then, releasing her hand to wipe his face. "Why did you run?"

Kat blinked at him, unable to comprehend the question.

He turned back to her, his eyes now ablaze, something dangerous in them that made her weak. "Don't you know me well enough by now that I wouldn't—"

"I was attacked."

The blood left his face. He opened his mouth to speak, but no words emerged. His eyes closed, and in his expression she saw anguish.

It was worse than blaming her for running away.

He blamed himself.

Vadeem opened his eyes, and fury pulsed in them. "Who was it?" he asked tightly.

"I don't know." She tunneled back to the bulk in the forest, scraping for identification. It seemed his voice had been familiar. "I don't know," she repeated.

He pushed the hair from her face. His gaze gentled, his caress telling her exactly how he felt about what had happened. "I'm sorry."

She squeezed his hand. "Am I okay?"

"For now." He leaned his forehead on hers. Stress or weariness had streaked his eyes red, and she felt his breath, so close, so unsteady, as if he was still wrestling with emotions. His smell embraced her, leather and sweat and strength. Almost unconsciously, she reached up and traced the hollow of his neck where dark hair peeked out from his black shirt. He drew back, his eyes in hers. His gaze traveled to her cheeks, her jaw, her mouth, and came back to her face. "Kat."

Before her common sense could catch up with her, she gripped his shirt and pulled herself up to him, brushing her lips on his, gentle, like a whisper.

He made a sound at the back of his throat, something that made her warm from head to toe, and moved into the kiss, tasting, testing, with a controlled urgency and a devastating gentleness that curled her toes and erased every ache.

"Kat." He drew back, close enough to touch her, far enough to look in her eyes. "Kat, you kissed me."

She nodded. "I caught that." She ran a hand down his face, thick with dark whiskers. "I wasn't sure I'd see you again." She saw the echo of her words in his wretched expression. "But God saved me." Oh, yes, God had saved her. Her racing pulse testified to that fact. She was very alive and perhaps even falling in love. She ignored a sharp stab of guilt and clung to the feeling of joy that swept through her. "Think you can get me out of here anytime soon?"

A smile creased his face, and teasing came into those blue eyes that held so much mystery. "Promise you'll kiss me again sometime, maybe when I know I won't hurt you?"

She felt a blush start at her toes and work its way up. "It didn't hurt, and. . .maybe."

He ran a finger tenderly along her jaw line. "I'm sorry I wasn't there to protect you." The look of grief in his beautiful eyes made her want to cry.

"It wasn't your fault, Vadeem. I—" She couldn't tell him she'd seen him outside the church, wrestling with some unseen anger. Her abduction had already stripped him down to his most intense feelings. She couldn't dig deeper when he looked so raw. Instead, "He wanted Anton's book."

Vadeem sat back, disbelief in his blinking eyes.

"That's not all. He told me he'd killed that monk. That young one we met at the monastery."

Before her eyes, Vadeem's face changed, darkened. He swallowed, and the hardness she'd seen on the train from Pskov entered his expression. She tensed and let go of his hand.

"Yeah. I'm going to get you out of here. You just sit tight."

Why did she have the feeling his *here* meant farther than the Blagoveshensk hospital?

W ere you followed?" Dog-tired, Ilyitch turned up the collar on his coat. His eyes burned, and he was achingly aware that someone could be watching him destroy the cover he'd erected for the last decade.

Grazovich gave him a glare. "Hardly."

Ilyitch had to admit, the glitzy casino, eerily aglow with disco lights and packed with gyrating bodies, seemed the perfect place for a clandestine face-to-face. A dull haze of cigarette smoke and the odor of too many sweaty bodies had his head swimming. The thought that the general probably had a dozen or so bodyguards on the payroll, watching their backs, gave little comfort. Ratting out his comrades in his own backyard never made the beer settle in his stomach.

He slapped the book onto the bar table and slid it across to Grazovich. He had to shout over the din of a Russian rapper. "I'm tired of chasing all over Russia. It's your turn."

"This is the journal?" Grazovich reached out and fingered the worn book like a gilded Ukrainian egg. It looked newer than Ilyitch supposed, but perhaps Timofea had taken good care of it.

Ilyitch shrugged. Like he'd read it? That was Grazovich's job. He was the rare art dealer, the one who knew how to dig up Russia's treasures. Ilyitch ran the money.

"What happened to the girl?"

"She got away." Ilyitch glared at the general, just daring him to comment.

Grazovich met the look without flinching. "I see." A bleach blond wearing less than a simple black dress sashayed up to them and leaned on Grazovich. A sick smile crossed the general's face as he snaked an arm around her. Ilyitch looked away, preferring the sight of a couple clenched on the dance floor to the general's gruesome habits.

"Refill?" A barkeep sliced through Ilyitch's disgust, indicating the spent beer bottle. Ilyitch passed him a ten-ruble note. "A bottle of Smirnoff." Tonight, he'd celebrate the sweet victory of a job nearly completed. The bartender screwed off the top and handed him the bottle. Ilyitch took a swig right from the bottle, just getting started.

Grazovich flipped through the book, his face expectant, the girl forgotten although she hung on his shoulder, moving her hips to the music, leaving nothing to the imagination. It took only a moment for Grazovich's expression to change. His face mottled with anger. "You're an idiot." Grazovich swore, adding to his opinion.

Ilyitch blinked like he'd been slapped.

"This is a Bible. A fancy American Bible." He flung it onto the bar toward Ilyitch. It upset a bowl of pistachio nuts, spilling them across the wooden bar. Grazovich's eyes narrowed, and for a split second, Ilyitch smelled the odor of evil that trailed his terrorist bedfellow. Ilyitch grabbed up the book and stared at the pages. Disbelief, then frustration, clenched his stomach.

"Get the girl. Bring her to Pskov. I'll meet you there, and we'll see if we can unearth Anton's little secret. This is your last chance. Don't make me sorry I saved your hide ten years ago."

Ilyitch took the book and tucked it away in his pocket, not rising to the threat. He had more going for him than this greasy

Abkhazian thought. Much more. He wasn't about to let it slip through his fingers. "Where are you going?"

"To see what treasures Moscow holds for a weary traveler." He wound a finger around the blond's hair and tugged. Ilyitch left before he saw the rest.

From Kat's vantage point, Pyotr seemed her last link to hope, and even that was dissolving quickly under the heat of Vadeem's bluntness. "She's in danger. She's leaving."

Vadeem paced the departure lobby like a panther, waiting for their flight to be called. Kat had never seen him so unstrung, but then again, she'd only known him for five days. Theirs wasn't a lengthy relationship.

But it felt like it. It felt like she'd known this man for the better part of her life, or at least wanted to. He climbed right into her heart, nestled there, and she'd forgotten, or at least abandoned, every teaching about not falling for an unbeliever.

She was in more danger than Vadeem even realized.

Maybe he was right. Leave. Run away before her heart got totally skinned. Depart before the emotions that had begun to build started to take on nightmare proportions. She had even spent time duping herself into believing he could love her back. Those blue eyes that looked right into her soul with unmasked delight, that lopsided smile, even those strong arms that held her, had made her wonder, and hope he could, possibly. . .

Kat swallowed back a sudden wave of heartache and picked up her suitcase. She nearly crumpled.

"What are you doing?" Vadeem instantly curled a hand around her waist, holding her up with a tight grip. "You aren't carrying anything, and if you don't behave, I'll carry you."

A smile tugged at his mouth, and she wanted to give in to his joke. . .unless it wasn't a joke. She grimaced, not sure. Visions of Matthew forced to walk her home or even the argument that had finally led to their official breakup flashed through her mind.

"You aren't going to Russia, and that's final."

Bossy. That was the way Matthew treated her. And suddenly Vadeem had acquired all sorts of Matthew attributes. Like carrying her in his arms out of the hospital, with Pyotr hot on his heels at the crack of dawn, despite the fact that her legs worked just fine. Or calling a taxi and driving straight to the hotel, where Vadeem unceremoniously packed her bag. She'd been red-faced and not a little furious as he ordered her to sit in a chair. He hadn't been too polite about it, either.

The poor Watsons. They'd been left in the lurch, waiting in the lobby, aglow with hope, dressed to pick up little Gleb and welcome him into their family.

"Not a chance," Vadeem had barked when John Watson pleaded with him.

Thank the Lord, Pyotr had diffused the situation by agreeing to take them to the orphanage and help them collect their son. Even now, his tall presence soothed her fragmenting heart. Tears pricked Kat's eyes when the pastor enveloped her in a hug. He was so solid, strong, and wise, and all she could do was stutter, "Thank you."

"I'm sorry you never got a chance to talk to my mother," he said, not looking at Vadeem, who stared out onto the tarmac, watching the gray sky like a meteorologist. Kat almost wished for a cyclone. Anything to let her stay.

If she were a stronger person, perhaps she could stand up to Mr. Menace. But confrontation had never been her forte. Ditching was more her style. The thought played through her mind and made this sudden jaunt east bearable.

"Me, too," she answered Pyotr. "Maybe someday."

Vadeem glanced at her, but she deliberately ignored him and planted a kiss on Pyotr's leathery cheek. "God bless, Pyotr, and thank you for your help with the Watsons."

"Anything for a sister in Christ," Pyotr said, warmth in his rich brown eyes.

Kat's eyes filled. Pyotr, mercifully, didn't comment.

"Let's go." Vadeem stalked up to them and grabbed Kat's suitcase. She bristled at the chill in his demeanor.

"Thanks again, Pyotr." He held out his hand.

Kat caught the look of genuine concern that crossed the pastor's face as he took Vadeem's grip. The two men stared at one another, one filled with compassion, the other hiding from it. Kat could almost hear a conversation being played in their silent expressions. Then Vadeem let go and tucked his arm around Kat, his face grim but unyielding. Kat's hope took a final dive.

"Vadeem," Pyotr said, reaching out and grabbing his arm. "If you ever want to. . .talk, I'm in Moscow now and again. . . ."

Vadeem shrugged away from him. "Thanks, Pastor, but I don't have anything more to say."

Kat saw the way Pyotr pursed his lips, reining in further comment. But he didn't nod or agree. Kat's heart sank. Somewhere, in the back of her mind, she'd given herself permission to believe Vadeem was just a lost believer needing the guidance of a man of God in his life. But she'd seen the truth in his eyes. Yes, Vadeem was a believer all right. He believed so much that it was eating him alive. He didn't want anything to do with God.

Or maybe he did.

Maybe that was what the crying, the rage outside the church was all about. Spiritual battle.

Before sympathy could temper her anger, Vadeem propelled

her toward the exit.

The doors whooshed behind them as they ran across the tarmac to the plane. Vadeem took her elbow as they started up the stairs, then practically pushed her along the twenty-passenger aisle to their seats. Yes, definitely bossy.

And to think she'd kissed him. She called herself every kind of fool as the plane took off and Vadeem sat like a sentry beside her, unmoving, his hands cupping his knees.

Her heart dropped into the pit of her stomach and stayed there the entire way to Moscow.

The Moscow weather did nothing to lighten her mood. Gray, with low-hanging clouds and not a hint of sunlight, the sky spat upon the window of the taxi. Kat traced a finger down the pane, following a raindrop.

Vadeem was on his cell phone, making her travel arrangements.

She hadn't talked to him in two hours.

He'd tried. He'd asked about her family at home. Once commented on the airplane snacks. Even bought her a package of M&M's. That dubious kindness nearly did her in. It took a clenched jaw and a determination to stare out the window to get past her conflicting emotions.

Finally, with a sigh, he gave up.

And that's what hurt the most.

The taxi splashed past the Kremlin, toward the US embassy where, Kat had no doubt, Vadeem was anxious to unload her. They were probably already processing her new visa and passport to replace the ones she'd unwittingly thrown at her dark attacker, along with her Bible.

"Your flight leaves tomorrow at two P.M."

Kat stared out the window, trying to find words to confront his utter betrayal.

"I'll be by to take you to the plane."

To make sure you obey me. The hurt pushed tears into her eyes. "Please, Kat, don't cry." His soft voice stabbed at her heart. She turned her shoulders away from him, refusing him the satisfaction of seeing her tears. She could hardly believe that yesterday morning he'd woken up in her arms or that last night she'd reached out and kissed him. The idiocy of her open heart swept bitterness into her chest.

"This is the best thing for you. I'm just trying to keep you safe." He reached for her, cupping his hand under her chin, attempting to turn her face toward his. "Look at you. You look like you've been used as a punching bag. I don't want that to become a reality."

She swallowed back the lump of pain forming in her chest, pushing its way into her throat. Okay, she was ready to admit that someone was after her. . .but there were other options. Options that included him acting like a friend instead of booting her out of a country that held answers to questions she'd asked all her life. She felt as if he were ripping her future out of her hands, and the whimper she made sounded just like that.

"Kat," he responded, "this little quest is not worth your life." She felt the frustration in his low voice. He turned toward her, and she covered her face with her hands. She heard his fist land in the back of the driver's seat and shuddered. "What is so important that you'd risk your life? Over and over, I might add."

"Family." Her voice betrayed her in a wretched whisper. "Belonging."

The whir of wheels running on slick pavement filled his silence.

She closed her eyes, willing her voice steady. "I came here to find family because I have none."

"What are you talking about?" His voice hovered just above

a whisper. "What about the grandfather you keep talking about?"

She couldn't look at him. Wouldn't. Her eyes filled, and she clenched her jaw, fighting the tears.

"I'm not related to him." She lifted her chin and stared out the car window at the chipped, graying building, an appropriate backdrop to her despair. "All my life, I knew I was different. I even look different. My family all has dark hair, green eyes. But I've got amber eyes and light brown hair. Why? I don't know, and that's the problem. My parents were killed when I was ten, and I grew up with my grandfather." Kat leaned her forehead against the window, the cool glass a balm against her skin. "What they all don't know, not even Grandfather, is that I know the truth."

"The truth?"

Rain spit on the windows as the pervasive cold drilled into her bones, and she began to shiver. "I don't belong to any of them. Not Grandfather, not Grape-Granny, not the hordes of cousins, uncles, or aunts. No one."

"Kat, I don't get it—"

"I got my tonsils out when I was eighteen and had some complications." She cleared her throat of the gathering tears. "I had to get a transfusion, and I discovered I had AB negative blood—a pretty rare type. My grandfather has type O positive, which is a universal donor for anyone but those with type AB neg." She closed her eyes, remembering the day in first-semester biology at Nyack when she'd realized her AB negative blood couldn't come from Grandfather. Genetics said that his dominant O positive genes would have been passed down to her mother and then to Kat. It had only taken some scientific sleuthing to realize true Neumann blood could never have run in her AB negative veins. Or her mother's.

"My grandfather is not related to me by blood. Which

means, I have no idea who I am."

He touched her hair with his hand. "I know who you are. You're Kat Moore, American. Stubborn. A brave and beautiful distraction in my life who is trying to get herself killed." She stiffened, fighting the urge to lean into his words.

"Don't send me home, Vadeem. Please."

"Kat, I know all about what it feels like to need to belong to something. . .or someone," Vadeem said in an achingly gentle voice. "But it's not worth risking your life."

She turned and saw his eyes glisten. It chipped at her fury. "The risk is worth it to me. Let me find Magda or at least Anton's secret. You know it's important, or someone wouldn't be trying to get his book."

He wove his hands together on his lap, white fists against his black jeans, as if making a point not to touch her. It felt like a slap. "I can't be a good cop and let you stay. You. . .you'll get hurt. And it'll be on my conscience."

"Well, pity you!" She clenched her teeth. "Heaven help you if you have to baby-sit me one day longer."

"Kat, I didn't—"

"I never asked you for help, as I recall. You just tackled me, by way of introduction, and you've been hounding me ever since." She didn't care that the harsh words burned in her throat. Anger pushed her past compassion, past civility.

"I don't need your help or want it, and you'll have to drag me kicking and screaming to the plane and throw me aboard to get me out of here."

His voice was deadly calm. "If I have to."

She closed her eyes. Tears spilled down her cheeks. "No, don't bother. I don't ever want to see you again. Tomorrow isn't soon enough to say good-bye."

Her chest tightened when he said, *"Ladna.* I'll send Ryslan to pick you up. I won't bother you anymore." His voice turned ragged, the only indication of the man she'd seen weeping at her bedside the night before. "But you *are* getting on that plane, and you're going home. And never coming back."

"Fine. Good." Her throat closed. "Give me my book back."

He played the perfect innocent. "What book?"

She nearly hit him. "Anton's journal. The one I nearly got killed for while you were supposed to be protecting me." She stopped short of blurting, "While you were basking in your own pity by the side of the road," but she couldn't go that far. She knew, by the way he flinched, that she'd inflicted enough pain. "It's all I've got, Vadeem. Please."

His face twitched, and he paused just long enough to look as if she'd driven a fist through his heart. "No. Not until you're on the plane. You'll get it as soon as you go through customs."

She thought at that moment that she might hate Vadeem Spasonov.

<hr />

Kat had slammed the door in his face.

He deserved it. He knew what he was doing to her, and it just about ripped his heart out of his chest. *"Kat, forgive me,"* nearly tripped through his lips too many times to count during the agonizing two-hour flight home. But it never cleared, stopped dead by her icy I-can't-stand-you posture. He'd traced her tightened jaw with his eyes until he had it memorized. And the imprint of her wretched expression as she stared at him through the glass doors of the US embassy, her suitcase weighing down her arm, her sodden hair dripping onto the collar of her white shirt, would be with him long after she flew home tomorrow.

Long after. Forever.

He rested his forehead against the wooden bar and covered his head with his arm. Outside, the rain hissed in the streets. Traffic whished through puddles and killed any desire to leave the darkened pub, go home, and face two empty rooms.

"Are you going to drink that or just stare at it all night?" The bartender, a wide man with arms like timber who did double duty as bouncer in this hovel, leaned on the bar and eyed Vadeem like he was a rabble-rouser. Vadeem had squatted space for roughly two hours without touching a drop.

Vadeem shrugged. He hated vodka. It tasted like kerosene and turned a man's body into a muddle. So what made him think that sucking down the stuff and crawling into a corner in the local FSB hangout was going to soften the pain in his chest? He took the drink, sniffed it, felt his stomach lurch, and set it back down. Maybe later. He had only worked up to a twelve on the misery scale. Maybe he'd wait until he reached fifteen. Another dance into the not-so-distant past, recalling the taste of Kat's kiss, the sound of his name on her lips, her heart-crushing story tearing out his heart should do it.

Vadeem groaned.

He picked up his cell phone and dialed. Again. Ryslan wasn't answering. He left a curt message on his partner's voice mail. If his current luck held, the man was out collaring Grazovich at the moment, cursing Vadeem's ineptness. The vodka called with a soft coo.

Kat Moore had to leave Russia. He had no choice. He had a job to do, and he'd conveniently tossed that aside to chase after. . .what? He could hardly say the word to himself. *Love.* He'd known the woman for less than a week, and she'd tunneled under his skin and turned him inside out. So maybe he was starting to love her. Maybe the feelings that surfaced when he thought of her made him want to cry and scream and dance and laugh and sing. She had to leave. Because, if he never saw her again, if she got killed on his watch, he just might crumble.

He knew that feeling all too well.

"I am the resurrection and the life. No one comes to the Father except through me." The words Pyotr had quoted hit him like a brick. Vadeem winced. The problem wasn't that he didn't believe. . .it was that he did. He believed in God so strongly, it hurt. Ate him alive. His faith in God had slipped through his fingers as his father lay dying, as his mother was sentenced to a gulag, as he was sent to the orphanage and his brother to the army. As his family disintegrated.

All because Vadeem had longed to belong to a brother-hood. Because he'd betrayed them to his so-called comrade. Because he trusted the untrustworthy. Faith destroyed. Vadeem put a hand on his chest, pushing against a flash of pain.

Perhaps he understood exactly how Kat felt.

Her journal hung like a brick in his coat pocket. He put a hand on it. Her wretched tone rang in his mind. *"It's all I have."* He'd come dangerously close to cutting out his heart and slap-ping it down in front of her like a sacrificial offering, wanting to answer, "What about me? Don't you have me?"

No, she didn't have him. He'd made that pitifully clear in the way he'd dumped her off like trash at the local embassy, a *das vedanya* dying on his lips. So what if she'd been the one to slam the door in his face? He knew he'd been the betrayer in their short-lived relationship.

Vadeem reached for the vodka and held it to his lips. The liquid spilled out in his trembling grip, burning his tongue.

"Don't, Vadeem."

Vadeem dropped the shot glass onto the counter like a man who'd been sucker punched. Pyotr slid onto the stool beside him. The man wasn't smiling. "Thought I might find you here."

Vadeem struggled for breath, his chest knotted. "What are you doing in town?"

"I accompanied the Watsons to Moscow. They needed some encouragement."

"How'd you find me?"

"I called your office. They gave me some ideas." Pyotr obviously had no problem walking into a den of thieves and drunks after a lost man. Vadeem licked his lips, scraping up composure.

"So, you're just going to let her go?"

Vadeem hung his head, running the shot glass around in the puddle he'd created on the bar. "It's the best thing. For her. For me."

"Well, faith is contagious, and you'd hate to let her get too close. It just might rub off."

Vadeem closed his eyes. "Not now, Pyotr. Faith isn't going to help me figure out what an old monk and Kat's ancestor have in common. Nor will it help me figure out how an art smuggler from Abkhazia is going to fence a four-million-dollar religious icon."

"A religious icon? How about sell it back to the Russian church?" Pyotr raised a finger to the bartender. "Mineral water."

"Oh, we'll get it back. That's the problem. We spend a mint trying to track down these artifacts instead of feeding our people. The smuggler finds the goods, takes it out, and holds it ransom. And Russia pays. Why? Because the country is fragmenting before our eyes, and holding onto our past is our only way to save the future. Unfortunately, said funds are used to purchase AK-47s and missile launchers. . .even tanks. Pieces of the Russian arsenal, legal and not. Our problem is, we can't find the link. Who's the middleman? Who's marrying our antiquities smuggler to the weapons dealers? More than once the shipment has gone out the same day as the ransom is paid. Someone knows the pay schedules and our inventory."

Pyotr popped open the cap on his bottled water and held it in one wide hand. "Sounds like an inside job. Someone's a traitor."

The word brought bile up into Vadeem's throat. "Yeah."

"A Wrecker, I guess you'd say."

Vadeem glared at him. "You don't know how to back off, do you?"

Pyotr twisted the bottle in his hand, watching it sweat. "You know, some of the members of our own church body were sent to gulag as Wreckers. Just because you're labeled something doesn't make it true."

"How about a believer? Can a person be called a Christian and not be one?"

"Of course. It's a heart issue. Only God knows a person's heart. Only He can see if they've been saved from sin."

"And if they haven't?"

"Well, if someone is a Christian, they have. And if not, they haven't."

"But what if. . ." Vadeem looked away, running his finger along the edge of his shot glass. "What if someone once called themselves a Christian and. . .doesn't now."

Pyotr began to pick at the label. "You know, the important thing isn't whether or not you made a confession of faith one day long ago during a foxhole moment, but rather if Jesus is your Lord today. Do you love God, this moment, this day? Instead of wracking your brain over what you said or did yesterday, you should take a look at your heart right now."

"What about a person who. . ." The words burrowed in Vadeem's chest, unable to surface.

"Is so angry at God he can't see past his pain to trust or love God?"

Vadeem looked at him but didn't nod. Pyotr continued to

pick at the label, tearing it off in tiny sheets. "You ever heard the story of Job, Vadeem?"

Vadeem nodded slowly.

"Job's error wasn't that he was angry at God. Job's error was that he wanted to hold God accountable. Job wanted answers from God. God never said He'd give us answers for our troubles. He only said He'd be our light in the darkness. That He would give us the strength to hold on and help endure, even set us free from the pain." He turned to Vadeem. "I have a feeling, Vadeem, you're like the blind man. . .stumbling around in darkness. Whether or not you were a Christian before, you need Jesus' healing now. I don't know what kind of horror you've seen, but I do know that only God can save you. Like the story of Lazarus. . ."

He reached out and gripped Vadeem's shoulder, staring at him with shepherd's eyes. "Jesus weeps for your pain. And He can raise you from the dead."

Vadeem closed his eyes, hearing his father's voice echo from the past. *Hold onto your faith, Son. Only then will you see the glory of God.* Perhaps. . .

"Isn't it time to take off your grave clothes and be set free?" Pyotr reached over, took the shot glass, and slid it down the bar.

Vadeem watched it go, wishing he could send his despair sailing with it.

"I don't know, Pyotr. I always thought it would be easier to have faith in God, that He would reach out of heaven and send me a sign that He was there, that He cared. Help me believe in Him or something."

Pyotr smiled, the expression slowly creeping up his face into delight, his eyes twinkling as if with a secret. "Well, He sent you Kat, now, didn't He?"

CHAPTER SEVENTEEN

Kat carried a cold bottle of Diet Coke, the sum of her breakfast, and padded down the carpeted hall of the US embassy, looking for John Watson and his wife. Cityscapes of Los Angeles, New York, Chicago, and Washington, D.C., hung in black metal frames on the wall, reminding her of exactly what she'd left behind. She could barely hear the tangle of street traffic outside, and the sweet redolence of a fresh bouquet of lilacs filled the hall.

She felt light years from the rustic accommodations of the Hotel *Rossia* or even the Yfa Intourist. She should have slept well in the lush comfort of the Moscow Hilton, paid for by Senator Watson and his family, but she couldn't expunge Vadeem Spasonov's handsome, betraying face from her mind and embrace blissful unconsciousness. She'd seen his wretched expression when she'd slammed the door, and an aggravating mix of regret and iron determination finally drove her from her bed to pace the night away in a swath of frustration across her carpeted floor.

Perhaps putting him a thousand or two miles behind her was for the best, even if she didn't have the slightest intention of leaving Russia. She'd arrived at that decision somewhere around five A.M., and she wasn't above hiding in the bathroom from whatever thug Vadeem planned to send to drag her onto the plane. They'd just have to throw her in the slammer.

Her own thoughts whisked the breath right out of her chest. What was she thinking, going up against the FSB? Exhaustion had obviously lulled her into thinking she was some sort of James-Bondish super agent, racing through Russia to save the world. Well, at least her world.

She couldn't leave, not yet. Not when there were still answers lurking out there. Answers that felt so near she thought she might be able to reach out and touch them. She may have lost the key, her Bible, and her picture, but she still had God on her side.

That, she was sure of. Long after she'd crumpled with frustration in her room, crying and even sending her boot into the wall with an unsatisfactory thump, she'd turned to the Bible. Thankfully, the Hilton had some faithful Gideons who had thought ahead and stuck a Russian-English New Testament and Psalms translation in the nightstand. It opened right to Psalm 100, like a beacon in a dark night. "For the Lord is good and his love endures forever; his faithfulness continues through all generations."

God was faithful. She believed it in her heart even before the Almighty chose to save her, scrape after scrape, in Russia. And if they booted her out of the Motherland and barred the doors, God would still be faithful. But the yearning to dig into her past and find her family now burned like a bonfire inside her and she had to believe that God wanted her here. The peace overwhelmed her, nearly made her giddy in her wee-hour exhaustion.

She wasn't going home. Not unless they gagged her and threw her in the luggage compartment.

Not that she would put it past Vadeem, the FSB pit bull. She'd have to get out of here soon to dodge him or his just-as-sinister cohorts.

Kat opened the waiting-room door and stopped short at the delightful sight of Sveta Watson playing with her new son. Gleb had turned into a full-fledged American, complete with denim overalls, a rugby shirt, and adorable little hiking boots. His eyes were wide, but a grin had broken out on his face as his mother played patty-cake with him. Kat had seen many a new mother turn into a pile of nerves and doubt, but Sveta took to it like a mama bear to her cub, knowing exactly how to coax a smile out of the frightened toddler. Delight radiated on the woman's face as she made baby sounds, bonding with her son despite their language barrier, proving to him that finally he had a family. Someone to belong to.

This is why Kat had come to Russia. To find her family. To belong. The clarity of it rushed through her, making her gasp.

She could nearly hear Grape-Granny's voice. "You've always been different. I blame it on your grandmother. Edward should have known better than to get involved with such a woman. Risked her life the entire pregnancy, and I have no doubt that thrill of adventure leaked right into her womb and infected her offspring. Look at your mother. And now you."

Kat had frozen, completely undone by Grape-Granny's mysterious, telling words. Her burning desire to find her ancestors, starting with unraveling the covert story of her courageous Russian grandmother, ignited right then. She wondered what other secrets ran ripe in the Neumann home. Instead of pointing out the obvious, however, Kat buried that truth deep inside the recesses of her heart, preferring not to dismantle the only family she'd ever known. She would find the mysterious Magda link, find her blood relatives, and the truth would never shatter the Neumann family.

She swiped a betraying tear and approached the Watsons. "I see Gleb is doing okay. How are you?"

Sveta didn't need to answer. She radiated joy. John stood as Kat sat down on the plaid sofa opposite them. "Thank you so much for your help, Kat. I'm so sorry for what happened to you in Yfa. Did the FSB find the guy who attacked you?"

John looked so worried, it made Kat hang her head. She hadn't stopped thanking the Lord for saving her, but suddenly she added gratefulness that, through the tangle of events, the Watsons still managed to bring Gleb successfully into their family. She swallowed the lump forming in her throat and answered his question. "No, not yet."

"Are you leaving today?" Sveta picked up Gleb and bounced him on her knee. A baby's giggle filled the room and brought a smile to everyone's lips.

"No, I have some more work to do in Russia. I'll be staying a few more days." The truth was, she was flirting with the sudden desire to put down roots, perhaps in Blagoveshensk, where she could help them run their adoption program, maybe get to know Pyotr's mother. She had a gut feeling that unearthing her past, especially without her picture or Anton's journal, might take longer than her visa allowed.

"Are you sure that's safe?" Sveta had the "mother" look as she glanced at Kat. "You look. . ."

"Pretty rough, I know." Kat didn't have to look in a mirror to see she looked like she'd wrestled a badger and lost. A yellow bruise scraped down her face. Scratches webbed her neck. Thankfully, her lip had shrunk to its normal size. She'd indulged in some makeup at the Hilton gift shop and, besides the stiff muscles and fatigue, felt like she had pulled herself together. "I'll survive."

"Look us up when you get Stateside," John said as he sat down next to his wife and joined in playing with their new son. His attention was already lost to Kat. She smiled, delighted that she'd seen the birth of this new family.

"God bless you," she said quietly as she stood and slipped from the room.

Kat had few possessions to gather and had already purchased a new shoulder bag. She stopped by the office of her only other friend in town, Alicia Renquist, and picked up the bulging bag, leaving her suitcase stowed behind the door. "Thank you, Alicia," Kat said to the petite brunette, who had nearly cried at Kat's condition when she met Kat in the embassy lobby the day before.

Unfortunately, the US government hadn't been able to find a drop of information on Magda Neumann inside Russia. "The only thing we could find was the marriage certificate in Schenectady."

"Yes, I know," Kat said and ruled out any hope of embassy assistance.

Alicia had spent the better part of the morning trying to convince her to head home as the FSB instructed. "You haven't broken any laws, but it would be against my better judgment to allow you to continue your tour here," Alicia said, as if tempted to launch into her previous sermon. Instead, she handed Kat her passport and visa. Kat noticed the exit date hadn't been changed. She still had three weeks left on her tourist visa. "Good luck, anyway, Kat." Alicia smiled, warmth in her eyes.

"Thank you." Kat slung the bag over her shoulder.

Alicia walked her to the door. "Call me if you need anything. And Kat, be careful."

Kat gave her a quick hug and hightailed it to the lobby. Ten o'clock wasn't too soon for Vadeem to send his army to muscle her out of the country.

The locked door to the embassy offices whooshed closed behind her. Kat tucked the backpack over her shoulder and strode across the lobby. Coast clear. No leather-coated FSB agents hanging around like wolves at the entrance.

She strode past the security gates and burst through the doors, tasting freedom and her future in the damp Moscow air.

Kat scattered a group of pigeons as she walked quickly down the street. *Train station, here I come, and then straight to Pskov.* She didn't know what she'd find there, but she'd start with a visit to the monastery, at least to pay her respects to the young monk who'd been murdered.

A shiver hissed up her spine at the grim thought. She clamped down on her fear. She had few choices—return to New York empty-handed or dive into the murky unknown, a prayer on her lips.

She'd take the leap of faith.

"Please, God, help me," she said, gathering speed. She wasn't sure when the train left, but she hoped to be on it before Vadeem sent his bloodhounds to the embassy.

A hand clamped on her shoulder, hard and tight.

Kat whirled, nearly jumping out of her skin. She recognized Ryslan, Vadeem's partner standing behind her.

"Good morning, Miss Moore."

***

"You do this often?" Vadeem gripped his knees, hauling in searing breaths, sweat pouring down his face, his heart thumping through his chest. The clammy breath of midmorning Moscow made him feel even stickier than he was after running five kilometers.

"What?" Pyotr asked, also hauling in breaths beside him.

"Follow people around."

"Oh, you mean people who invite me to stay at their apartment or challenge me to a foot race?" Pyotr smiled, looking not at all like a man who'd wrangled out the wretched story of a sinful man until 3 A.M. in a dimly lit apartment. Sweat ran in rivulets down his wide face, and his tawny blond hair stood up in spikes. "I'd say my army days paid off."

Vadeem half-glared at him, not wanting to admit how well the man had kept up. . .and how much he enjoyed his company. He wasn't ready to call the pastor *friend* yet, but the moniker skimmed close to actuality. What would he call a person who knew the demons that ravaged his soul and didn't flinch at them?

A shepherd, perhaps.

It felt somehow freeing to be able to unload the story onto Pyotr and see the man's eyes fill with tears. To know that someone else grieved the loss of Vadeem's family and to hear the kind words, "It wasn't your fault."

It felt like his fault. Vadeem had brought it on by not listening to his father, by clinging so desperately to the need to be a part of something bigger than himself. He should have realized the importance of family.

Instead, he had betrayed them.

Just like he'd betrayed Kat.

He'd been running from that fact for the past five kilometers and in his thoughts for most of the night. He'd betrayed the woman God had sent him. The gift meant to spark in him a little faith.

Pyotr's words had found a soft place, burrowed deep, and grown like a sweet-smelling fragrance over the past twelve hours. Kat, with her ever-present smile, her unconditional love, her buoyant faith, had been sent by God to remind Vadeem he was not alone. No, not by a long shot.

Perhaps he wasn't the stone-hearted traitor he'd always labeled himself. Perhaps redemption waited for him if he would find the courage to ask. Maybe he'd even find a woman to whom he could belong and whom he could cherish as his own. The thought stole the breath right out of his chest. He leaned against his apartment building, cooling down, stretching his calf muscles, and listening to regret rush in its wake.

He had to send her home.

Or did he? Her words rang back at him. *"You could help me."* He yanked open his apartment door and started up the stairs, Pyotr breathing heavy on his heels.

Maybe Vadeem *could* help her. There had to be other clues out there, things they hadn't yet considered. Anton Klassen had been clever enough to leave behind a journal. What if he left behind something else, something that could lead them to the Crest of St. Basil?

Find Grazovich's prize and make Kat's dreams come true in one turn. The idea sent new adrenaline coursing through his legs.

"Vadeem, Pal, slow down." Pyotr huffed a flight below, hanging on the stair rail.

"I have to stop Kat before she leaves." Vadeem shoved his key into his apartment door lock.

Pyotr trudged up the stairs. "That's what I've been hanging around all night to hear."

Vadeem headed for his telephone while Pyotr dove into the shower. Pacing, Vadeem listened to the embassy phone ring. A sweet-voiced operator picked up and told him she had no listing for the American he was trying to find.

"Of course not, she's a guest there." He described her, thoroughly enough to make it obvious, even to himself, that he had her pegged down to her hiking boots. He guessed he didn't have to add that she smelled so sweet it made a man cry, but he wanted to. The woman put him on hold while she searched, and he listened to a potpourri of wordless American tunes.

Finally, "I'm sorry, Sir, but she has already left."

Vadeem slammed his hand into the counter. "Do you know who picked her up?"

"Just a moment, please."

Vadeem's heart pounded out the seconds, dread pinching his chest. She'd probably ditched him. Again. Without a thought to her own safety, she'd most likely hightailed it to the nearest train station and was en route to Pskov, headed smack dab into the arms of one very bloodthirsty smuggler. Vadeem nearly pulled the cord out of the phone socket and tried to calm himself by bracing an arm against the wall.

"Sir? My name is Alicia Renquist. Can I help you?"

Ragged breath through his lungs, then, "Yes, I'm looking for Kat Moore."

"She left awhile back. She, um, was going to go to the train, but. . ."

"What?" He knew it. He just knew it. She'd ditched him.

"Well, someone came in after she left, one of your FSB officers. I think he picked her up. She should be en route to the airport by now." He thought he detected a tone of relief in her voice. "I can send a message for you with the Watsons. They are leaving soon. They'll be taking the same flight home."

He fought the sudden lump of regret in his throat. This was for the best. "No, that's okay," he said and put down the receiver. Ryslan had picked her up. Odd, since he hadn't asked the guy to do it. Especially odd since his partner hadn't returned even one phone call.

But then again, he was Vadeem's partner. And partners had a bond that went beyond words. Too bad he hadn't noticed it until now.

Vadeem was leaning against his kitchen counter, drinking an orange juice and contemplating this new revelation when Pyotr emerged from the bathroom, looking like a bear, his hair spiked in all directions. "Did you find her?"

Vadeem shook his head. "She's already headed to the airport. I guess my partner picked her up." He held out the carton of juice to Pyotr, who poured himself a glass.

"I thought you couldn't get ahold of him."

Vadeem shrugged but didn't ignore the strange expression on Pyotr's face. Their confusion knotted into a tense silence.

"I've still got Kat's book," Vadeem said at nearly the same moment Pyotr suggested, "Maybe we should head out to the airport and say good-bye to the Watsons before they take off."

Vadeem didn't even slow down to shower.

CHAPTER EIGHTEEN

I 'm not going anywhere with you." Kat said it for the second time, but she failed to halt Ryslan's pace or wrench herself from his vise-grip on her arm. Obviously, Vadeem had been serious about having her hauled off like a sack of grain to the airport. She sent a couple of help-me looks to passersby, hoping someone might meet her eyes and have mercy on a woman tripping down the street.

Muscovites were clearly used to the oddity on their city sidewalks. Besides, the struggle didn't last long. Vadeem's hulk of a partner threw her into the backseat of a white Toyota Camry and slammed the door.

All four locks clicked while he crossed over to the driver's side. Kat clutched her bag on her lap and swallowed her heart back into place.

Ryslan unlocked his door and climbed into the car, parked conveniently outside the US embassy, where he'd stopped in to complete the mission on which he'd been sent.

She suddenly much preferred to have had the chance to say good-bye to the one FSB agent she actually cared about. She really had wanted to say good-bye. She couldn't believe this was it. Her quest was over. Deep inside she'd been harboring hope that Vadeem would come charging after her, book in hand, furious, of course, but with delight in his eyes, glad to see she'd disobeyed him and would be sticking around.

She couldn't believe that the man who she had prayed would be in the hallway when she opened the door wasn't going to come to her rescue and be the hero she wanted him to be. Not the bossy, arrogant FSB cop, but the man who'd sat by her bedside and cried, the man who'd kissed her gently, igniting a blaze of hope in her chest.

The man she was starting to love.

"Where's Vadeem?"

Ryslan said nothing as he started the car and pulled away from the curb, his meaty hands gripping the wheel.

She fisted her hands in her lap and clenched her teeth. She didn't know what made her angrier, that Vadeem hadn't valued their budding relationship enough to see beyond yesterday's slammed door to the woman who needed him or that her heart had run out ahead of her, betraying her to fall for the one man she could never have.

Tears stung her eyes. She blinked them back, watching the buildings ramble by as they made their way toward the Kremlin. . .and away from the airport.

"Where are we going?"

Ryslan filled the front seat with bullish presence and a profile that made her wince. Clearly freshly shaven, she noticed scratches along his neck as if he'd wrestled a broom and come out the loser.

She blinked at him, not believing the thought she'd conjured up, praying it couldn't be true. She leaned forward in her seat, noticing for the first time a silver ring on his right hand. Then he exhaled, and she got a good whiff of his morning beverage.

She didn't have to close her eyes to know where she'd smelled that before. Nor did she have to invoke the memory of the low growl that still made cold fear rush down her spine. He confirmed her worst suspicions himself.

"Now, where were we when you so rudely took off?"

❧

Vadeem stood at the gate, watching Pyotr hug the Watsons. The pastor mimed his feelings, severely handicapped by the language barrier. If it weren't for Vadeem's stakeout near the customs booths, Vadeem would be over there interpreting.

If he could force words out through his fury.

What he'd never told Kat was that he knew every nuance of her language, courtesy of the Red Berets. If only she hadn't so easily adapted to his. . .that one talent could be ensnaring her in trouble this very second.

He turned away from the happy farewell scene and scrubbed a hand through his still-sweaty hair.

Either Ryslan had forgotten the way to the airport or Kat had decided to ditch them all again, just as John Watson had suggested. "She told us she had more work to do," he'd said confused, when Vadeem nearly pounced on the couple at the departure gate. Vadeem couldn't imagine what kind of work that could be when he had Anton Klassen's diary weighting his jacket pocket. That Kat, she was a bomb, a messy explosion in his life. He found himself hoping Ryslan had found her, wrestled her into the car, and was just horribly late.

He'd already scanned the departure lobby on the other side of customs. No feisty American with caramel-colored hair sat pouting in an airport chair.

He continued to battle the cold feeling of dread that had started to sneak up his spine, and he dialed Ryslan's cell phone again. No answer. Vadeem nearly threw the unit across the room. Instead, he calmly closed it, dumped it into his pocket, and resumed his pacing. The Watsons filed past him, John clamping him on the arm as he shook Vadeem's hand in typical American style.

Vadeem choked up a polite smile. "Did she say where she was going?" He hated the desperate sound to his voice.

John Watson shook his head. "I hope we see her on the plane."

Vadeem couldn't agree more. He didn't know what he was going to do if he found her stalking the train platform to Pskov. "Thank you, John."

The Watsons filed through customs, little Gleb on Sveta's hip and clinging to her like a dazed puppy. He knew how the kid felt. Vadeem's heart sank, watching them go.

"I think I'll stick around Moscow a few days and check into our denomination's headquarters here." Pyotr held out a slip of paper. "My cell phone number."

Vadeem stared at the number, unable to dredge up words. A sick feeling piled in his chest.

"If you ever need a friend, call me."

Friends were in precious short supply at the moment. "Thanks, Pyotr."

An hour later, Vadeem stalked into HQ in no mood to sit reading the decrypted Internet messages piled on his desk or sift through mug shots, hoping he might find the thug who'd beaned him in Moscow four nights past. Vadeem's head throbbed just thinking about it. And if Denis didn't stop prattling on about the recent corpse down in forensics—

"Can't believe somebody murdered a monk, especially this one."

"What was that?" Vadeem swung around in his swivel chair, rubbed his eyes, and blinked at Denis. The rookie looked like he'd hadn't slept in a week. Brown hair poked in all directions, his gangly body drooped in a rumpled brown uniform, and bags rimmed his eyes. "What did you say?"

"The monk. From Pskov. They sent us his autopsy report, thinking he might be connected to Grazovich. The guy was stabbed, military style, in the lungs, so he couldn't make a sound. I thought it was a little strange, so. . .look at this." The kid held out two sheets of paper, copied passport and visas. He grinned through the fatigue. "The guy has two names."

"Let me see that." Vadeem grabbed the copies, "Misha Papov. . .and Akhmed Rakiff."

"From Georgia." Denis crossed his arms. "Why the alias?"

"No, I'll bet he's Abkhazian," Vadeem said, his mind racing. "It's a breakaway territory of Georgia. They splintered off about ten years ago and pulled Russia into a nasty war. We had comrades fighting on both sides of the line, depending on their preference. Abkhazia technically won, but the skirmishes continue." He scanned the copies again and squinted at the youthful face. "Abkhazians are pretty faithful to their tribal traditions. What was this kid doing serving in a Russian Orthodox monastery?"

"He'd only been there two years. I got to wondering about that, too, and found this." He whipped out another sheet of paper, this time with a familiar face copied on the front.

Vadeem got a sick feeling. "Grazovich."

"See the list of aliases?"

"I don't need to read it. Ali Rakiff." Vadeem's heartbeat pumped up a notch.

"They're related. Looks like they might be cousins."

Vadeem winced. "Of course they are. All of Abkhazia is related. And blood runs thick there. Practically everyone in the new government is related."

Denis pulled up a chair, obviously bursting with news. "I think I figured out what Grazovich is doing here. His brother's execution date got bumped up—two weeks."

"The Georgians are finally going to do it?" Hunan Rakiff, Grazovich's older brother, had been decaying in a Georgian prison for the better part of a decade, living through three escape attempts and the subsequent Georgian punishments. "When did you get this news?"

"TASS news wire. I did an Internet search and found out the date was rescheduled about a month ago after the hit attempt on Georgia's former president here in Moscow."

"So Grazovich is desperate."

"I'd say he's looking to spring big brother soon." Denis looked like a ten year old with the news of a loose tooth. "And did you know that the annual Omsk International Exhibition of Land Equipment and Armaments is next week?"

Vadeem wasn't at all happy that the weaponry that had once protected the *Rodina* was now available for public auction by Internet catalogue. The FSB had their hands full sifting through the terrorists that infiltrated the country through Omsk. "What's on their inventory list this year? Anything interesting?"

"How about a T-725 rocket gun tank?" Denis rubbed his hands together. "Asking price, a cool four mil, American bucks."

Yeah, that was about right. Four million for the crest in trade for a tank, something that could mow down Center Street, Tbilisi, Georgia, right into a prison compound. Vadeem's brain ached right between the eyes.

"Good work, Denis. Go home and get a shower."

Denis smiled like he'd won the gold. "By the way, Ryslan called."

Now that was good news. Maybe he'd gotten Kat on a plane and had her successfully winging her way to New York. His pushed down a wave of regret. "Yeah, what did he want?"

"He's still in Pskov. He says Grazovich hasn't moved, so you don't need to rush out there."

Vadeem opened his mouth, but no words came out.

"He said to keep tracking Fitzkov in Novosibersk, and let him know if he even flinches." Denis gave a huff of laughter.

Vadeem felt slashed across the chest. "He's in Pskov? Are you sure?"

Denis ran a hand through his mussed hair. "Sure. Called me this morning on the cell phone."

Vadeem braced a hand on the corner of his desk. "Then who, if anyone, is with Kat?"

───

"What are you going to do with me?" Fear pinched Kat's voice whisper thin. Recognition had rushed over her like nausea. Vadeem's partner was the biggest man she'd ever seen, even in shadow, and without asking, she knew he was the hulk who had tracked her down in Blagoveshensk and stolen her backpack, her Bible, and her picture. The man who had killed Brother Papov.

Perhaps even the man who had freed her from the interrogation room in customs.

But why?

"Did you steal the key, too?"

She looked pointedly at his hand, remembered the cold scrape of a ring on her neck, and knew her answer.

He laughed.

"Why? If you wanted it so badly, why didn't you take it the first day I was here?"

His eyes narrowed in the rearview, and Kat clamped her mouth shout.

They'd cleared the city, having passed the Kremlin and the

train station. From the gray clouds ahead and the sun climbing to her back, she knew they were heading east. Clumps of birch and pine bordered the highway on either side. She examined the pavement as it screamed by and knew her next move was going to hurt.

She dove for the door. The handle moved but the door didn't release despite the added *umph* of her shoulder into the window. Her heart sank like an anchor. So much for a painful escape. "Let me out!"

"When we get to Pskov. I need your help," Ryslan said in a quiet voice.

"Never," she ground out. "I'm not going to help someone steal from their own country."

"What do you care?"

"I'm Russian!"

"Good for you," he snarled. "Then help your fellow *narodina* dig up the past."

"What are you looking for?" Panic pushed her voice higher than she preferred.

"Like you don't already know?" His gaze flicked to the rearview mirror, and it held just enough menace to turn her weak. "The crest. Four million dollars of gold and jewels. Hidden by your great-grandfather."

"I don't know anything about it." She fought to still her thundering heartbeat as she eased her satchel off her shoulder and gripped the strap in two hands.

He harrumphed. "You'd better know, or you're going to die."

Kat tried to ignore his words. "Why are you doing this?"

His fingers whitened on the steering wheel. His jaw tensed. "Freedom."

"This isn't going to give you freedom. Vadeem will find you. He'll never let you get away." This much she knew for certain.

"He'll track you down, no matter where you are. You'll never be free." Bracing her feet, Kat inched forward.

He laughed cruelly. "I'm not afraid of Vadeem."

What he left unspoken was whom, exactly, he feared. She pounced on it. "But you *are* afraid."

"*Zamolchi, doragaya,*" he said, his tone dangerous. "It would be wise if you learned to shut that mouth of yours."

Kat swung her satchel wildly, praying she'd hit flesh—his.

He swore and jerked the wheel. The car screeched across the lane. "You want to get us killed?"

The question seemed inane coming from a man who had wielded precisely that threat.

She clenched her jaw as he pulled the car over in a cloud of dust. Her heart rammed into her throat when he turned. His eyes had the dark ring of hate. "Give me that bag."

She trembled as she handed it over. "I'm sorry," she said, forcing a humble tone. Every self-defense lesson she'd ever taken, at Matthew's urging, had told her that she had to slow this down, to think it out, to watch her attacker and discover his weakness.

She wanted to live. Why, oh why hadn't she listened to Vadeem? Why hadn't she curbed her irrationally impulsive urges?

He threw the bag down onto the front seat and gunned the car out on the highway.

Oh yes, she was going back to Pskov. For the first time in four days, she wished she were on a plane home.

***

Vadeem's meager breakfast was about to come back up right in his office. He even grabbed the metal waste can once but gulped enough deep breaths to keep sane, for the moment.

Ryslan wasn't in Pskov. Vadeem had given up trying to get

ahold of the guy and gone right to Pskov FSB HQ. No, he hadn't been there.

At all.

Never.

Vadeem braced both hands on his desk. His breath scraped against his ribs.

Denis, the poor kid, had nearly gone white when Vadeem suggested they dig a little into the activities of Ivan Grazovich, cross-referencing them with Ryslan's cases. Bingo.

It was a sweet, smooth operation, one that took someone with Ryslan's brains and history. A growing slush fund, operations, and expenses for the recovery of Russia's stolen treasures. A fund with significant withdrawals, which, when lumped together, equaled disturbingly large amounts. Amounts that could purchase a trainload of AK-47s. Or Bizon-2 submachine guns, or even a T-725 tank. Weapons that Ryslan, a former soldier with friends in every branch of the military, would know how to get his hands on legally or otherwise.

Vadeem went cold. Sell it back to the Russian church, indeed. That is exactly what Ryslan and Grazovich had been up to. . .for the last five years at least.

He'd found his middleman.

And the man had Kat. Vadeem knew it in his gut. Except he knew where they were headed. He dialed his cell phone as he headed out the door for the airport.

If he ever needed faith in a God who could raise people from the dead, it was now.

<hr/>

Grazovich was late. Ryslan stared at the woman, waxed white from the pale fingers of moonlight that filtered into the cave. He didn't dare leave her to go hunt for the smuggler. The woman had enough cunning in her petite frame to sneak out under his nose—had already tried twice—and he'd been forced to bind and gag her. He wasn't about to let her get a head start. He'd already lost a footrace to her in the wilds of Yfa.

Ryslan checked his watch, then took another slug of his vodka, having decided about two hours before that beer just wasn't strong enough to kill the frustration churning in his gut.

Wind rustled the shadow of trees, and the fresh, crisp smell of the Velikaya River, not far away, snuck into the cave. The walls felt damp, the cave dark, and it hid too many secrets. Ryslan had taken two wrong turns before he found it. . .just where Grazovich had directed. He supposed it would be just as difficult for Vadeem and his cronies to find it as well. Yes, it was the perfect place to hole up while Grazovich and Miss Moore dug into the past, and he whittled a cool four million from the books in expenses. Ryslan's only prayer was producing the crest. Then he'd get out of Russia and put a healthy distance between himself and Grazovich and his gang of bullies. He'd bury himself in some South American country, deep enough so that the tendrils of the Russian government would never track down a traitorous mercenary who fought against them in the Georgian-Abkhazian war, should Grazovich decide to spill his secrets.

He took another swig. The vodka burned as it went down. Ryslan breathed into the cuff of his shirt, deadening the bite of the alcohol.

Moore watched him with wide, doe-brown eyes that betrayed more than a hint of fear. He smiled. "Vadeem thinks you're touching down right about now at JFK in New York. Are you going to miss him?" His voice lifted in sarcasm as he thought of Vadeem jumping a plane to Yfa as if it had been his own, brilliant idea. Thankfully, Vadeem's daily check-in calls had been just what Ryslan needed to keep him in pocket. Only half the time, Ryslan had been staring at him from across the room while they talked.

He laughed at that.

She turned away, and he saw a tear hanging on her eyelash.

A crack, like the snap of a twig, brought him to his feet. The room spun slightly, and he gulped a breath before throwing the bottle across the room. Cursed drink.

He stumbled out of the cave but didn't call out. Grazovich knew where the grotto was located. Still, every hair prickled on the back of Ryslan's neck. He heard the rush of wind scrape the darkness. The ground crackled beside him.

He turned.

Not fast enough.

"Good-bye, Ryslan Ilyitch," Grazovich growled.

White-hot pain speared into Ryslan's neck. He opened his mouth, but his voice box had been severed. Blood clogged in his throat. He fell to his knees, his meaty hands clawing at an arm clamped over his eyes. Wet soil seeped into the knees of his pants. Then warm blood spilled down his shirt, and he fell forward, flopping like a freshly hooked fish who knew he'd flirted with the bait for far too long.

Grazovich's FSB tails were both dead. Their windpipes severed, their eyes wide with horror. Vadeem watched as the FSB forensics team went to work, fingerprinting, photographing, taking blood samples. He stood in the hall outside the room above the grocery store, his hands in his leather coat, gasping for calm.

It wasn't hard to guess how Grazovich found them. The man was a soldier, after all, the leader of a small but lethal group of religious fanatics who made killing an honorable way of life and dying a glorious sacrifice.

And now the smuggler was AWOL. Vadeem had spent the better part of the last hour tearing apart the man's room. Literally.

Grazovich had left behind nearly everything he owned, which probably duped the two FSB guards into thinking he wasn't creeping into their perch across the street to slit their throats. Dirty socks, grimy wool pants, sweat-stained shirts, and a garbage can of vodka bottles made the guy seem human. But Vadeem knew he was nothing of the sort. Not when Vadeem surveyed the grisly trail Grazovich had left behind.

Vadeem had spent the better part of two hours visiting the monks again. The father had been overly accommodating, shaken by the recent death of Brother Papov. But either he was a consummate liar, or he truly hadn't seen a hulk of an FSB officer dragging a terrified woman through the monastery grounds.

It was worth a try. Vadeem had a gut feeling that, whatever Ryslan and Grazovich were after, it could be found somewhere near that monastery. He'd have to start thinking like a cop—and fast—if he intended to save Kat's life.

Get the crest. That one thought drilled through his mind like a jackhammer the entire high-speed drive to the airport, during the white-knuckle flight in the FSB-owned AN-2, and even now as he paced the hall like a jackal. The missing crest gave Kat's life value, and the treasure in Vadeem's very capable hands meant he had some barter power.

But how was he supposed to find something hidden successfully for nearly a century? Yes, he still had Anton's diary, but that had only illuminated the path to his own lack of faith, dangling the concept of peace before him like a spicy bowl of borscht to a starving man. It didn't point the way to any secret treasure, despite local lore.

Vadeem braced a hand against the wall and clutched the back of his neck. His muscles were as tight as *balalaika* strings. He needed something he could hit, hard. Something more substantial than Grazovich's duffle bag.

His cell phone trilled in his pocket. Digging it out, he knew he'd hit exhaustion by the sound of his voice.

"Spasonov."

"You'll find your friend at the grave of my dead cousin."

Vadeem's heart lurched in his chest. "Grazovich?"

"You have until dawn to find the crest. Then the girl dies."

"Wait, how am I—" Oh no, his voice was shaking. The last thing Kat needed was for him to betray his fear to Grazovich.

"And don't bring any of your FSB friends. I'll be watching, and she'll pay."

The phone went dead.

Vadeem nearly threw it against the wall. *Grazovich had Kat.* Vadeem fought for breath, in and out, while the forensics team murmured in the background and the smell of death hovered in the dusty hall. Why hadn't she listened to him? He clenched his jaw and closed his eyes. His chest felt so tight, he thought he might suffocate.

How was he supposed to find the crest in six hours? And even if he did, Grazovich wasn't a man long on promises. Vadeem knew he could very well find Kat with her own beautiful neck slit, if he found her at all. A wise agent would bring a squad of FSB sharpshooters to watch his backside. Grazovich's warning echoed in his ears. Vadeem hit the wall hard with his open palm. The sound died in the cement, ineffectual in its catharsis.

Friends were exactly what he needed. Unfortunately, he had not a one.

Or did he. . . ?

CHAPTER NINETEEN

Kat had always thought the expression "paralyzed with fear" a cliché until Professor Taynov, her hero from the airport, suddenly appeared, his hands freshly dipped in blood. He'd morphed into Genghis Khan. Her muscles actually refused to engage as the barbarian dragged her out of the cave and threw her into Ryslan's car next to the pale, bloody corpse of the man who had been Vadeem's partner. She started praying then and never stopped, even after Taynov parked outside the monastery cemetery and, grunting under the weight of the bullish Ryslan, dragged the corpse to a mound of dark earth. The moon draped the body in a ghastly glow, and Kat berated herself for not listening to Vadeem when she'd had the chance.

A smart person would be on a plane to America right now, a piece of her past safely in her pocket along with, perhaps, the happy memory of a friendly good-bye from a handsome cop who'd been trying to save her life.

So Vadeem had been a little bossy. Wasn't that his job? A job she desperately hoped he was good at. "Oh God," she moaned under her breath. "Only You can save me. Give Vadeem wisdom."

She'd listened to the telephone call the professor had placed, her heart frozen in her chest, and knew without a doubt she would die at dawn.

How would Vadeem find the Crest of St. Basil's if Professor

Taynov, supposed master of history, couldn't figure it out? Or was he lying about that also? The accusations and stories Vadeem had dredged up about the sinister identity of the professor haunted her memory. Terrorist. Smuggler. *Murderer*. What had Vadeem said his name was? Not Professor Taynov. A general. . . Grazovich. An ice-cold shiver started at the top of her spine.

Vadeem needed help. Tears pricked her eyes as she thought of him beside himself with anger or panic. She remembered the pain she'd seen in his eyes after they'd been attacked in Moscow and when she woke up in the Yfa hospital. Oh, why hadn't she listened to him? Why had she been so stubborn?

"I just want you to be safe." His words rushed back to her in a voice that cracked with unspoken emotion, and suddenly she knew. *She knew* and couldn't believe she hadn't seen it before. Snapshots of Vadeem filled her mind: Vadeem laughing at her eating habits on the train, his low, sensuous voice calling her *maya doragaya*—my dear one. Vadeem pulling her close on the darkened streets of Moscow, his breath in her hair, relief betraying him in his racing heartbeat. Vadeem tucking his jacket over her shoulders in his busy office and running a gentle finger down the wound on her face, his eyes glistening with unshed feelings. Vadeem standing in her hotel lobby holding out a pack of M&M's like a peace offering. Vadeem crouched outside her hotel room, eyes glued to her door like some sort of superhero. Finally, Vadeem, shoulders slumped and wretched regret written on his face, as she'd slammed the door in his face at the US embassy.

Vadeem showing her without words that he cared. *"I just want you to be safe."* Could he be really saying something else?

And she'd mocked him. Not only that, she'd sacrificed her future to dig up her past. A past that was about to get her killed.

She felt sick. Kat made a noise that matched her stomach, and terrorist-Grazovich turned in his seat, eyes narrowing.

Quickly he reached over and tugged on her gag, pulling it down. "Behave yourself," he snarled.

She looked away, out the window to the dark forest. The wind moaned as it brushed the car. Dread swept though her, and she trembled. Somewhere out there, the man who had traipsed across Russia to help her uncover her past was scrambling to keep her alive.

She stiffened when Grazovich turned and hung his elbow over the back of the seat. "So, Miss Moore, we have some time to kill. What do you say we get to know each other better?" He reached out and took hold of her hair, rubbing it between two long fingers. His eyes darkened, those aged eyes that told her he'd seen a lifetime of pain and war, and she saw something lecherous. She bristled, doubting that murder alone played on his mind.

Vadeem, please hurry.

She swallowed a rush of panic and tried to think on her feet. "Why is this crest so important? What is it exactly?"

Grazovich smiled, his eyes dark as obsidian, glittering with amusement. "You Americans really don't pay attention to world history, do you?"

Kat forced a casual shrug. "If you're going to kill me for it, I'd like to know. . ."

Grazovich let go of her hair and clasped his hands on the seat back, enacting the pose of professor he claimed himself to be. "The Crest of St. Basil's is much more than even Russia realizes. That's the beauty of this little adventure. Legend has it that the crest was forged here in Pskov by a master monk and presented to Czar Ivan IV—you call him Ivan the Terrible—when the architects from Pskov were asked to build the great church of St. Basil's the Blessed. But the rest of the story makes it one of the most valuable religious artifacts in history."

Kat enacted a smile while she worked at the twine that

bound her wrists. Her skin burned, but she had begun to make progress. She leaned forward, as if mesmerized, and even allowed him to touch her hair again without flinching.

"The history of the crest dates back to the start of Christianity in Russia, with the conversion of St. Vladimir, Emperor of Kiev around 990 A.D. The crest was a wedding gift from Basil II, emperor of Byzantium, where Turkey now sits, to his sister Anne, on the occasion of her marriage to Vladimir."

"So it's over a thousand years old?" The surprise in Kat's voice was real and even more so as she worked the twine halfway down her hand.

"No, it's even older." Grazovich's voice heightened, aroused as he was by his own tale. "The Crest of St. Basil was presented to Leo, the son of Basil I, emperor of Byzantium, as a gift of good faith from Rome around 890 A.D. when the union with Rome was reestablished. The Roman church hoped to bring about peace and draw under their wing the country of Byzantium, the eastern 'New Rome,' as they called it. Perhaps you ignoramuses in America have heard of the capital of Byzantium—Constantinople?"

Kat jerked her hand free but held it tight behind her back. Her eyes narrowed appropriately at Grazovich's sneer. "Yes, of course. But I thought Byzantism, the religion that started in Byzantium, was the foundation of the Russian Orthodox Church. And they claim to be separate from the Roman Catholic Church."

Grazovich smiled, as if happy with her knowledge. "Constantinople had a love-hate relationship with Rome. Eventually, after years of crusades, she broke away from Rome's control. Vladimir, the emperor of Kiev, decreed that all Kievans were to become Christians, and Russian orthodoxy, through Byzantium, started to spread across Russia. When Constantinople reestablished a relationship with the Roman Church around 1450 A.D., the Russians rebelled and established Russia's own order, the Russian Orthodox Church."

"So what happened to the crest?" Kat slid the twine off her other hand and closed her fist around it. She would find a way to slam it into his smug face if he kept on playing with her hair. Her stomach knotted.

"After Vladimir, it worked its way up from Kiev, surfaced in Pskov, and passed to the czars until it finally disappeared at the hands of Anton Klassen in 1918."

He ran a long, sweaty finger down her cheekbone. "And will be recovered with the help of his great-granddaughter eighty-some years later." His voice held a dangerous lilt that cut right to Kat's soul.

Kat stiffened and pulled away, her courage dissolving through her chest. Tears sprang to her eyes. "I don't know where it is."

He cupped her chin with his hand. "The Vatican has been waiting for over one thousand years to reclaim their lost treasure. Let's see if you can help them."

Kat closed her eyes and prayed.

✦

Vadeem found Ryslan lying on the grave like some sort of sacrificial offering. Blood darkened his neck and matted the hair on his wide chest. Vadeem swallowed a wave of revulsion as he approached the body, his Makarov pistol drawn. *I'm watching you.* Grazovich's words stabbed at him, and he squinted at the clutch of forest, dark and foreboding, on the far side of the monastery. The moon bathed the ground in luminescence, a surreal and pale landscape to his nightmare.

Kat was going to die because he had no idea how to find the crest. None. Zip.

And that made him nearly rabid with frustration.

He crept up to the corpse and noticed a glint of light against the mass of darkness. He nearly cried when he saw the key, hung like a cross around Ryslan's neck. Grazovich, smuggler, warlord, and murderer had a shred of decency. That, or the man really believed Vadeem could find this mythical icon instead of simply playing an agonizing game of finders-keepers.

He had the key. And the book. Vadeem's breath chafed his lungs as he fought to keep calm. Oh yes, he needed a friend, and for the first time, he was considering seriously the words Pyotr had spoken to him only two nights ago: *"There is a Friend who sticks closer than a brother. . . ."*

The urge to pray, to scream out for help, filled his chest and made him gasp with its ferocity. Scraping up control, Vadeem opened Anton's journal. Answers. Obviously, Grazovich believed there were answers in this ancient text, and Vadeem had no choice but to scour the pages in desperation, with the faint hope he might discover the treasure they were all searching for.

It was too dark to make out the words, and the deadly odor of his recently deceased partner soured Vadeem's stomach. He scrambled to his feet, gave another look around, and dashed toward the chapel that had held so many terrors during his last visit. Maybe tonight it would revive answers instead of heartache.

The musty cave chapel chilled him to the bone. He found matches and lit a candle, then two, three, and more until the tiny church glowed with flickering light. Standing before the cross of Jesus, he stared up at the artist's portrayal of the Divine on earth, and his heart felt huge in his chest. Jesus hung there, His fingers curled in pain, His eyes downcast, thorns on His head, an unusual expression of peace on His face. Mesmerized, Vadeem saw for the first time something beyond the pain. *I am the Resurrection and the Life*. Eternity beyond the grave. Joy despite earthly suffering.

Vadeem's throat tightened, and he was transported back through time and grief and stood beside his father.

> *"Father, I'm sorry, I'm so sorry!" Vadeem's knees were wet in the snow. "It's my fault, Papa. . . . I'm sorry!"*
>
> *Papa reached up, his big hand on his cheek, his breath coming in gasps. "This is not forever, Son. Lift your eyes to heaven and God will show you the light. Trust Jesus, and you will see God's glory."*

Vadeem hadn't looked up. Not once. He couldn't, not after they buried his father, not after they scattered his family. Light didn't inhabit a communist orphanage. . .and despair had taken its place in his dark soul. A soul so accustomed to the darkness that, when light arrived in the face of Kat, it hurt. Vadeem rubbed his chest, feeling the knot of anguish tighten.

"We have a choice, Brothers and Sisters. When we walk in the darkness, we will stumble. But we can lift our faces to the light and trust in the One who will never forsake. He who weeps." Vadeem closed his eyes, hearing Pyotr's sermon, trying to breathe past the wad of pain in his throat.

Faith destroys.

No, faith is a gift. Faith starts with gratitude. Vadeem forced his gaze up, to the cross. *"He who believes in me will live, even though he dies; and whoever lives and believes in me will never die."* The verse filled his chest and found fertile soul. Hope could be found in the Savior's face. . .not only hope, but joy. Eternal joy.

This was God's glory. The defeat of death. Forever. A man who walked in the light would never know eternal defeat, despite the darkness around him. A man who walked in light radiated joy.

Like Kat. She knew what it meant to trust in God. Perhaps it made her foolish, but above all, Kat radiated joy. Vadeem winced, seeing for the first time indeed that God had sent Kat to remind him of the Almighty's constant love. A friend who never forsakes.

Maybe now was the time to walk in the light. He needed God now more than ever before. And a wise man considers his options.

Faith is a choice. Pyotr's words resonated in the recesses of his mind.

Vadeem dropped to his knees, trembling. "God, please, I'm begging you. Give me faith. Help me look to You for hope, for strength. I know I've failed You. I know I've forsaken the healing and the comfort I could find and instead embraced despair. Please forgive me."

The book dropped onto the floor with a thud as Vadeem sunk his face in his hands. "I don't know what to do. Help me find Kat. Please."

The echo of his desperate words in the conclave made him shudder. But in that moment, he drew breath, and it was not his own that filled his lungs. Supernatural, ethereal, and thick with hope. Vadeem gasped and put a hand to his chest. Tears glazed his eyes. Yes, this is what he'd missed. The presence of God holding him up, helping him take one step at a time.

He sucked in ragged breaths, the tight band of despair that had encircled his chest breaking, tearing, ripping to shreds. Vadeem's chest expanded to breathe in grace. The lightness of forgiveness swept through him, and he tingled down to his toes. Tears pushed into his eyes and his throat thickened at the immensity of the emotions welling within. "Thank You," he whispered, looking at the statue of his Savior. "Thank You for weeping, for sacrificing, for setting me free."

He leaned forward, climbing to his feet, and his hands fell on the book. Anton's words whooshed through his mind. *His light has illuminated my dark paths. He has set me free. Peace can be had for those who have faith.* Yes, he understood those words. Vadeem's heart thundered as he scanned through the pages for the passage, written by another, voicing Vadeem's own joy.

> *July 1918*
>
> *Banya with Timofea. I cleared my soul as we sat as brothers in the Lord. He understands. He is a good friend and will help carry my burdens. He says God will find a way to keep His promise. I know it now to be true. I tucked my past into the darkness, then turned toward the light. I even found a verse upon which to cling. John 11:9. His light has illuminated my dark paths. He has set me free. Now, my prayer is that Timofea will keep his promise in due time. Only God knows the future, and I am trusting in His Word. Peace can be had for those who have faith.*

He has set me free. Vadeem breathed deeply, feeling like he intimately knew this man, this ancestor of the woman he loved.

Kat. Wild, impulsive Kat, who could run like the wind and had an iron will to match his own. Quick-witted Kat, who could spot escape and nab it like a rabbit. Kat, a woman who had come to Russia armed only with a key and a picture, in search of her brave, quick-witted ancestor—an ancestor who knew what it was like to bear burdens, to be imprisoned in despair.

An ancestor who had been set free. *John 11:9.* Vadeem suddenly longed for a Bible. It only took a moment to find an ancient monastery text sitting on a shelf beside the altar. Vadeem flipped through the pages until he found the verse.

"Jesus answered, Are there not twelve hours in the day? If any man walk in the day, he stumbleth not, because he seeth the light of this world."

But Anton had a light. A light in the darkness.

Vadeem slowly stood and turned. Banya with Timofea. Fulfill the promise. Whose promise? God's or Anton's? What light would Anton have seen in the darkness?

Vadeem stumbled out of the cave into the moon-bathed cemetery and knew.

***

"Don't touch me." Kat pushed herself back into the seat, yanking her hair out of Grazovich's slimy grip. She spit at him.

His face darkened.

She'd learned in basic self-defense training that a woman in danger should be as disgusting as possible in order to repulse her attacker.

She was ready to do just about anything, and the first thing wouldn't be too difficult. Her stomach was already rolling.

She smiled, just barely.

Grazovich's eyes narrowed.

Then she saw him exiting the chapel. Kat's heart nearly leaped out of her chest with hope, delight, and not a little panic when Vadeem stepped out into the moonlight, the wind skimming his hair, his face to the heavens.

She gasped. "Oh no."

At the sound, Grazovich turned. And saw her hero.

Her breath clogged in her chest when the terrorist said, "Let's go for a little walk."

***

Vadeem stumbled along the perimeter of the monastery walls,

digging through his brain files for his research on the Pskov monastery. What had the monk said? It had been built in the fifth century, the cliffs and caves used as the first chapels. *Timofea had loved the grottos and spent much time here, preferring it to the monastery grounds.* Vadeem scanned the ring of caves, dark mouths open without words. Anton had known Timofea well enough to take a *banya* with him. Shed his secrets. Vadeem closed the book, the passage already memorized. *Banya* was a place where men talked in low tones under the cover of steam and a cathartic layer of sweat. In the early 1900s, where would the monks have built the *banya?* Somewhere outside the grounds, perhaps. Or in a cave? Vadeem scanned the grounds, the array of grottos that looped in a semicircle along a jagged shoreline. A *banya* in a cave would have ventilation or a pipe of some sort.

Long since removed. . .

And a path that wound down to the river, perhaps. He started for the caves, then realized his mistake.

Timofea had helped carry Anton's burdens. Could one of those burdens be the crest? Timofea had to be the key to the entire puzzle. He not only had the real key. . .but the crest as well.

Where would Timofea hide Anton's most precious treasure?

Vadeem blew out a breath. He knew where he'd keep his treasure. Close. Close enough to keep his eyes on it. Where he should have kept Kat. Vadeem forced the thought away. *Okay, Timofea, where would you hide a religious icon from the Communists?*

His cell? Vadeem scanned the dark caves. Yes, Timofea had relished the caves. . .could he have been checking on the crest, keeping it tucked away all these years? But which cave?

I tucked my past into the darkness, then turned toward the light.

The light. The moon, the bright crest of the wee morning hours, blazed a glorious path from behind him, alighting the row of caves like a spotlight. *I have seen the light. It has illuminated my path. . . .*

Vadeem tucked the journal into his pocket, turned, took a guess, and strode toward a darkened cave, carrying a candle from the chapel. *Please, oh God.*

The dark grotto mocked his assumptions as he stood in the lip of darkness, firelight pitifully striping the cave wall. Shallow and wide, the cave's gloom left him cold and discouraged. Vadeem took a quick tour around and moved to the next one. Again, pitch darkness filled the well made by the spoon of God ages past.

He'd been hoping to find a swatch of light in the dark folds of the sandstone. Somewhere. Anywhere.

He searched each cave, praying he might find some clue to Anton's cryptic words. He dragged his hands along the rough walls until they were dirty, nicked, and sore, searching for a crack, a hole where a monk might hide a priceless gem.

The moon's power waned thin as Vadeem's desperation grew. The futility of his efforts rose like the dust, mocking, choking him, until nothing but desperation drove him to the next dirty sandstone hole. His candle finally flickered out, leaving only his fear to direct his search.

The alcove pushed musty, dry dust into his lungs. The mouth was wide enough for a cot, perhaps even a table. But it tunneled back quickly into darkness. *Keep your eyes on the light.* Vadeem angled back, hope pressing him into the shadows. He squeezed between a pinch of rock, and his eyes made out a swath of moonlight filtering in through a hole in the sand-stone roof.

Vadeem began feeling the walls of the grotto. Hard, jagged rock, grooves and curves, crevasses. Nothing big enough to hide a lock box or a precious necklace. He worked his way farther back, feeling in turn each side, high and low. Nothing.

Frustration pinched his nerves. The moon had begun to pale. Dawn wouldn't be long behind. *I tucked my past into the darkness, then turned toward the light.* Vadeem stood in the wash of lunar light, looking up through the crack. The moon hovered in the lightening magenta backdrop; a beacon of majesty pointing to God's ever presence breaking through even in life's darkest hour. Deliberately, Vadeem turned his back to it and put his hands against the far wall.

He reached into a crack, nearly up to his armpit, and felt something solid. Metal. Wedged tight.

He plunged the other hand in. His cheek grazed the rock as he felt around in the furrow of shadow. Catching a fingernail, he wedged the tips of his fingers around something sharp and cold. Sweat beaded on his forehead as he tugged. Grunts bounced against the grotto walls, but hope kept his fingers on the object even when dirt came loose from the walls and sanded his eyes. He thought he felt a creature crawl up his arm under his coat sleeve but kept at the task until. . .it budged. A screech and then more tugs past jagged rock. The skin scraped off the back of both his hands as Vadeem dragged the box out.

It released with a final grating tug against rock and fell into his arms. He cradled it appropriately, like Anton or even his faithful friend, Timofea, might have. A burden of incalculable wealth. A treasure that could redeem the life of Anton Klassen's great-grandchild, a lady beyond worth. A lady used by God to remind Vadeem about the pearl of great price—salvation in Jesus Christ.

The breath whooshed out of Vadeem, and he realized he'd been holding it, counting his heartbeats. He set the box gently on the floor, nearly weak with relief. Fumbling for the key, he dropped it, then scraped it up and fitted it in the gnarled lock.

It turned.

He opened the box and inside found a dingy gray cloth. Slowing drawing it open, he could see even in the milky moonlight the dazzle of rubies, sapphires, and amethysts. He released his breath as he pulled the necklace up by its golden chain.

The Crest of St. Basil. It glimmered, catching the moonlight, radiating mystery and awe. How had this treasure come into the possession of Anton Klassen, and why had he chosen to hide it in a cleft of rock? What secrets had the walls of this cave heard as Anton spilled out his secret to the then-young Timofea? What images had that monk held onto until his deathbed?

The crest dangled in Vadeem's grip, twisting slightly. It was everything he'd imagined, the fulfillment of every myth, the dazzling icon of faith and hope once worn by Czar Nickolas, and every czar before him from the thirteenth century. The emblem of salvation.

But whose? A rush of indecision swept through Vadeem. He could surrender this treasure into the hands of a murderous smuggler and forfeit everything Anton Klassen, Timofea, and even Kat had suffered for. Or he could leave now with the crest tucked in his coat and run straight for Moscow, turning it over to the church and restoring the tradition, the glory for which it was made.

The thought made him ill in the pit of his stomach. Was he still so selfish, so driven to self-honor, that he would sacrifice the life of the woman who had turned to him in trust? *Oh God, forgive me!* Vadeem pressed the crest to his forehead as tears bit into his eyes and ran down his grimy cheeks. Yes, this crest was an emblem of redemption. Vadeem's redemption from his traitorous past.

And at dawn, the crest Anton Klassen had so carefully hidden would be used to redeem his great-granddaughter's life.

CHAPTER TWENTY

Kat wrestled with the iron fingers clamped over her mouth as Grazovich manhandled her out of the hiding place behind a gravestone. He dug his fingers into the back of her neck and hissed, "Quiet!" as if he hadn't been holding her down and gagging her with his gloved hand for the better part of two cold hours, forcing her silence.

Satisfaction swept through her when she managed to connect her heel to his shin. She didn't care that pain knifed up her leg.

The blunt end of a pistol, an icy finger just below her ear, made her freeze. "Don't cause any trouble now, or your boyfriend is dead, too."

She couldn't think of enough choice adjectives for the terrorist as he hauled her, tripping and stumbling, toward the cave where Vadeem had disappeared fifteen agonizing minutes earlier.

Her breath caught as she drew closer and saw Vadeem emerge, a necklace dangling from his grip. Even twenty feet away, she caught the luster of gem and gold.

The Crest of St. Basil.

General Grazovich stiffened, as if shocked by his good fortune. "Be good," he growled in her ear.

She had no intention of doing anything to persuade him to put a bullet into her skull. On noodle legs, she allowed Grazovich to push her forward until she stood in the ring of light a step outside the cave.

Vadeem looked up, saw her, and jerked as if he'd been slapped. The general must have had an "I am serious" look on his face because Vadeem swallowed audibly. Kat didn't miss the anger Vadeem tried to keep flushed from his face. She knew him too well, had seen that look used on her too many times not to recognize it.

"You found it." Excitement strummed in Grazovich's voice. "Congratulations."

Vadeem's chest rose and fell as he glared at the thug. "Let her go. I'll give it to you."

"Drop your pistol first," Grazovich said.

Kat winced when the weapon clattered on the cave floor. Then Vadeem looked at her full in the eyes, his sorrowful gaze communicating everything she'd dreaded. *I was just trying to keep you safe.*

Somehow, she found comfort in those unspoken words. She knew them now for what they truly meant.

I love you.

She would have to be blind not to recognize the truth. Emotion piled in his gaze, spilling out as he stepped forward, his hand outstretched, holding the necklace. As he did, she knew. . . .

He was betraying his country to save the life of the woman he loved.

She saw it on his agonized expression, and it rocked her to her bones.

She couldn't let him do it. He would live branded as a traitor for the rest of his life—something, she had a feeling, he already wrestled with. She ignored Grazovich's threat and let desperation drive adrenaline into her veins.

"No!"

Her outcry startled Grazovich. The kidnapper loosened his grip.

Kat found flesh and bit hard.

Grazovich cursed. Kat jerked away and stomped on his foot. She lunged toward the man who wanted so desperately to protect her. "No, Vadeem!"

Grazovich caught up fast and cuffed her, connecting with the back of her head. Kat slammed against the lip of the cave entrance. Pain exploded in her shoulder, then down her neck as the general pulled her up by her hair. "Good try."

Tears burned her eyes as Kat scrambled for footing. Grazovich yanked her head back and jammed his pistol under her jaw.

"Not a step closer, Spasonov."

Vadeem froze in midleap. She saw fury gather on his face and bunch his muscles. He didn't look at her, and the icy glare he leveled at Grazovich turned her cold.

"One move, and she's dead." Grazovich screwed the gun into her jaw for emphasis. Kat denied him a whimper, choosing instead to ball her fists against the pain.

"Now, you're going to put that necklace down. Gently, over there." Grazovich jerked his head toward the clearing behind them where the moon turned the grass an eerie yellow. "And then you're going back, good and far away. When I'm tucked in my car, snug as a bug, I'll let her go."

Kat winced as Grazovich shuffled backward, out toward the light, his hand wound into her hair.

Vadeem spoke through clenched teeth. "You're not going to get out of Russia. Every FSB agent from here to Kiev will hunt you down."

Grazovich laughed. "Right. Ryslan wasn't the only one who understood our cause."

Vadeem's eyes narrowed. "Ryslan didn't believe in your cause. He believed in cold American greenbacks."

"Well, so do I. Now move."

HEIRS of ANTON

Kat cried out as Grazovich let go of her hair and twisted her arm behind her back. Vadeem's face contorted with her pain. He didn't hesitate. She watched in agony as Vadeem paced out and set down the necklace in the puddle of moonlight.

Then he backed away, his eyes holding hers with every step.

"C'mon, Miss Moore, I have a plane to catch." Grazovich pulled her toward the necklace, keeping her wrenched arm tight as he scooped up the precious relic and let it drop around her neck. It hit her skin and made her shiver.

She had no doubt now that Grazovich had every intention of killing her. She'd seen the lecherous look in his eyes and knew as the weight of the jeweled crest hung on her neck, she'd never see Vadeem again. Grazovich inched away, his hand now fisted in her hair, towing her roughly behind him.

No, this was not happening. She'd lived her life around men bossing her around, taking charge of her life, making her feel helpless. She wasn't going to let this terrorist steal everything she'd come to Russia to find and more. She wasn't going to let him kill the future she'd once seen written on the now-agonized face of her would-be protector, the FSB captain who'd captured her heart. She didn't care that the muscles in her neck bunched around the death end of a gun or that her scalp burned from Grazovich's grip.

God had never left her before. He wasn't going to do it now, regardless of what happened.

God, give me courage!

Kat erupted in fury. She slammed her boot into Grazovich's loafer, fell to her knees, and jerked away. She stifled a scream as she left a wad of hair in the terrorist's hand.

Vadeem leaped like a panther.

The two men hit the dirt with a grunt. Grazovich let go of her as Vadeem wrestled with the man's gun hand. Kat rolled away, not sure if she should run or get in a lick.

"Run, Kat!" Vadeem yelled between grunts.

That decided it. Vadeem didn't need her help, obvious from the way he shook the gun out of Grazovich's grip and followed with a one-two punch that made even Kat's teeth rattle.

Her legs took control. The last thing Vadeem needed in a sudden reversal of fortune would be to have her near enough for Grazovich to threaten.

She sped out toward the road, gulping chilly air into her burning lungs, not daring a look back. One idea drove her—dive into the car, lock it, and wait for Vadeem to show up, her hero.

She never made it.

A bulky figure moved out from beside the car, tall and dark and arrowing straight for her. She veered away, and a scream left her ravaged lungs a second before two timberlike arms crushed her to a solid, unforgiving chest.

Vadeem heard Kat's scream just as Grazovich pulled out Ryslan's pistol from some well inside his coat. He shoved it in Vadeem's face, and Vadeem backpedaled, fast. Grazovich, ghost white and bleeding from the mouth and nose, struggled to his feet. A smile creased his face. "I should have done this a long time ago."

Vadeem heaved in hot breaths, wondering how fast it would take to dig up the pistol Grazovich had dumped in the tall grass.

The moonlight waxed Grazovich's twisted face a bone-chilling yellow. The thug smiled and leveled his gun. "With you out of the way, just think how much fun your girlfriend and I will have."

Rage poured into Vadeem's muscles as he hurtled himself toward the Abkhazian terrorist.

Shock washed Grazovich's face. He pulled the trigger.

The shot sent Vadeem wheeling back as the bullet grazed across his arm, burning like a branding iron. He landed in a splash of pain and braced himself for the fatal follow-through shot.

In a blur of motion, Grazovich slammed into the dirt. He swore loudly, dazed and knocked silly by the bear of a man straddling him.

Vadeem blinked, his heart in his mouth.

"Sorry I'm late," Pyotr said as he drove his knee into Grazovich's spine. He easily jerked the weapon from his hand. "I had a hard time finding the place."

Vadeem gulped back relief. He had never been so happy to see a pastor in his entire life. "No problem. Your timing is perfect."

Grazovich suddenly roared in fury. Pyotr shoved his face into the dirt. Vadeem quickly snapped a set of cuffs on the man, ignoring a barrage of Abkhazian curses.

"You okay?" Pyotr asked as he hauled Grazovich to his feet.

Vadeem clutched his arm, exploring the shredded leather where the bullet had grazed him. His hand came back sticky with blood. "Good thing his aim was off. He almost got me in the chest."

Pyotr grinned even as he wrestled Grazovich into a submissive position. "I don't know, Pal. I'd say you got a direct hit right in the heart." The pastor looked past him, grinning.

Vadeem followed his gaze and saw Kat, face white, her hair a tousled nest, her amber eyes wide and glistening, holding her breath in with a cupped hand over her mouth.

"Direct hit," he echoed. He didn't even have the chance to climb to his feet before she barreled into his arms, burying her face in his neck, sobbing.

He soothed her, crushing her to his chest. "Are you hurt?"

She shook her head in the well of his neck. He felt his relief build in his eyes, turning them moist. "Sorry I scared you."

She sat back. Fury filled her expression. "Next time you decide to send me packing, I'd sure appreciate it if you'd do the honors yourself."

Vadeem's lips parted in shock.

A smile tugged at her lips. "I missed you." Her voice broke, and he read everything he'd hoped to see in her wounded eyes. "I thought I'd never see you again."

He traced her face lightly with his finger. "You just had to have a little faith, Kat. That's all you needed."

Her face twitched. "I thought you said faith destroys."

He leaned close, his forehead to hers. "Oh, no, Kat, faith leads us to the treasure we've always longed for. Salvation. Forgiveness." He cupped her cheek with his hand. "Hope."

She leaned into his touch as the wind tangled her hair and swept her fragrance to him, embracing him with the joyous gift that was Kat. God's gift. Vadeem nearly cried at the magnitude of it.

"I'm in love with you, you know." He whispered the words, forced as they were from the darkest corner of his heart.

She smiled at him, a full, encompassing grin that was so sweet it made him ache with happiness. "So, you're not sending me home on the next plane?"

"I'm sorry, Miss Moore, but you're not going anywhere."

She raised her chin. "You know, I hate it when you tell me what to do." Teasing glimmered in her eyes.

"Well maybe that's more of a. . .request." He wove his hands into her hair. "Maybe I can give you a reason to stay." He kissed her gently, testing, and discovered that she had moved beyond the tentative stage to acceptance. Her lips were sweet and warm and full of that unconditional love he'd always longed for. Full of Kat.

No, she wasn't going anywhere.

Now this is Moscow at night." Vadeem tucked Kat under his arm. As they walked down the cobble-stones of Red Square, he felt mesmerized as much by the wonder of her nestled close as by the star-strewn sky. It glittered like diamond-studded velvet against a jeweled crescent moon. In the lunar light, the church of St. Basil the Blessed glimmered red, blue, green, and gold—the colors of the crest that had been safely delivered back to the Russian Church.

The glory of it seemed as surreal as the fact that he'd been nominated a Hero of the Motherland. A medal of merit pended approval by the Duma during that legislative body's next session.

Except the hero status Vadeem truly longed for was in Kat's eyes. Vadeem led them onto the bridge that spanned the Volga River. Kat hummed contentedly, stirring within him a well of emotions still unfamiliar to his thawing heart. Each time, it brought a fresh wave of amazement and often a wash of betraying tears. He managed a shaky breath and blinked them away.

"Thank you for taking me to the ballet," Kat murmured. "The Bolshoi Theater is more beautiful than I ever imagined."

"You're welcome." Vadeem stopped and watched the river as it flowed, its ripples peaked silver as the moon kissed them. He leaned against the rail, pulling Kat close, and played with her hair as the wind teased it. He loved its silky feel through his fingers. He could stay here forever, drowning in her enchanting aroma, surrendering to the magic in her smile. Tonight, dressed a black velvet skirt and a short, brown wool coat with a furry lamb's wool collar, her amber eyes shining, Kat looked downright regal. Especially against the deep red backdrop of the Kremlin, the fortress of the czars. Not for the first time, Vadeem knew he'd found a princess, someone with royalty running through her veins. A daughter of the King of Heaven. Vadeem touched the key, now hanging by a gold chain around her neck, amazed at all it had unlocked for him. For her. "I'm glad you're here to share it with me."

Emotion clogged his throat as he drew his arms around her, pulling her close. Her fingers ran through the hair at the nape of his neck and sent a warm shiver down his spine. Oh yes, he could stay here forever and longer. He smiled, his gaze going to the heavens in silent gratitude.

If Kat had taught him one thing over the past four weeks—the first week spent trying to keep her alive, the next three enjoying the fact that he'd succeeded—it was that his darkest moments could be survived if he kept his eyes on God, on the light. Vadeem did that now, smiling at the stars above and the moon in its mysterious, eternal radiance. Like the moon, always there, never absent—even when he couldn't spot it with the naked eye—God would never leave him. As if to add an exclamation point to that truth, God had given him Kat, his precious *Katoosha*, an explosion of light in Vadeem's life. A delightful, invigorating, sometimes exasperating reminder of God's love.

Now, if he could just pass muster tomorrow. "What time is your grandfather arriving?"

Kat threaded her fingers through his. "Two o'clock." She drew back from him, leaving her fragrance in her wake, then she smiled and wiggled her brows. "Nervous?"

Nervous? He was about to meet the illustrious Grandfather

Neumann, the equivalent, or perhaps worse, of Kat's father. Nervous didn't begin to describe the way his stomach turned inside out or the general *kasha* quality of his knees. "A little," he said.

"Don't worry. He'll love you." She pressed her forehead to his, her gaze in his, close and hypnotic. "Just like I do."

He couldn't help but kiss her. She was so full of life, of hope, and when he pulled away, he felt it all on his tingling lips and the explosion of joy in his heart. He swallowed, still trying to get used to tugging vulnerable words from his chest. "I love you, too."

He kept that moment in the forefront of his mind the next day at Moscow's Sheremetova 2 Airport as he stood, shifting weight from one leg to the other. "Which one is he?"

Kat jumped up and down like a preschooler. "Tall, white hair, lanky."

Oh, the one holding a briefcase, walking like an athlete? The one with piercing dark eyes who looks like he could eat me alive? Vadeem's courage careened to his toes, and he grimaced. Kat didn't notice but flung herself into her grandfather's arms. The old man braced himself well, obviously used to her exuberance. Vadeem waited until Kat had hugged him enough to make up for her adventure and the next few Christmases, then extended a hand.

"Vadeem Spasonov, Mr. Neumann. Welcome to Russia."

The man's grip clenched his own, and his eyes warmed, despite his curt nod. "So, I guess you're the one who kept my granddaughter alive, huh?"

Vadeem opened his mouth and wished for words.

The old man winked.

Perhaps her grandfather wasn't so different from Kat as Vadeem thought.

Vadeem flagged down a cab, then rode with them to the Hilton, Kat's hotel of choice, listening to the two catch up and Kat spin tales of bravery that Vadeem viewed in a completely different light. He'd have to get the grandfather alone and set the record straight. Still, he liked the way esteem seemed to be building in the man's eyes. Perhaps he'd let things lie.

"Okay, Grandfather, I know you've had a long trip, but I have lots of questions, and I want answers." That was what Kat had planned to say to him. Had planned it during the week since she discovered he wanted to fly over on the pretense of bringing a suitcase of her personal effects to help her get settled as she searched for the Klassen family relatives. The KGB *did* have files—and Vadeem had promised to help her dust them off and trace them forward. Hope tinged their every conversation. The fact that Grandfather had decided to join the search felt some-how. . .healing. And she wouldn't have to dig far under his offer to help discover ulterior motives, namely curiosity. Grandfather wanted to run Vadeem through the ringer.

She didn't care. Not only could Vadeem stand up under the old man's scrutiny, Grandfather came armed with answers, and if the book in her possession didn't trigger him to spill them, well, she planned to turn demanding. To ask the Lord for some of that grit she'd unleashed on a smuggler with murderous intent.

Instead, what came out when Grandfather closed the hotel room door behind them was, in a horribly squeaky tone, "Can I. . .did you. . .um. . .I still have some questions."

Grandfather Neumann turned those gentle, sometimes stern, eyes on her. "In due time, Kat. Right now, I need to rest my weary bones. I am nearly eighty years old, you know."

Kat nodded, disappointment rising up in the form of tears. "Can I just ask you one question?"

Grandfather sighed, but he nodded, his strong hands coming to rest on her shoulders.

"You said you came back to Russia once. Why?"

He pursed his lips and stared at her a long time. Sorrow rose in his eyes, alive and flickering, as if he were reliving fresh grief. "I suppose I was on the same quest you are."

Kat opened her mouth, but no words emerged. Grandfather had come looking for Magda's ancestors? Questions knotted her brain, and she frowned at him, suddenly furious that he'd kept so much of her past locked away. Thirty years seemed an eternity to wait for answers. She stepped away from him. "I found her father's journal, but I never found anything about *her*, Grandfather. I hope you can help me."

Grandfather Neumann nodded and pulled her to his chest. "In time, Kat. In time." She hung on tight, eyes closed, feeling suddenly like the eight year old who had seen a broken stranger in a hospital bed and wondered who he was beneath the bandaged exterior.

Grandfather finally released her, sat on the bed, and patted it for her to join him. "Now *I* have a question." He searched her face, those green eyes as piercing as she'd remembered them. "Do you love this man?"

Kat sat down and leaned into her grandfather's shoulder, the only grandfather she'd ever known, her true grandfather, woven into her heart. "Yes. He's the one I've been waiting for all my life."

She had unearthed so few answers in Russia. But wrapped in Vadeem's arms, the strong masculine redolence of strength and safety rushing through her on a wave of delight, the touch of his whiskered cheek on her face, she knew she'd found a different answer. Perhaps God's special answer for her. Six-feet-two-inches of answer with curly dark hair that begged a woman to muss it, muscled arms that held her without hesitation, and a heart that was just beginning to learn what it meant to walk with God.

She couldn't wait to stick around to see that happen. Yes, Vadeem Spasonov was an answer she'd journeyed to Russia to find.

Grandfather tucked his arm around her with a strength that never diminished regardless of his age. "True love is a rare find, Kat. Hang on tight and never let go."

She wondered at the tremor in his voice.

"Now, go downstairs and keep your young man company. He's tied up in knots." Grandfather gave a wry chuckle. "Tell him not to be so nervous. I like him. He reminds me of a dear Russian friend I had once named Pavel."

Kat popped her grandfather a kiss before she left the room.

Vadeem *was* in knots. Pacing a figure eight on the floor. Kat laughed at his mussed hair, the worry in his eyes. "Vadeem, calm down, he likes you."

Vadeem smiled wryly. "Well, I hope so, but I'm not the only one who's worried about meeting him."

Kat frowned.

Vadeem gestured with his head toward the lobby seating area. Pyotr stood and smiled, lopsided, not at all looking like the rugged man who had saved Vadeem's life, but the gentle pastor who had tended his soul. Kat walked over to him and then noticed his mother, sitting tall with a bright amber-eyed gaze on Kat.

Kat slowed her pace, confused.

"My mother has something to tell you, Kat. . .and I hope she's telling the truth." Pyotr's eyes apologized again, and Kat traveled back to their conversation. Obviously, he'd taken the woman's wild ramblings seriously enough to drag her onto a plane to Moscow.

"Hello, Baba Rina." Kat reached out gently, like she might do to a frightened child. Rina startled her by climbing to her feet and holding her hand in an iron grip. Fire blazed in those amber eyes, so strong Kat felt it to her toes.

"The name is Marina Antonova Klassen Shubina Dobrana."

Kat froze, her heart thumping like a hammer against her rib cage. *Grandmother?*

"I came to thank you, Child. You have done it, Kat. You have fulfilled the promise. Anton's promise."

Kat frowned at the old woman. How much had Pyotr told her?

"My father, Anton, made a promise, and you, through your bravery, have kept that promise to bring the crest safely home."

Kat scraped up gentle words for this woman speaking in riddles. "I don't understand. You're Marina Klassen? I thought she died. How do you know me? How do you know my family?"

She smiled, and for the first time, Kat noticed her amber eyes, deep and twinkling. Eyes that stared back at her in delight. Eyes she recognized as her own.

"Give me the picture, Child."

The ancient picture. Kat felt Vadeem sidle up beside her as she fumbled for her Bible, safely rescued from the glove compartment of Ryslan's car. She retrieved the picture, and just to make sure her ears weren't playing a horrible joke, she checked the name on the back. Klassen. Her hands trembled as she handed the photograph to the babushka. *My babushka.*

Marina took it, and suddenly years dissolved from her face. She smiled, and recognition, even longing, filled her expression.

"I've missed my picture. When you showed it to me at the house. . .well, it was as if my past had reached out and grabbed me." Her voice fell. "I simply couldn't believe my eyes."

Kat's pulse roared in her ears. Her voice betrayed her as a thousand questions knotted her mind. As if in understanding, Marina reached out and touched Kat's arm. The soft grip sent waves of warmth through Kat. "I suppose you read the verse on the back?"

Kat managed to nod.

"You see, God kept His promise, too. His faithfulness continues through all generations. He brought the Klassen family home"

Kat froze as the woman touched Kat's face, her hair, examining it as a mother might a newborn child. Thankfully, Vadeem's arm, warm and steady, curled around Kat's waist and held her up on her trembling legs.

"Sixty years ago I met a man with whom I fell in love. He helped save our Motherland, but together we committed a terrible crime. His name was Edward. And he called me by a Hebrew name that means strength."

Kat caught her breath, seeing the truth, the hope, the joy resonating in the woman's expression as she smiled and said, "He called me—"

"Magda."

The name came out in a strained puff of shock, the voice constricted by disbelief and perhaps pain. Kat turned and saw time melt away on her grandfather's face. His voice warbled as his emotions caught up with it. "I thought. . . They told me. . ." His Russian struggled against years of disuse, and Kat ached to fill in the gap for him. He swallowed, his Adam's apple a ball of frustration bobbing down in his throat. Then those green eyes that had churned with unspoken sadness for so many years ignited and blazed. "But I knew. I *always* knew."

Kat took a step toward him, suddenly fearful of the passion building in his voice. Vadeem's grip around her waist tightened.

"I came back once and searched for you. . . ." Grandfather's face twisted, and he seemed to be fighting a wave of memory. "I'm sorry I left you behind."

The voice of the woman behind Kat came out thick with emotion. "You had to, Edick. It was God's will. And because of your courage, you saved our family." Magda moved past Kat and reached out her wrinkled hand.

Grandfather clasped it, his face shining, tracing hers with a gaze that spoke of pure devotion, pure love. It pulled at Kat's heart, and tears laced her eyes.

What had happened that had forced Grandfather to abandon the woman he so obviously loved? And what will of God had Grandfather summoned the courage to fulfill?

How had Kat and her mother ended up in America? And who was her mother's biological father?

The questions—and answers—would have to come later, when joy wasn't gluing the words to her chest, when her heart wasn't swelling to three times its size watching her grandfather draw the frail woman, Pyotr's mother—her grandmother!—into his arms and hold her as he would if a soldier returning home from battle.

Magda's voice emerged, buoyant and betraying the fear, the confidence, the inner war she'd waged for over half a century. "I hoped, from the day you left, that you'd return. And you took care of my hope, just as I knew you would. The day you carried me from the flames, I knew God had a plan for you. I just needed to trust Him."

Grandfather kissed the top of her head gently, like a man might his beloved bride, then looked at Kat. His eyes brimmed

with an unfamiliar radiance. "God has answered so many promises," he said in English. He tracked his gaze to Vadeem and
smiled. His tone turned fatherly, and this time, his Russian
came out perfectly and said all Kat could have hoped. "I think
His blessings are just getting started."

A wave of warmth started in Kat's toes and crested
through her until tears streamed down her cheeks. She looked
at Vadeem, who met her gaze.

"Oh yes," Vadeem said in a whisper that sent a ripple down
her spine. "His blessings are just getting started."

*Those who know Your name will trust in You, for You, Lord,
have never forsaken those who seek You.* The words of David's
psalm filled Kat's mind like a whisper. "Praise the Lord," Kat
said softly. She glanced at Pyotr, who had braced his arm
against the sofa, his face a few shades lighter than it had been.
"So that makes you. . .my uncle?"

He might have nodded, but the answer came in the tilted
smile and the light twinkling in his eyes. "I knew I liked you. I
should have recognized that Klassen spunk."

Kat looked away, feeling a blush crawl up her face, but
Vadeem hooked his finger under her chin. "She's got spunk
all right. She's my *Katoosha*. My explosion of delight. . .*Maya
Doragaya.*"

Then he kissed her, right in front of her grandfather, the
kind of kiss that hinted of so many of those blessings he'd
mentioned.

But when Vadeem released her, Kat noticed that her grandfather wasn't paying any attention. He had his face buried in
Magda's hair, his shoulders shaking, sobbing as he peeled back
time and pain to embrace the joy they'd all come to Russia
to find.

SUSAN K. DOWNS

Susan served as the Russian adoption program coordinator for one of America's oldest adoption agencies prior to her decision to leave the social work field and devote herself full-time to writing and editing fiction. Through her adoption work, however, she developed a love for all things Russian and an unquenchable curiosity of Russian history and culture.

A series of miraculous events led Susan and her minister-husband to adopt from Korea two of their five children. The adoptions of their daughters precipitated a five-year mission assignment in South Korea, which, in turn, paved the way for Susan's work in international adoption and her Russian experiences. The Downses currently reside in Canton, Ohio. Read more about Susan's writing/editing ministry and her family at www.susankdowns.com.

SUSAN MAY WARREN

Susan May Warren and her family recently returned home after working for eight years in Khabarovsk, far east Russia. Deeply influenced and blessed by the faith of the Russian Christians, she longed to write a story that revealed their faith during their dark years of persecution and a story of their impact on today's generation. *The Heirs of Anton* is the fruition of these hopes. Now writing full-time in northern Minnesota while her husband, Andrew, manages a lodge, Susan is the author of both novels and novellas. She draws upon her rich experience on both sides of the ocean to write stories that stir the Christian soul. Find out more about Susan and her writing at www.susanmaywarren.com.

Don't miss the next book in the

HEIRS of ANTON

family saga.

NADIA

By Susan K. Downs and Susan May Warren

ISBN 1-59310-163-5

COMING SEPTEMBER 2004

Wherever Christian books are sold

CHAPTER ONE

Moscow, 1970

Anyone looking at her might see a woman lost in the jazz, swaying to the sassy tones imported from America and emulated, often poorly, in a dingy underground nightclub on the south side of Moscow.

No one would recognize her as Hope, aka "Nadia," Moore, seasoned CIA agent, now poised on the edge of desperation. She gripped her stool with both hands and crossed one booted leg over the other, moving her foot to the music of Aretha Franklin sung by a longhaired Muscovite with an ear-aching accent.

Hope slung her gaze across the shadowed room, searching. No, he hadn't arrived. And no one had made her cover. Yet.

She sighed and leaned back against the bar. The low murmurs from clumped conversation groups tugged on her ears and competed against the racket on stage. These clandestine forums oozed information that might further the cause of the United States against its Cold War nemesis. She'd been a habitual eavesdropper for too long and logged miscellaneous information in the recesses of her brain.

Over the dark room that stood maybe twenty meters square hovered a cloud of smoke—cigarette and otherwise. Thankfully, Russia didn't have near the drug problem that ravaged the youth across the ocean. Still, possession of illegal substances netted a gruesome sentence in the gulags to the north—a prospect guaranteed to crash the highest high. Russia's drug of choice centered on the state-sanctioned firewater, vodka, and this close, its acrid scent cramped Hope's empty stomach.

Oh, yeah. Food. She'd been too busy to eat. Too intent on

sneaking into Russia. Too focused on saving the only man she'd ever loved.

She glanced at the timepiece that hung from a long chain around her neck. Aranoff was now over an hour late. Had he received her message? She'd left it in their former dead drop. Fear found a foothold and dug at her courage. She was an idiot to think he still checked his PO Box or the chipped-out brick behind the Dumpster at his cousin's flat. She fingered the piece of jewelry, a wedding gift from Mickey. The backside contained a small compartment for microdots and other clandestine information she might transport.

Not today. This trip was about her. About Mickey.

About baby Ekaterina.

For the thirteen thousandth time in the last twenty hours, she called herself crazy, and her courage knotted into a hard ball in her stomach.

Crazy Hope. That's what she had.

Crazy Hope. That's what Mickey had called her when she'd snuck them into a General Assembly meeting of the Duma, or when she'd secreted her way onto a Leningrad train and into the private berths of General Lashtoff. Her crazy, sometimes fantastical missions—and accomplishments—had earned her legendary status in the company. But even she knew that springing Mickey out of Gorkilov Prison or evading the KGB in this dimly lit underground cabaret might be a feat above Crazy Hope's abilities.

But she wasn't going to let Mickey die without demanding the truth from him.

Hope breathed out hard. Sweat beaded underneath her long, black wig. Twenty hours enduring its weight made her neck muscles scream. She should have waited to don her disguise until the Moscow airport. Then again, wouldn't it have seemed strange to see a blond in the conservative shirtdress of a mother enter the bathroom and a young, hip brunette with waist-long hair and a beaded necklace exit? No, she needed the guise of American student and war protestor to get her into the mass of society. Let customs officials see nothing more sinister than a free-love hippie with a peace agenda, and they'd let her pass without a blink. But a mother of one, a savvy woman with fluency in three languages and the ability to move around Russian society like a mouse? They'd have her under the bright light in the KGB bowels faster than Solzhenitsyn.

Once inside Russia, she'd beelined for the *Zhenshina Belaya Nocha*, her old stomping grounds, snuck in the back entrance, and changed into a more conservative, Russian-style dirt-brown polyester skirt, turquoise blouse, and suede jacket. Still hip. But tame enough to blend into the Soviet crowd.

Please, Aranoff, find me.

She turned around to the bartender, a gaunt man with an Adam's apple the size of Brooklyn, and ordered a tomato juice. He eyed her, perhaps a moment too long, and slid her the drink.

She drank it down in one gulp and felt it saturate her aching stomach with nourishment. Once on a mission to dig through files in the inner office of a high-ranking party secretary, she'd gone without eating for more than two days.

She would gladly never eat again if it meant Mickey might live.

A new song by a new jazz singer. This time the music of John Coltrane filled the room. The shaggy heads of Moscow University students, pushing the party line with their neck-length hair and fringed leather jackets, stared at the musician. No movement. No swaying of heads. No feet tapping in time to the music.

Even in their attempts to reproduce the West, they couldn't break free of stoic Soviet culture. Hope stopped her bobbing foot. Her heart sank. How quickly she'd forgotten her training, relaxed her instincts. If the KGB hadn't spotted her yet and weren't rounding up a posse outside the *Belaya's* doors, it would only be due to God's mercy.

She hoped God was especially generous with said mercy on this trip.

Aranoff, where are you?

She stood, walked over to the wall, leaned one shoulder into it, and surreptitiously scanned the room. A blond tucked, stage left, in the shadows caught her attention. Hope's heart skipped when she noted the woman had her in her sights. No smile, her eyes fixed. Recognition slid over Hope like a chill.

Lena.

Mickey's friend.

Or should she say. . .*girlfriend?*

Hope clenched her teeth and fought the anger that welled at the back of her throat. Lena should be wasting away on death row, in Mickey's place. And if Hope could figure out a way to make the swallow—the KGB femme fatale—pay for her crimes, she'd invest a lifetime into bringing her to justice.

Focus. Hope blew out a breath. She was here for Ekaterina. And she wouldn't jeopardize her mission. Even for revenge.

Where was Aranoff?

The fear that he'd been arrested flickered across her brain and she winced. No. She would have heard. Aranoff was too valuable to disappear without a ripple in the community. Even her father, as angry as he still was over her marriage, would have eased his stance and conveyed the news that one of her best friends had been betrayed.

No, only Mickey was doing the betraying these days. A fact that her father, spymaster Edward Neumann, took every opportunity to drive home.

She held up her glass, hoping for one last taste of juice, and noticed her hand shook. Her own softness rattled her. Two years out of the field, and she reacted like a rookie.

Maybe she was. Maybe she'd been out of the game so long that this attempt to salvage her future was sheer suicide. Then where would Ekaterina be?

An orphan.

Hope closed her eyes and let the image of her one-year-old—the baby-soft chestnut hair, the amber brown eyes, the droolly smile—wax her mind. A softness started in her heart and spread out through her body. No. She wouldn't fail. She'd bring home Kat's father. And then, somehow, she'd start being the mother she should be.

Whatever that meant.

Somehow, she had to believe that yanking Mickey out of this mess held the key to her questions, to this sudden floundering for identity. Ever since she'd held her red-faced squirming daughter in her arms, an unfamiliar feeling had sizzled in her chest.

She'd finally named it. *Panic.*

She, the woman who knew how to sweet-talk the German Stasi into allowing her into a covert restaurant for party officials, the same operator who could unlock a closed door in less than ten seconds, felt just a little weak every time her daughter toddled up to her, arms out, toothless mouth grinning.

She needed this trip, if only to find her footing. Resurrect the confidence that had shattered into smithereens on the floor of a Nyack, New York, maternity ward.

She put the glass down and crossed her arms over her chest, pushing her fear into a cold ball. She would refuse to believe the rumors until she could confront her lying, traitorous, two-timing husband face-to-face.

So maybe she believed the rumors more than she wanted to admit.

Two minutes out in the back alley with the woman across the room, and Hope would have the hard, cold facts.

Somehow, that only sent a ripple of pure fear up her spine.

No, she'd wait until she could look square into Mickey's light green eyes, see past the legends, the cover stories, and uncover the truth.

And maybe if she really kept her wits about her, she'd be

able to withstand his intoxicating charisma long enough to convince him to return home. To her.

To Kat.

Don't expect loyalty from a career spy, Nadezhda. Her father's voice took out a chunk of her heart with one swoop, and she gasped. No. She'd pledged to trust Mickey.

And she would.

Even if his girlfriend sat across the room like a minx, oozing elegance and charm and 120 percent deceit.

Oh Mickey, how could you?

As if in some mythical trance, Hope couldn't rip her gaze off the woman, off her long blond hair, the way she laughed with others at her table. Hope felt a hot ball ignite in her chest when the woman looped an arm through one of her companions and whispered into his ear. Lena still had the poise of a ballerina, the figure of Marilyn Monroe.

Lena Chornova obviously hadn't given birth to a nine-pound baby within the last year. Hope felt downright pudgy in her dingy skirt. Little wonder Mickey had moved on.

No. He'd pledged to love her too.

Hadn't he?

She pushed off the wall when Lena exited during the rhythmic applause following a Duke Ellington tune. Hope eased over to the opposite door, and her heart in her throat, she debated tailing the little tramp. Aranoff hadn't shown, and Lena was a sure link to the only man who could help Hope. Suddenly Hope couldn't bear another moment of not knowing.

"Nadia Neumann. Welcome back to the USSR."

Hope turned, and her heart jumped into her throat. Dressed in head-to-toe black garb and smoking a cigarette stood the very picture of her nightmares.

*Komitet Gosudarstvennoy Bezopasnosti. . .*the KGB.